FLASH *OF* *FURY*

LEA GRIFFITH

sourcebooks
casablanca

Copyright © 2017 by Lea Griffith
Cover and internal design © 2017 by Sourcebooks, Inc.
Cover art by Paul Stinson

Sourcebooks and the colophon are registered trademarks of Sourcebooks, Inc.

All rights reserved. No part of this book may be reproduced in any form or by any electronic or mechanical means including information storage and retrieval systems—except in the case of brief quotations embodied in critical articles or reviews—without permission in writing from its publisher, Sourcebooks, Inc.

The characters and events portrayed in this book are fictitious or are used fictitiously. Any similarity to real persons, living or dead, is purely coincidental and not intended by the author.

All brand names and product names used in this book are trademarks, registered trademarks, or trade names of their respective holders. Sourcebooks, Inc., is not associated with any product or vendor in this book.

Published by Sourcebooks Casablanca, an imprint of Sourcebooks, Inc.
P.O. Box 4410, Naperville, Illinois 60567-4410
(630) 961-3900
Fax: (630) 961-2168
www.sourcebooks.com

Printed and bound in Canada.
MBP 10 9 8 7 6 5 4 3 2 1

Prologue

Beirut, Lebanon

"HEY, YOUR HIGHNESS?"

King sighed. His men loved to jack with him on helicopter missions.

"Oh, Your Hiiiighnessss…"

King lifted his middle finger in a salute and kept his eyes closed, concentrating instead on breathing.

King didn't do helos. They were cramped, squatty birds with fragile metal "wings." He preferred C-130s with their big, rounded girth shooting through the sky at high altitudes. Helicopters went down easily with nothing more than gunfire. It took a hell of a lot more than a bullet to take down a C-130 transport plane.

Alas, they weren't engaging a HALO approach tonight. Instead of a high-altitude, low-opening jump, tonight was all about fast insertion—getting in, getting out, and not being seen while doing it. They'd come here to destroy a weapons pipeline depot belonging to Horace Dresden. The man was both a traitor to the United States and a warlord to the rest of the world. His illegal arms trade funneled millions in money and even more in weapons to zealots who killed innocents. Dresden had to be stopped, but because of his close association with Lebanon, the U.S. couldn't send in military. Lebanon was sovereign and wouldn't appreciate a U.S.-sanctioned operation to take out an ally.

So Dresden would have to deal with Endgame, and King was fine with that.

"Seriously, sir, Ella wants to hear about Serbia." Jude Dagan—the only other man besides King within Endgame Ops who had once called SEALs home—was angling for something. King realized it was going to take more than a middle finger to keep Jude from pestering him the entire flight.

King felt the rumble of the rotors above them. The *thump-thump-thump-thump* of the blades whisking through the air left an indelible impression, a deep thud in the region of his stomach. Something about this mission seemed off. It wasn't anything he'd voiced to himself, but something niggled at him and refused to give him enough peace to ignore the helo ride.

Maybe it was the helo itself. Goddamn helos. Nothing good had ever happened for him on a helo.

He opened his eyes and stared hard at Jude. Jude grinned and pointed to Ella Banning. King flipped on his communication unit. "Jude, you're a pain in my ass."

"Sir, if it's—" Ella began.

King held up a hand and shot Jude a look. Jude was unperturbed.

"It was fifteen men, Your Highness. You were pinned down behind a building in the middle of the country, and you fought with nothing but a—"

"I know the damn story, Jude," King said firmly.

"I'm just saying," Jude began, "It's a damn *good* story."

A beep sounded over their comm devices, and King gazed over at his men. And one woman. Women on missions were a new thing. For all of them.

Endgame had been born in the mind of a man who

knew the value of black operations. On paper, they were a consulting agency to military contractors. The world was rebuilding, so Endgame provided security for the Grayfield Incs., Dalton-Strattons, and Crayor Corps of the world. These large companies were responsible for protecting oil fields, diamond mines, and other assets. They were the reassemblers of infrastructure in a world torn apart by war.

Off paper, Endgame Ops was something else entirely. Sometimes commissioned military couldn't do the dirty jobs. Sometimes they had to be done in the darkness of the black-ops world, and this is where King's team operated. King had signed on with a man he called the Piper. King knew the man sat on the Joint Chiefs of Staff. Other than that, all King knew was that the Piper held the strings and sometimes you had to dance.

He wondered what Ella Banning had to pay for. She was one of Endgame's three CIA liaisons. A bright, beautiful, up-and-coming analyst, she held a world of information in her tiny hands, and in Endgame's business, information was power. It hadn't taken long for Jude Dagan to stake a claim, and yeah, it bothered King.

Not because he wanted her, but because romantic entanglements were a weakness warriors couldn't afford in battle. And Jude was barely on the reservation most days as it was. Add another stressor, and he was likely to snap at a moment's notice.

But even Jude, with his caustic brand of humor, had a place on this team. *Family*.

King breathed in deeply, tamping down his panic as the bird shifted and angled to the right. Once he'd caught his breath, he began to check his men again.

Rook Granger, his face camouflaged by paint, nodded at King. A former Army Ranger and a better soldier King had never seen. He remembered his first meeting with Rook outside a bar in North Carolina. King had been nursing a beer; Rook had been nursing a grudge.

A soft, feminine voice slid along their communication links. "Ten until touchdown, boys. I'll be linking your pilot so you know coordinates."

King smiled to himself. Vivi Granger was also a CIA analyst, though she only had half a foot in the Company now. She was also Endgame. Vivi had taken care of Rook's grudge. Good thing too. Rangers were almost as batshit as SEALs.

King let his gaze drift down the line—Harrison Black, British MI6. A truly dark, inhospitable man. Danger whispered around Black, which was fine by King. He hadn't co-opted the Brit for his witty banter. He'd invited Black in because he had resources in the dark underbelly of the world that Endgame needed if the playing field was going to be even.

Next to Black was Micah Samson, formerly a combat rescue officer with the United States Air Force. He continued to snooze, though surely he was hearing everything they said because Micah never missed anything. Rescue operations were his forte, but he was a mean son of a bitch when riled. King had never trusted anyone the way he immediately trusted Micah.

Beside him in the cramped quarters of the helo was Brody Madoc. *One big-ass dude for sure*, King mused. Brody and the man to his right, Chase Reynolds, had been teammates in a Marine Force Recon unit. Marines were the toughest sons of guns King knew.

He'd never, *ever* tell them that—come on, a SEAL telling a marine he was tough?—but it was probably true. Marines never stopped, and if channeled the right way, the instincts they possessed—by nature or cultivated through training—could be a huge benefit.

King's gaze landed on the dark eyes of Jonah Knight. Those eyes held secrets.

King remembered when he'd first met Knight. Rook had brought him to Port Royal, South Carolina, their base of operations, and sat down in front of King, saying only that they needed him. King had been in the service for nearly fifteen years by that time. He'd joined at the tender age of eighteen and though he thought he was relatively young at thirty-three, he was a seasoned soldier, a vetted leader, and they'd made it clear that's why he'd been sought out.

When Knight had finished speaking, King had agreed. It had escaped none of their notice that all three of them had chess-related monikers.

Endgame was for good, but Knight knew the bad and how to traverse it clandestinely. He was a hard man, the air around him tinged with a bitterness King couldn't place, but he was loyal and King now considered him a friend.

These men and women were King's responsibility. He was their leader, and while each of them held the traits of a leader themselves, King had put this team together after much research. That made them all his. His men and women. The word *family* whispered through his mind again. They'd trained for a year and a half to become a solid unit. Living together, eating together, drinking together, fighting together—they were the epitome of a family.

"Five minutes until touchdown, boys and girls," Vivi informed them.

Even Ella and Nina were Endgame. Nina had remained at base in Port Royal headquarters, doing her thing as information gatherer. She had initially been picked for this operation in Beirut but had fallen ill. Over Jude's protests, King had chosen Ella to go with them.

Ella spoke Lebanese. None of the others did.

"Two minutes until insertion," the pilot relayed.

"What the hell is that?" the copilot asked suddenly.

Ice skittered down King's spine. "What is what?" he asked.

"Bogeys in the air! Repeat, bogeys in the air!" the pilot yelled over the comm links.

King felt more than heard the percussion of anti-aircraft fire hitting the bird. This wasn't supposed to happen. Sure, there was always a chance of discovery, but they'd mined this area for months before preparing to insert here. No one outside their team knew of this op.

The rumble of the rotors rocked King as they shuddered to adjust to the pilot's evasive maneuvers.

He looked at his men, pulled down his helmet, and watched them do the same.

"In, out, protect yourselves. Remember the alternate extraction point," he ordered. "Ella, you're on my six, behind me at all times, you understand?"

She nodded. Jude's eyes narrowed.

"You got something to say, Jude?" King asked harshly.

The other man shook his head and pulled his visor down.

"We're hit! We're hit!"

King went hot, then cold. The bird swayed in the air

and then began a death spiral. He grabbed on to anything he could find and knew his men were doing the same.

"We're going down, Your Highness!"

Chase's voice was loud in King's ear mic. The dying whine of the bird's rotors screamed through his mind.

"Brace for impact!"

The helo fell rapidly, and hell unleashed as they hit the ground. King's world split apart as flames shot to the sky above him. The air scorched as the smell of burning fuel invaded his nostrils. He tried to locate his team, tried to maneuver, but he was held in place by his seat buckle. Smoke writhed around him, covering everything until he was blinded by it. And in the midst of his blindness, the pain made itself known, twisting around his mind until it was almost all he knew. The darkness called him and he fought for precious seconds.

The last thing he heard was Vivi screaming for Rook to answer her, and then there was silence.

Chapter 1

Douala International Airport
Cameroon, Africa

ALLIE FEARED SHE WASN'T GOING TO MAKE HER FLIGHT, and damn but she really needed to be on that plane. She weaved through the throngs of people in the main terminal, dodging hysterically crying children and obstinate old folks, and trying not to knock down anyone else who refused to get the heck out of her way.

"Final call for Air France flight 1701 to Paris, France, boarding now," the gate hostess said in a lilting, accented voice over the intercom.

Allie was flying to Paris and then catching a flight to DC. Home was eighteen hours away if everything connected properly. She pushed her heavy blond hair out of her face, breathed deeply, and smiled at the woman as she handed her the boarding pass. The woman shooed her through. *So close to home.* Exhilaration pumped through Allie's body, a sweet, cooling relief. She pulled her carry-on behind her down the loading ramp. The *tick, tick, splat* of rain on the dock's tin roof reminded her that it was monsoon season in Cameroon. She definitely wouldn't miss the rain. The people were a different story. She'd miss them like crazy. But she'd be back.

She stepped into the plane and nodded at an attendant.

"Welcome aboard, mademoiselle," the flight attendant said with a smile.

She would miss that too—the sound of French and all the beautiful dialectal diversity in this country. But home called and she couldn't wait.

Visions of manicures, pedicures, and McDonald's french fries danced in her head as she practically skipped down the aisle of the 747.

Allie found her seat, lowered the handle of her carry-on, and was beginning to lift it to the overhead compartment when a large, tanned hand covered hers and took the bag.

Shock—that was the word that came to her mind. The man had shocked her, a current running from his hand to hers. Allie shivered.

"Let me help," a deep voice rumbled. The man had been seated in her row next to the window. She'd noticed him at a distance as she walked down the plane's center aisle.

Now, she sighed in relief, grateful for his presence as she allowed her gaze to drift up the man's arm, to his neck, to his...sweet little baby Jesus in a manger... his *face*.

He was quite possibly the hottest man she'd ever seen. She stood there in awe as she took in his mink-brown, wavy hair. Her palms itched to brush it from his eyes. High cheekbones balanced a square jaw darkened by a five-o'clock shadow.

Her gaze lowered, once again noticing the strong column of his neck and the breadth of his chest, the width of his shoulders. She had the irrational urge to raise her hand and request permission to continue staring at him.

Then she slammed right into his gaze, and Allie almost swallowed her tongue. His eyes were the green of an Irish hillside and his lips, curving at her perusal, begged sin. All kinds of hot, sweaty, lick-me-all-over, then-dive-back-in sin. The thought had her stepping back.

His eyes smoldered before he blinked. That single instant of reprieve allowed her to get her shit together—okay, almost together.

"Thanks," she murmured as she quickly sat her behind in the aisle seat of her row. She tried to concentrate on breathing evenly. The sexy bastard had stolen the oxygen from her lungs. Allie wasn't a believer in insta-love, but insta-lust? She'd just become very familiar with that concept.

"We'll be leaving shortly. Please make sure your seat belt is securely fastened and all carry-on luggage is stowed underneath the seat in front of you or in the overhead bins," a flight attendant said over the speaker.

To distract herself from thoughts of Mr. Lick-Me-All-Over, who continued to stand in the aisle beside her, Allie focused on her go-to fantasy—McDonald's french fries. She closed her eyes, imagining the crisp, salty goodness. She took a deep breath, and all thought of french fries disappeared. She smelled evergreens and mint. Her body tightened and she looked up.

"Excuse me," Mr. LMAO said. The acronym had her snorting, to which he raised an eyebrow.

"Um," she stammered. "Yeah?"

"Are you okay here?" he asked in a deep baritone that seriously rearranged pieces inside Allie's abdomen. "If you are, I need to get past you to my seat."

His hand rested on the seat behind her head, and

as she moved so as not to crane her neck, her cheek brushed his hand.

The zing she felt in the pit of her stomach was ferocious. More like a lightning bolt. Similar to the jolt she'd experienced earlier, only way more intense. She really didn't need intense right now. Fries. She needed fries.

"Uh, well, sure?" She was a mess in the face of all that hotness.

He smiled, which was the most beautiful thing she'd ever seen on any man—ever.

"I think what I'm asking," he began and sighed as if he had the patience of Job, "is do you want the aisle or the window?"

She stared up at him, and his brows lowered. Then it hit her. "Oh! Aisle is fine, thanks," she murmured as she started to stand so he could sit down.

His face tightened as if he'd argue, but then he brushed by her to his seat and there it was—the holy grail of backside views. She thought she heard angels singing and somebody yelling, "Hallelujah." Allie shook her head. Her palms itched again, and she rubbed them on her jeans.

She couldn't sit beside him. Not Mr. LMAO, with his minty, evergreen smell and his Irish eyes a-smilin'. No, no, no…

"Mademoiselle?"

She turned to the attendant vying for her attention. Oh, it was a mighty struggle because while Allie was looking at the attendant's lovely face, her mind was all over the finger-lickin' goodness beside her.

"Mademoiselle?" she prompted again.

Earth to Allie. "Yes?"

"Time to buckle up," she said with a shy smile.

Allie sighed. "Geesh. Pull it together already."

"*Pardon*?" the stewardess asked with a raised brow.

"Oh, sorry, not you," Allie hurriedly assured her.

She took her seat and buckled in, but when her arm brushed against his (which was damn near impossible to avoid because the dude was huge), she burned. Allie jerked her arm away and felt more than saw his chest rising and falling.

The jerkface was laughing at her. Okay, that could totally kick this insane lust in the butt. *Please laugh at me some more*.

He didn't, just went stone-cold still. She shivered. The buckle-up sign continued to flash, and the flight attendant began to run through the myriad rules for riding in a plane. Allie drowned it out by thinking of McDonald's fries.

Yeah, the Golden Arches had some thirty thousand locations worldwide, but not one Mickey D's had graced the country where she'd devoted the last three years of service. She was lost to the dream of salty goodness, her eyes closed, so the *rat-a-tat-tat* took her by surprise.

A large hand pushed her head down. "Don't move!" he bit out.

"Hey," she objected, but her comment was directed to her knees. She tried lifting her head, but his grip on the back of her neck was solid.

"We've got trouble. I need you to keep your head down, 'kay?" he whispered in her ear.

Trouble? *Understatement*, she thought. Shots fired were a *bit* more than trouble. Yet still, in the midst of obvious danger, she noticed his warm breath sliding down her neck.

A chill swept through her at another round of *rat-a-tat-tat*, which was definitely automatic weapon fire. Children and adults were screaming, and over it all, a hard voice demanded that everyone sit down.

Gunshots. *Well damn*. All her day needed was gunshots. "All I wanted was a mani-pedi and some hot, salty McDonald's fries," she muttered.

"What?" the man next to her asked.

Then every thought left her brain as a woman screamed. It was a scream Allie had heard too often—*fear*. Her instincts kicked in, and she reached for his hand to remove it from her neck.

"I said to stay down," he urged.

She twisted his hand in a move her father had taught her, and he released her immediately. She'd surprised him with the move. When she lifted her head, her gaze found chaos. At least five men were holding AK-47s and shouting orders to people in heavily accented, broken English interspersed with…*Arabic*? Oh damn. That was so not good.

"Where is the woman?" one of them yelled as he shoved his gun in the face of a flight attendant.

She screamed, and the man lifted his rifle and shot in the air. The bullet punctured the aircraft, the projectile ripping a hole big enough for rain to begin dripping through. They wouldn't be traveling in this plane any time soon.

Another man glanced up and down the rows, searching each one.

"The woman with white hair—where is she?" the

first man shouted in heavily accented English. "I know she is on this plane!"

Babies cried, women sobbed, and still the men shouted orders in Arabic. Boko Haram, Allie thought. It had to be. Her dad had been worried about that particular terrorist group's presence in Cameroon. Each of his communications had asked her to watch out for her safety. She had.

The one she'd identified as the leader pulled up a child by her hair. "You have three seconds, white hair, before I shoot this child between the eyes. Three," he yelled.

"Do not stand up," the man beside her murmured.

She'd managed to forget about him for a second. Allie turned her head and met his gaze. She heard his warning, felt his intent to protect her. Crazy how in the midst of everything *that* stood out.

"Two!" the leader yelled.

"I have no choice. They're looking for 'white hair.' Don't know if you've noticed, but I'm the only white hair on this plane," she whispered a split second before she stood. "I'm here," she called out.

"Don't!" Mr. LMAO said and then followed that with a harsh "Fuck me."

The leader spotted her, and Allie glimpsed evil. His eyes blazed with malevolence. This man was beyond her realm of experience.

"Ah, good. It's the white hair. What is your name?"

"Why do you need my name?"

The leader's eyes went flat, and then he calmly turned to the child's mother and unloaded a single round into the plane beside her head. The child screamed, and the woman grabbed her, pushing past the gunman and Allie as she ran toward the back of the plane. The gunman let her go, then raised his rifle and aimed it directly at Allie. She raised a hand to her mouth to hold back her own scream.

"Allison Redding," she garbled out. "My name is Allison Redding."

His brows lowered as confusion tattooed his face. He didn't like her answer, but as quickly as the confusion appeared, it was gone. "Come to me, Allison Redding," he demanded.

Allie didn't hesitate, something telling her that if she did, the man would make sure the next bullet hit someone. The man searching the rows moved back to the leader and stood there, his threat implicit in the way he held his rifle. Hell, there were at least five of them, maybe more in the cabin ahead. Each of them with really big weapons and intent that colored the air black around them.

She came to the leader, stepping very carefully. "What do you want?" she asked the man who'd turned her world upside down.

"Oh, it's really very simple," he said. He stared at her with a grin that showed perfectly straight, white teeth. It was macabre how white his teeth were in his dark, gaunt face.

She met his gaze and her stomach rebelled. She was going to lose it. *Keep your shit together, Redding.* She waited, fear freezing her feet to the spot and her breath in her lungs.

"I want your head."

Chapter 2

GOD SAVE HIM FROM A STUBBORN WOMAN! KING HAD no idea what the hell she was thinking. He did however have a pretty good clue who had just hijacked their plane. Boko Haram. And wasn't that just another surprise in a long list of them today!

He'd been waiting on this plane for a woman with blond hair, blue eyes, and a mole at the side of her mouth to board. The woman was alleged to be Vasily Savidge's courier. King had been prepared to follow her all the way to France just for the chance of nabbing Savidge.

Apparently, everybody else in Cameroon was looking for the woman too—okay, maybe not everyone, but for sure King and the terrorists now holding AK-47s. What a mess. Just once he wanted a mission to go according to plan. Just fucking once.

Another shot pinged through the top of the plane, and King took a deep breath, pulling air into his lungs as he readied himself. The need to get his hands on Allison Redding pricked his brain, demanding action.

The lead terrorist was still yelling. King peeked around the corner of the seat in front of him and prayed the woman would keep her mouth shut. Yet even as he prayed, he knew it was a useless entreaty. Bravery like she'd just displayed was a commodity in most situations. In this one, not so much. Most people didn't venture into deadly situations like they were invincible. Even though he wondered at her insistence to tread where others feared to follow, she'd damn sure taken his breath when she stood up.

Hell, who was he kidding? She'd stolen a lung from him when he met her gaze moments ago. He'd not known blue that color existed. What'd you call that? Cornflower blue? Sky blue? Kick-me-in-the-nuts blue?

Because that's what she'd done—kicked him straight in the balls with that wide-eyed gaze. Then she'd smiled and junk-punched him again with the curving of her mouth.

He rubbed a hand down his face. The interior of the plane was growing warmer. The pilots had turned the plane completely off. Rain pelted the aircraft outside.

He could feel death stalking. It was everywhere now. Instead of waiting until the plane was in the air to hijack it, they'd done so on the tarmac. What was their goal? Why did they want Savidge's courier?

For that matter, why did King want her? Was she really his lead to Savidge or would this wind up being another dead end? Too many questions, and he had no clue what information she held. By her demeanor, lack of guile, and that damn bravery, she was an innocent. No way was she mixed up in Endgame Ops shit. But all arrows pointed to her—or at least his intel had. She had to be the courier, and if she wasn't, well then, he was doing her a service by saving her ass.

If she was working with Vasily Savidge, Horace Dresden's second-in-command, then King was doing himself and his team a favor.

Another discharge of a weapon, and King peered around the seat again. There was a third hole in the roof of the plane. The woman still faced the leader, legs shaking, shoulders stiff as if prepared for a blow.

Too brave. She'd be the death of him.

Think, King, think. He was weaponless but that in no way made him powerless.

The leader murmured quietly to the woman. The child she'd stepped in front of was weeping softly a few rows up from King.

"Tell me," the leader demanded as he moved within inches of her.

"I don't know," she said with a slight catch in her voice. "My name is Allison Redding."

The sound of a fist meeting flesh, followed by a sharp inhalation, rang in King's ears. His hands fisted. Rage swept in a red wave through his body. *Control.* He couldn't relinquish control. It's what made him the best at what he did.

"Who is your father?" the terrorist demanded.

Unease skated down his spine. What the hell did it matter to these men who her father was?

"White-haired bitch," the leader spat. "Tell me who you really are!"

No more playtime, then, King thought. It was about to go down. He really needed a weapon, and as he glanced around, he decided he'd have to pilfer one. His gaze fell on a small African man huddled against the side of the plane.

King motioned to the man, whose eyes widened. He shook his head furiously.

Time to be a hero, buddy. King peered around the seat again and waited until nobody was looking his way. He slid into the small guy's row and took a deep breath.

"I need you to yell, okay?" King said a split second before he acted like he was about to punch the man in the jaw.

The man let out a startled yelp, the woman in front of them screamed, and then, thank God, one of the men holding a rifle came to investigate.

"What you do here?" he asked brokenly.

"I didn't do anything," King answered in a very low voice. The man leaned down, getting into King's face just enough...

King struck, punching the terrorist in the throat, incapacitating him—okay, *killing* him—silently and without the bastard being able to call for help. He situated the terrorist in the seat between him and the small guy and checked the man's weapon. Empty. Son of a... It was useless. King sat back and waited.

Silence had taken over the back of the plane. He didn't meet anyone's gaze, just kept his eyes straight ahead, cataloging sounds.

"You are American?" the small guy whispered. "You save us?"

King swiveled his head, held up a finger to his lips to signal for silence, and then nodded. The man visibly relaxed. And the leader continued to demand an answer to his question.

Another strike, another sob followed by a moan. Oh, that son of a bitch was going to pay. So hard. The woman, Allison, cried out again. That had King peeking down the aisle. She had turned partially in his direction. The leader held the gun to her head now.

King knew the man wouldn't shoot her. Whatever the bastard wanted couldn't be obtained from a dead woman.

"Turn around, and get on your knees," the leader demanded, roughly shoving her until she did as he demanded.

That left her facing King. He met her gaze, and the rage he'd capped seconds ago threatened to overflow. Her cheek was bruising already. But her eyes, those gorgeous blue orbs that had danced with interest earlier, smoldered with defiance.

He stared at her, and in a move so subtle he doubted what it was, she nodded at him. And there was zero fear in her eyes. Okay, that was different. And certainly not the action of a woman innocent to the ways of subterfuge and warfare.

The leader pressed the gun against the back of her head, and there was the fear. Then it was gone as quickly as it'd come, and her eyes cleared as her jaw clenched.

The bastard pushed the barrel into her skull, and she tumbled forward. He pulled her up roughly by her hair. She winced and hissed in pain.

King needed a bit of a distraction to get things going. She licked her lips as he stared at her. His eyes zeroed in on the bruise forming on her cheek. Something tightened in his gut, vicious and undeniable. *She's hurt.* He pushed the thought aside. Now was the time for action.

"Who is your father?" the leader demanded for what had to be the fifteenth time.

Even King wanted to roll his eyes. Allie actually did. Goddamn it. She was crazy.

"Abdul?" one of the leader's men called out and handed him a phone.

"Yes?" the leader, Abdul, said into the phone. "But he said…"

Silence reigned, and Allison's eyes widened slightly as the leader continued to hold the phone. Her gaze shot up to meet King's. What was she hearing?

Abdul tossed the phone, and it clattered to the floor. King wanted to know who'd been on the other end. Badly.

There was a galley at the back of the plane, which meant there was a door to the outside. If he could herd her back there, she'd be safe.

Adrenaline flooded his system. Her eyes remained on his, even while Abdul grabbed another handful of her hair and yanked her backward.

"Wait!" King yelled as he stood up.

Every rifle in the place turned on him.

"Sit down! Sit down!" one of the terrorists yelled.

She moved then, reaching up and grabbing Abdul's head while she smashed her own against his. Bastard never saw it coming. She'd knocked him out cold. Instead of allowing him to fall back, she pulled him forward, slightly over her shoulder, as she straightened and began making her way to the back of the plane, using his body as a shield. Abdul hadn't been much bigger than she was, but she managed to pull him with ease.

It all went down so quickly that it took the remaining terrorists a moment to figure out what had happened. By that time, King was there, grabbing Abdul's gun and firing in rapid succession, quickly eliminating all targets. He located the phone the terrorist had discarded, scooped it up, and turned to her.

"Get to the galley. There could be more," he said in a low voice.

"Who the hell *are* you?" she asked softly as she stood rooted to the spot for an endless moment.

"Get to the galley at the back and open the door. Do it quickly. Do it *now*."

Children screamed, while grown people shouted as they all clamored to get out of the front of the plane. Panic was in the air, but no more gunshots rang out. If the terrorists had help, they didn't yet know what was going on.

King reached over, pushed Abdul from her grip, and his gaze narrowed again on her cheek. He brushed over the growing mark with his thumb. "He hurt you."

Confusion clouded Allie's face and she cocked her head, staring at him as if she'd never seen anyone quite like him before.

He shook his head, the sight of her big, blue eyes almost undoing him. He motioned her to the back and said simply, "Go."

He reached for the small guy he'd almost clocked as the man tried to pass and said, "Tell them what happened but stay vague about us. Do you understand? Tell them all"—King motioned over the plane's fleeing occupants—"to remain vague about us."

It was unlikely that the two-hundred-odd passengers would keep silent about the blond who'd head-butted the lead terrorist. Or the giant American who dragged her away. Chances were that his and this woman's faces would be all over the local news. But if even a few of the passengers negated the story, that mixed intel might buy them a bit of time.

The guy nodded and King took off. He rounded the corner of the attendants' galley and noticed Allie had the door open. Rain sluiced in, wetting everything in its path. She stuck her head out and peered down, then pulled her head back in, spearing him with her gaze.

"It's a long way down," she said mournfully.

"Drop and roll, darlin'," King responded. "Drop and roll." Then he was out the door, dropping like a stone and rolling once he hit the ground. He pushed to his feet and glanced around. Security was pouring out onto the tarmac, and sirens could be heard in the distance. A luggage transport machine was rounding a corner, and they didn't have much time.

He looked up at her, held out his arms, and yelled, "Jump!"

She didn't hesitate. Good thing she was tiny because she fell right into his arms.

"Thanks," she murmured.

He didn't respond, just put her on her feet, grabbed her hand, and hailed down the luggage cart. He told the man they needed a ride to the terminal. The airport employee didn't even blink — like random Americans came up to him every day asking for a ride in the middle of the pouring rain. He dropped them as far as another plane and told them they had to walk.

Instead of walking, they ran. King moved to an abandoned airport security truck, and they hopped in. He hot-wired the vehicle and had them on the move in under a minute.

"Get down," he ordered.

She did as he directed. There was hope for her yet.

A gunshot punched out the back glass, and King ducked. He could see no one behind them, but obviously someone was back there shooting. He hung a right and took off around the terminal, passing planes and looking for the airport parking lot.

He'd have to ditch this truck and get them out into the city of Douala quickly.

"Who are you?" she asked and then grunted as she was thrown against the door.

King had just broken through a fence barrier to the airport parking lot and managed to shed the fence that tenaciously clung to the bumper. He picked a row of cars and barreled down it.

"King," he replied succinctly.

She snorted. "Okay, now really, who...*oomph*... holy... Could you stop... Son of a..."

He slammed on the brakes. He winced when her head bumped against the glove box. "Sure."

King hurried out of the truck and picked the first car he came to. He didn't need flashy; he needed operational. Flashy had alarms. Operational could go undetected.

Fortunately, the first one he came to fit both bills. A Yugo. It just kept getting better and better. The car was unlocked and he slid in.

"A Yugo?" she asked, standing beside him now. "Seriously?"

"In the car and don't talk," he demanded.

Her brows lowered and her mouth tightened, but she decided to throw in her lot with him. She rounded the car and got in. King lowered the sun visor, and the keys fell into his lap. The Yugo's only saving grace was that he wouldn't have to expend the energy to hot-wire it.

The piece-of-shit car cranked, and King squealed out of the spot, though he slowed down as he approached the exit gate. "Act normal," he said. "And don't look anyone in the face."

Allie didn't say anything, but she didn't have to—the anger pinching her features spoke volumes. He almost, *almost* laughed. They were both soaking wet, but for some reason she looked even more beautiful.

"You laugh at me, and I'll get you back," she said from the corner of her mouth.

Spunk. He hated spunk. Oh, and bravery. He hated that too. "You already have," he responded and enjoyed the way her eyes widened.

Blue, soul-sucking eyes. Her presence was enough of a payback.

"I didn't. But first chance I get—"

King held up a hand. "Yeah, yeah, yeah…whatever. Now be quiet and lower your face."

The woman actually *growled* at him. And it was sexy as hell. The smile that tugged his lips caught him by surprise.

He pulled up to the exit gate and grabbed the stub someone had hung on the Yugo's rearview mirror. He'd done the owner a favor by stealing this tin can. He lowered the window and handed the attendant the stub.

"Fifty francs," the woman said and held out her hand.

The car wasn't even worth that amount, but King calmly took out a twenty-dollar American bill, which was about two hundred times the amount due, and paid her, telling her to keep the change. Then he rolled up the window, saw the flashing lights in the mirror, and even more calmly pulled out of the lot.

He turned onto the main thoroughfare and began heading out of the city.

"Can I raise my head now, Your Majesty?"

Oh, she was a viper-tongued bit of sexiness. "No,"

he said just to be contrary. Something inside him really liked it when she was riled.

"Soooo going to get back at you when we stop," she huffed.

He grunted.

They drove an hour, and he was grateful she didn't ask questions. Eventually, she sat up straight and leaned her head against the headrest. She didn't look at him once. During that hour, he made plans, checked their six while driving all over Douala, and came to the conclusion the little Peace Corps volunteer from Virginia wasn't who he'd been told she was.

Information carrier, my ass. But King could not shake the sense that she'd been trained. Her calmness in the middle of the plane fiasco had sent his thoughts on that path. Her ability to take on that terrorist drove his theory completely home.

When the mission in Beirut had gone to hell, he'd not listened to his instincts. It had cost him three operatives. Nine had gone in; six had come home. It had been a miracle they'd all survived the crash, but he could still hear the gunshots that had taken Samson, Madoc, and then Ella to the afterlife. The helo crashing had been the least of their worries. Dresden and Savidge had been waiting for them.

King had regrets, but not listening to his own instincts that day was one of the greatest. And it had all led him here—to this woman.

Beirut had only been the opening sortie. Yes, Horace Dresden had been a target for Endgame, but he'd been much more. In the year since the debacle outside Beirut, Endgame had discovered Dresden was a tool for the entity looking to take down Endgame Ops, using whatever means necessary. King was determined to find and eliminate Dresden, Savidge, and that entity, no matter what the cost.

King pushed the past deep. Douala proper was fading in his rearview. They were close to their destination, but he'd have to take it slow getting there and then check it out before he took her in. This was an alternative safe house that only the current members of Endgame knew about. Still, he would be here an hour tops before they moved again. Nothing was truly safe anymore, and he wasn't the only one after her. There was no telling who was on their trail now. He pulled onto the side of the road so they could rest and allow a little time to pass. He needed to scout the safe house and determine whether it remained that way before he took her inside anyway.

He turned to her. "Who are you?" he asked.

She looked up at him, and there was it was again—that feeling she'd stolen something from him. His hands clenched as he fought the urge to rub the area of his chest where his heart was.

"Allison Redding," she replied. "My friends call me Allie."

He winced and shook his head. "Who. Are. You?"

"Who are you?" she queried, with a tilt of her head and a stubborn look in her eye.

"I told you…King."

"That's your name? *King*? Who has a name like King?"

He glanced at her, then back out the windshield, all while remaining dead silent.

"That's all you're going to give me?" she asked. "Huh, imagine that. Look, if you don't give me information, then I'm left to assume. And you know what they say about assuming…"

He remained silent. She sounded a bit desperate, and if he were to *assume* she was an innocent and not Savidge's courier, that was normal for what she'd just been through.

"Okay, you must want to know what I'm assuming. Here it is. I'm guessing your real name was horrible—oh, I don't know, something like Herman or Leslie or Gaylord—and little boys beat you up on the playground. You thought, *I'll go for a different name, please*. Something strong and manly, so you started calling yourself King."

"What's wrong with Gaylord?"

She raised an eyebrow. "I don't like…" she began.

He grinned, and then his smile disappeared. It didn't matter what she didn't like. He had a feeling that once she started, everything would all go downhill. He needed her to take a breath and be quiet.

"Come here," he urged, breaking into her brewing diatribe.

She leaned closer automatically. He smiled again, and damn if it wasn't the weirdest friggin' thing. He'd smiled more in the two hours since he'd laid eyes on her than he had in thirty-five years.

"I'm here," she said as if she couldn't quite believe she'd obeyed him.

And then he did what was needed. What the drumbeat of his heart was demanding. What any sane, though no less desperate man in his situation would have done.

He kissed her.

Chapter 3

As fine as he looked, the feel of his lips on her and the demand of his tongue sweeping into her mouth eclipsed that. It rendered her mute, maybe blind, possibly deaf.

Damn, he might be better than McDonald's french fries.

Allie sighed into his mouth. Oh yeah, she was pretty much feeling all the tingles right now. She recognized the wet silk of his hair under her palms. *How'd my hands get there?* He licked along the inside of her bottom lip, and she hissed. *Please let his tongue do that again.* He kissed like it was his mission to consume her, to devour every lustful dream she'd ever had and give them back to her, making them reality.

He took her over. Her mind blanked but for the smell of minty evergreen and the heat of his mouth. Over and over he plunged into her, his tongue gentle and then intent, stroking and then licking. He sipped at her lips, and she felt the sting of his hand tangling in her damp hair. Even that small bite of pain was welcome.

He was all around her, and the car wasn't big enough to hold the case she'd managed to develop for this man who called himself King. She should be put out at his daring. She should be confused at her own response. She was neither.

Yeah, she was screwed. Or maybe she'd just begun wishing she was.

King was there at her lips one second, and the next he was gone. Literally, out of the car like a shot, and all she could do was gape as he disappeared into the deluge that fell from the sky.

She leaned her head against the headrest and cursed herself. The rain seemed pretty determined to wash away everything in its path, and as she peered through the windshield, she wondered who the hell he was.

Because he damn sure knew how to shoot and evade. He had soldier written all over him, from the bottom of his Wellco combat boots to the hard glint in those amazing green eyes. His hands were big, strong, and callused. His breathing never changed, and his gaze never stopped roaming over his surroundings. He may not be dressed in camo, but Allie wasn't a fool. That preternatural stillness and the cloak of wariness that rode the lines of his body were dead giveaways.

She'd been raised around his kind her entire life. Had been taught a thing or two by some of them. King had military, more specifically black ops, oozing from his pores.

A big, dark shape appeared through the rain and he was there, opening the door and getting back in. The interior of the car was freezing. Maybe she was in shock.

"It's clear," he said and tossed her a veiled look.

She looked back at him solemnly. "I have no idea who you are or what is 'clear.'"

As she voiced her concern, a realization hit her in the solar plexus: She could be in even more danger with him than she'd been with the hijackers. Her dad would be disappointed. She should've throat-punched him the moment he kissed her.

Or, at the very least, immediately after. Because it'd been a hell of a kiss for sure.

King took a deep breath and put the car in gear. Ten minutes later, they were pulling onto a dirt road that led to a small clapboard dwelling. He stepped out of the car. She looked around, considered her options, and followed.

Between the car and the door, her clothes were soaked again.

He walked in first, pulled her in behind him, and left her there, heading to the back of the tiny house. She stood there, trembling, until he returned, bare-chested and offering her a towel. She took it and watched as he placed a bag on a small end table, then tugged on a black T-shirt. He pulled three different wicked-looking handguns out of the bag, chambering a round in each before he placed them carefully on the table. Her skin prickled as she watched him strap on a holster for each firearm, one at his back, one at his left side, and one at his ankle, before placing the firearms securely within them. He became a walking commando between one blink and the next.

He glanced at her and cocked an eyebrow. Allie swallowed her retort and used the towel to dry her hair before wrapping it around her head. Then she stood there shivering again. "Is there any heat?"

His gaze was a tactile stroke over her skin. Her nipples tightened and her core clenched. Her body was out of control.

"Seriously, I'm cold," she said plaintively.

He walked to her then, and oh good God in heaven... *his chest*. She held up a hand to ward him off, going so far as to take a step backward. She met the door and knew she'd lose the fight if he came closer to her with… with that…with that *chest*… Even covered in cotton, it was dangerous to her sanity.

He continued to advance, his face a tight mask giving her no indication of his thoughts.

"Thank you for putting another shirt on." She practically wheezed as she tried to pull oxygen into her lungs.

He smiled and her knees buckled. She would have hit the floor but there he was, pressing that broad expanse of tanned, smooth, now cotton-covered chest against her body. She was pinned to the door by his frame, and then he was pulling at her shirt, yanking it over her head, leaving her in nothing more than a soaking-wet bra.

King wrapped her arms around his torso, pushed her head to his chest, and stood there. It took seconds for his heat to begin soaking through her skin, warming places she'd never realized could be warmed and making her ache for all the things she'd never had. He smelled like everything a man was supposed to smell like.

"Shouldn't kiss again," she mumbled inanely into his breastbone.

His chest rose and fell repeatedly, but his hands tightened on her back. If she didn't know better, she'd say they were caressing the bare skin there. When she realized hers were doing the same thing to his back, she dropped them.

"We don't have much time, and this is the best way to warm you," he replied finally. "There're clean T-shirts in the other room, but I don't want you going into shock right now, and the rain doesn't help."

"We shouldn't kiss again," she repeated. It was her

mission in life to make sure he absolutely did not steal her mind with kisses anymore.

"You want me to agree to that?" he asked, but there was a hint of humor in his voice.

She nodded.

He lifted her chin with his forefinger. His gaze was intense, almost as if he were trying to ferret out all her secrets and leave no part of her untouched. "Well, I'm all about honesty, and I can honestly say that I cannot agree not to kiss you again, Allison 'My Friends All Call Me Allie' Redding."

She bit her lip but couldn't contain her smile. "Well, why not?"

The inside of the house was dark, and the rain outside afforded little light. His face was thrown in relief by shadows, but his eyes glittered dangerously.

"Because of this," he said a second before he dove back into her.

His tongue twined with hers, and eventually his kiss moved to her neck, her collarbone, and back up again. Good God, he actually licked the tiny mole at the side of her mouth. And boy did she like that. This was beyond madness. Beyond anything she'd ever experienced. Then he lifted his head and stepped away.

Her harsh breathing was the only thing she could hear. King stepped out of the room. It should have been a blow to her ego—that he could walk away from that so easily, and she was left a hot mess. But something about the tense line of his shoulders told her he was as affected as she was.

He returned again and handed her a T-shirt similar to his. She pulled it over her head and wished fleetingly for a pair of dry pants.

"There're no pants that will fit you, sorry," he said, clearly reading her face even in the low light.

She'd never had much of a poker face. She shrugged and headed to the room's only chair, falling into it and holding her head in her hands.

"I need to know who you are," he said from across the room.

She pulled the towel off her head and began finger-combing her hair. She sighed. Loudly. "We're back at this again?"

"Yes."

She'd known him two hours, and already she recognized that as his implacable, we-ain't-moving-'til-you-answer-me tone.

She rubbed her forehead and glanced at him. "I know we met under crazy circumstances, and I appreciate you getting me off that plane and everything—because come on, *terrorists*—but I'm not going to give you my entire life story. I mean, how can I trust you? Your name is King, for cripe's sake."

"What does my *name* have to do with anything?"

"See, it's not really your name, though I know I gave you a hard time about it." She smiled, attempting to placate him. "Sorry about that, by the way. But it's not really your name. It's what's behind it." She gestured to him. "It's you."

He raised an eyebrow and crossed his arms over his chest. "Me?"

"Yeah," she said around a sigh. "You." When he crossed his arms like that, it made her happy places stand up and want inappropriate things. Dirty things. Delightful things. With him.

"I'm not sure what you mean, and I feel like I'm pulling teeth."

"Welcome to my world. Until you tell me who *you* are and how *you* just happened to be on my flight — you know, the one that was hijacked by Boko Haram terrorists — I'm not going to give you another tidbit of information. Not a single word." She dropped the towel in her lap and crossed her arms over her chest, mimicking his action.

"They were looking for you. You're lucky I was there."

She shook her head. They had obviously been looking for her, which wasn't good in any way. Didn't mean she was going softly into that good night. "Not giving up anything until you do," she reminded him.

He stilled, as if gathering himself, and she felt more than saw the change in him. *Death*. It whispered in the space between them. She'd only seen one other person go that still — her father.

"You're a spook?" she asked and then clamped a hand over her mouth. She'd thought he was black ops, but maybe it was even worse.

He cocked his head, the tension dissipating with that single action. "No. But I'd be curious to know why that was your first thought, Ms. Redding."

She just shook her head at him.

He held up a hand. "My name is King McNally."

She tried not to let her jaw drop. It did anyway. "Your name is really King?"

He rolled his eyes and then smiled. Butterflies took flight in her stomach. Craziness.

"And?"

His brows lowered, and the smile was gone before

she'd had time to appreciate it properly. "What do you mean 'and'?"

"Why were you on the plane?"

He sighed and she wanted to smile. "Looking for someone."

"And?"

"They have information I need." He dropped that bomb but didn't say anything else.

"You think I'm this person?"

He gave her a curt nod.

"*You* think *I* have information? Why would I have information for you? I hadn't even laid eyes on you until about"—she glanced at her watch—"yep, two hours ago."

Anger flushed his cheeks. She knew it was anger because it tainted the air, malevolent and aimed right at her. "Don't screw with me. You carry information back and forth for your handler."

Her bones froze. "My handler?"

"What is up with repeating every word I say?"

She couldn't get past his "handler" comment. "I don't have a handler. I don't carry information. I'm not a courier. I volunteer for the Peace Corps. So whoever told you I carry information is dead wrong, Mr. McNally."

"I don't believe you, Ms. Redding. I saw you on that plane—watched you head-butt a man out cold and just keep moving. You kept your cool. You're trained."

"What you saw was luck. My daddy taught me a thing or two about taking care of myself. Besides, it got us off that plane. Now, I think it might be time for us to part ways," she said as she stood.

He was in her face in a flash. "You aren't going

anywhere until you tell me who you are and why the terrorists on that plane wanted you."

Fear trilled through Allie, as potent as the lust she'd experienced under his kiss. This man was hard, unrelenting. He was beyond her experience and, quite frankly, more than she'd ever wanted to handle. He had her lady parts and her brain at war.

Amazing kisser notwithstanding, he had just been crossed off her list. Allie had no idea why Boko Haram was looking for her, and she wasn't sticking around to find out. Frankly, it made her heart seize even to contemplate the reasons. As for her identity, this man was better off not knowing who she was. Ever.

"Maybe whoever gave you the information that I was a courier talked to them too? It's a small world in Spookville. Perhaps you should talk with your source," she told him.

"I'm not a damn spook," he replied.

"You know what? You don't scare me. Lose the macho, mean routine, okay? Didn't your mama ever teach you that you can catch more flies with honey?"

"My mama died shortly after I entered the world."

His eyes widened, and she wondered if maybe he couldn't believe he'd actually given her information.

"Well, um...damn... That's rough. God, I'm sorry—"

King held up a hand to cut her off. "Appreciate it."

His tone indicated it wasn't exactly an open wound. Allie nodded. "Just so you know, for the length of our acquaintance, I promise not to make any 'yo mama' jokes."

He made a sound halfway between a choke and a laugh. "I appreciate that too. Let's get back on track, shall we? Who. Are. You?"

"I'm quickly becoming real close with my feelings of frustration. Do you have that effect on a lot of people, Mr. McNally? I told you… I'm Allison Redding. Now, are we finished here?" At his silence, she tried to step around him. "Good. Excuse me."

He grabbed her arm but his touch, while limiting, was gentle and nonthreatening. His warmth seeped into her skin. It was…amazing. She closed her eyes and counted to ten.

"I—" he began before a shrill ring sounded. He reached for his pocket, though he maintained his hold on her.

Her skin burned where he touched it. She wanted him to let go. She might kiss him again, put him back on the list, if he kept touching her—and that was a big no-no.

King raised the phone to his ear. "Yeah?"

His gaze went flat, and the heavily accented voice on the other end sounded pissed.

"I've got her," King said, and there was that whisper of death again. An interminable minute passed and then, "You want her, huh?"

His gaze pinned her, hemming her into his world as surely as a chain-link fence with rolled barbed wire at the top. She wasn't built for this. She just wanted to go home. Mani. Pedi. French fries.

"I'll kill you, Kadar, and let the buzzards pick the flesh from your bones. You make a play. You go ahead and come after her. She's mine now. And I'll be waiting." King disconnected, removed the battery, and placed both back in his pocket.

Long moments passed while he continued to hold her arm but said nothing. He simply stared at her, and she stared back.

He knew. He knew the truth. There wasn't a hint on his face, nothing in the way he held her arm in the loose circle of his fingers. The knowledge was intangible, but she recognized the certainty of it.

"This changes things." His voice was deep. Dark.

She had to get away from him. If he'd been misled into thinking she was some sort of courier, she was on somebody's radar, and that wasn't good. Being with this man could possibly be worse than if Boko Haram had managed to steal her off the plane.

Deny, deny, deny. Her father's words rang in her ears before sinking like lead to the pit of her stomach. *Nowhere is safe. Nobody is trustworthy.*

Even as she heard her father, she knew she was caught.

"It changes nothing," she replied in a whisper.

"You should have told me."

She shook her head. "I'm a weight. Let me go. I can get myself out of Cameroon. Whatever you're involved in, soldier, you don't want any of what I'm bringing to the table."

He remained a rock in front of her. His face was as blank as his tone. "So just let you go it alone?"

"I imagine if you like breathing, that's probably your best bet."

He stepped closer to her, and her eyes nearly crossed at his heat. "Are you threatening me?"

Her gaze lowered to his lips. *French fries, french fries, french fries…lips. Damn. Back on the list.* She licked her own suddenly, desperate for his taste. "No," she said softly. "Not threatening. Making a statement though."

"I enjoy breathing, but I've never been one to let a lady in distress stay in distress. It's your lucky day, princess. I'm gonna get you to your daddy," he said softly as he traced the lip she'd just licked.

"I'm not in distress," she returned when his hand dropped. "And I don't need to get to my daddy."

"You aren't in distress *yet*. But I'm sure it's coming. I hate to keep bringing this up, but I wasn't the only one after your ass."

She cocked her head and refused to look away. "My ass can get itself home, Mr. McNally. I was doing fine before I met you, and I'm sure I'll be fine once you're gone."

His green eyes burned. "But that's the beauty of this, don't you see?"

She shook her head, sadly afraid that she most assuredly did not see.

"I was looking for a courier, and I found you."

Confusion beat a swift path through her mind. "I'm not what you wanted."

He nodded. "See, now that couldn't be further from the truth. Maybe not a courier, but something even better. You're the director of the CIA's daughter. And that makes you, Allie Redding née Broemig, the goddamn mother lode."

Chapter 4

KING ROLLED HIS SHOULDERS, CLENCHED HIS FISTS, and prayed the woman would remain silent. Since he'd told her that he knew who she was, she'd been dead quiet. He didn't know if that pissed him off or made him deliriously happy. He did know that if she licked her bottom lip one more time, he was going in for another round with the delectable Allie Redding. And that made him nervous.

She squeezed her eyes closed and then opened them, the blue of her irises bright in the falling darkness. "You think you know, but..."

He cocked his head, listening for any noise that would tell him more than that the rain was keeping them company. His head pounding, he rubbed his neck. Fareed Kadar was coming. He was a high-level operative within Boko Haram, so his involvement meant nothing good was headed their way. The terrorist group had direct ties to Dresden's organization, and King could feel the man's intent bearing down on them. There were now multiple players in a brand-new game King hadn't even realized he was playing.

Endgame Ops, Boko Haram, Horace Dresden, and now the CIA. Someone had put Allie Redding in the mix. Did she have a direct link to Dresden or his right-hand man, Vasily Savidge? The possibility settled in King's gut like a rock. He found himself hoping she didn't before he shied away from the thought. He didn't know her from Adam—didn't know her history or her present agenda.

So basically he could put all his hope in one hand and shit in the other because they'd probably be worth the same thing. This was such a clusterfuck. He'd been looking for an information carrier and was now stuck with the head of the CIA's daughter. It was looking more and more like he was either responsible for getting her to safety or… Yeah, there was another way he could use her presence.

He couldn't muster up any enthusiasm. None. Normally, people with connections like hers could be used as a bargaining tool. Not this time. He rejected the prospect before it could germinate. The CIA couldn't be trusted. They'd settled themselves into the middle of Endgame business and then proven unreliable on the Beirut op. There was a single CIA affiliate he could trust—Rook, or more specifically, Rook's wife, Vivi. Rook and Vivi were supposed to be in the Ukraine working a lead on Dresden. He'd have to tap them for information later.

King was looking for answers, a lead of his own, and not more problems. Sure as Hell was hot, Allie represented more problems. She sighed deeply, sounding all sorts of put out, which had a grin pulling at the corner of his mouth.

What was that about anyway? King never smiled. There was nothing funny about his life—not one thing.

"What are you carrying for your dad?" he asked into the silence. Maybe Director Broemig had a link to Savidge or Dresden. There was no way to know how high the treachery responsible for the death of King's team members reached. The Piper had told him people in the White House could be involved, so it was a short leap to believe the CIA was as well. Allie's dad was known for manipulating the entire world to suit his agendas.

King was searching for any way possible to clear her of being associated with Dresden's operations. When he noticed what he was doing, he frowned.

She lowered herself to the floor, sitting with her chin on her knees, her gaze pensive and drilling into the wall behind King. "I'm not a courier. You're insane if you think the leader of the largest, most efficient spy agency in the world would use his *daughter* to carry information."

Her lips twisted, and the action was mirrored in his gut.

He let a mirthless laugh escape. "You must be basing that hypothesis off the supposition that spooks have a moral compass. I know from experience they don't. They'll give up their mother, their firstborn... Hell, they'll shoot an innocent dog without blinking an eye if it gets them to their goal. Something I've learned the hard way, but learn it I have."

Her eyes widened, and for a split second, King wondered if she really was a simple Peace Corps volunteer, spreading do-gooder cheer all over the world. Then her gaze blanked, her lips flattened into a hard line, and she chuckled, the sound echoing in the room. Moments before, he'd strained to hear anything, but now the sound of her low laugh was strident.

The rain had lulled. It always rained in this fucking country. He hated the rain.

"I'm gonna kick my own ass for asking, but what's so funny?"

"You used the words *hypothesis* and *supposition*," she said with another deprecating chuckle.

"So?"

"I thought those words might be above your pay grade."

With *her* words, the reality came sliding home again. Her father was the director of Spookville. She could be anyone and no one at all.

King went to his haunches in front of her, his body coiled and ready to strike. Several long moments passed until finally she glanced up, meeting his gaze and even tipping her chin up defiantly.

"You have no idea, Allie," he murmured.

"Okay, I'll bite. I have no idea about what, *King*?"

He smiled. "I'm sure there was an insult in there somewhere, but, darlin,' there's something you need to understand pretty damn quick… I *am* the pay grade. And now you're stuck with me. Give me your satellite phone."

Her pupils widened and her breathing stopped. If she was a spook, she sucked at it. She might be able to hold her own, but subterfuge seemed beyond her. Oh, except that she'd managed to hide her identity from damn near everyone except the people who'd set Boko Haram terrorists on her ass.

"I-I-I don't—"

He stood abruptly and stared down at her.

She grimaced, rooted in the side pocket of her cargoes, and slapped the phone in his outstretched hand. He had to fight again to hide his smile at the hesitation pouring from her. He took the back cover off, pulled out the tracking device located in the bowels of the phone, and put the cover back in place.

He handed the phone back, taking a quick look at her

face. She stuffed it back where it came from. He shifted, dropped the tracking beacon, and stomped on it.

"Let's move," he said.

"Move? Move where?"

He turned and stared down at her lifted face. The heart-shaped contours were silky smooth. The bruise coloring her right cheek made his abdomen clench. He'd felt the slope of her cheek, tasted the curves of her lips, and wanted to again. For some reason, that made the anger rise once more—virulent and stifling.

This woman could take his much-touted control and demolish it. The cost of having to drag her along was one he didn't want to pay.

"This," he said as he nudged the broken pieces of the tracker in her direction, "was a tracker embedded in your phone."

She looked up at him, confusion lowering her brows and darkening her gaze. She bit the inside of her lip, the rounded curve disappearing for a moment.

King almost groaned. Instead, he shifted his body away from her while keeping his gaze locked on her upturned face. He took a deep breath as he fought the panic threatening to take him over. Having men and women under his command who knew the score and had been trained for evasive maneuvers was one thing; dealing with an innocent in a situation like this was another.

Allie hadn't even disabled the tracking beacon on the phone, which meant that whoever knew about her had been able to track her position with ease. Hell, she hadn't even realized there was a beacon on the thing. She was definitely no spook.

And he was now responsible for the beautiful woman with the kick-me-in-the-nuts eyes.

"What that means, princess, is that whoever gave you the phone has the ability to track your whereabouts."

Still, knowledge was slow to dawn.

He sighed. "How the hell do you think Boko Haram found you?"

She shrugged her delicate shoulders, which pressed her rounded breasts against the T-shirt he'd given her. The hardened tips mocked him. King cursed.

"Goddamn it, Allie, if your father could track you, so could anyone else who has the ability to hack into a computer system. Don't you realize that nothing—hell, nowhere—is truly safe anymore?"

"You're guessing with no facts. Nobody even knows I'm his daughter—" She clapped a hand over her mouth and closed her eyes.

He heard her words, but the sound of a vehicle pulling up the road in front of the house drew his attention from her to the outside.

"Expecting company?" she asked.

Her tone was hopeful, but the tremble at the end told King she realized they were being hunted now.

"Not this fast. But then I verified you had a sat phone embedded with a tracker and, well, company arriving sooner than anticipated became pretty fuckin' inevitable," he said as he moved to the front room and looked out the window.

A single shot broke through the small, foggy glass insert in the door, hitting the wall behind him with a solid thud. Glass cut his cheek, the sting small and inconsequential. "Get down!" he yelled.

He pulled his Kimber pistol from his waistband and took aim. At least six men were pouring from the back of a Land Rover near the gate at the front of the house. Two more got out of the front. King aimed and fired off four shots, taking out the four lead men.

One man dove behind the Rover but continued to pepper the house with shots. Another tracked to the back of the small house. King waited, patience his only claim to virtue, and was able to pick off one more before a muffled scream from the other room had him turning and diving through the doorway. He rolled and came to his feet, weapon trained on the area where Allie had been sitting.

What met his eyes had his blood freezing.

"Kadar says if you give us the woman, we are to let you go," said the man holding Allie by the hair and pressing a snub-nosed revolver to her temple. "He no want Endgame problems."

King lowered his weapon as he stood casually and circled to the other side of the room. This put ten feet between him and the man holding Allie. He didn't look at her face, too afraid her fear, or her bravery, would sway his focus. He needed his control right now. "How about this," he began. "How about you go back and tell Kadar he can shove his offer up his ass, and that because you let her stay with me, I let you live."

Sweat poured down the other man's face, and his smell could have knocked a horse down at fifty paces. His eyes were big and round, dominating a painfully thin face. His hands shook like a junkie needing a fix. None of that was good. The man wouldn't kill her on purpose, but by accident would leave her no less dead.

The grip he had on her arm had to be painful. King made a mental note to make him suffer for the bruises he was surely leaving on her skin. The men at the Rover must've realized King's attention was divided and were about to break through the door, so his wish would go ungranted. Sadly, this would be a quick kill.

"I go back without her, I'm dead anyway," the man stammered.

King nodded his head. "I thought you'd say that," he murmured.

His gaze narrowed to the spot between the man's eyebrows. One breath, and he tracked the drop of sweat from the man's hairline down his cheek. Two breaths, and King let his weapon become an extension of his hand.

Between his third breath and the next, he raised his hand and took a single shot.

The man fell back, dead instantly. Allie fell forward to her knees, grunted, and pushed up immediately before reaching for the dead man's weapon.

"How many rounds?" King asked as he pulled his backup weapon from his boot.

"It's not loaded," she replied mournfully, glancing at him, alarm riding her gaze.

"What the hell is up with these dudes?" He handed her his backup Kimber. "You know how to use this?"

She nodded, the motion jerky. His heart beat slow and hard as the urge to comfort her nearly overrode his need to protect her. This woman was dangerous—so very dangerous to his well-being.

"Good. There's a single room in the back. Get there now. You meet anybody on the way, use that." He glanced at her, adrenaline flooding his body, making his hearing and his sight sharper. Someone kicked repeatedly at the front door. They'd tried shooting the lock, but it was reinforced and hadn't broken under repeated attempts.

She didn't move.

"Now, Allie. You wanna live, right? Get to the room," King demanded, and something in his tone must have gotten through because she took off.

The door was about to give, leaving him a second to thank whoever was watching over them that Allie had vacated the room. King breathed through his bloodlust and rage. How dare they touch her? How dare anyone try to take her? His emotions were amped up by combat, but in the back of his mind, he acknowledged she'd gotten into a place inside him he'd never known existed. And she'd done it pretty fast.

The door finally crashed in and King fired a shot, felling the man where he stood. He turned and glanced down the hallway before he stepped back into the main room. There'd been eight men total. Seven were dead, and one remained unaccounted for. More were heading their way, he was sure.

He waited, allowing a smile to curve his lips when he heard heavy breaths and footsteps from the direction of the kitchen area. One more shot, one more kill, and King was moving.

He took the same path to the back room that Allie had. Once he entered, he locked and bolted the steel-reinforced door, closing them in and ensuring them an opportunity to get away.

Each Endgame Ops safe house had a war room. Filled with untraceable weaponry and electronics, the room was safeguarded by a retinal scanner and came with a getaway tunnel and a self-destruct mechanism.

"I hear another vehicle coming down the road," Allie whispered.

"Damn it," he ground out. *He* should have heard it.

King placed his eye at the scanner as his mind moved at Mach 1, concocting scenarios for escape and then discarding them just as quickly. He'd have to kill the men pulling up, blow this house to smithereens, and then haul ass out of this death zone. They'd have at least two miles to travel on foot before they could reach the backup vehicle he'd stowed two weeks ago.

In the game of war, nothing was ever fail-safe. He'd trained his men to plan for every eventuality. King had set this operation up himself. They'd received intel eight months ago that Savidge had a courier based in Cameroon. If King had found the courier, he and the courier would already be in that backup vehicle, heading toward the seaside resort port of Kribi.

Once the scan registered, another room opened up, and King turned to Allie. "Anybody comes in here, shoot to kill. Give me two minutes to gather everything we need, and then we'll head out."

"They can get in?"

He kept his gaze forward. If he looked at her, he'd feel the need to comfort her, and they didn't have time for that. "That's a steel-reinforced door, and these windows are bulletproof. But you should always be ready for anything. I've seen you knock a dude out with your head, and I watched you cock that gun like a pro. I think you've got this."

When she didn't respond, he entered the war room,

walking to the far wall. He lifted a shelf that turned over before collapsing into the wall and presenting a control pad. A moment later, a small door in the floor rolled back, revealing an abandoned irrigation tunnel. Dust filtered into the war room as King fit rounds of firepower into a knapsack. He'd been a sniper by trade as a SEAL. It had been mandatory that every Endgame Ops safe house have his preferred sniper weapon of choice, the M110 SASS with AN/PVS-10 Sniper Night Sight. His SEAL teammates had always teased him for using an army-preferred weapon, but those rifles killed really well.

And at the end of the day, that's what a sniper needed. A killer weapon.

He found the single M110 and broke it down, stuffing the parts into a different knapsack before strapping both packs to his back. He pulled another bag from a compartment and loaded it with protein bars, a first-aid kit, two changes of clothes, and rounds for the SIG Sauer P226 he was about to give her. It was a 9mm with a little less recoil than his Kimber and something she should be able to handle effectively.

"Get in here," he said.

He smelled her before he saw her from the corner of his eye. He closed his eyes and inhaled. Wildflowers— the scent reminded him of the field behind the trailer where he'd grown up. King shook his head, silently berating himself before he pulled out a headlamp and dropped to the floor beside the hole. He leaned over and shone the light into the opening, searching for any signs of occupation or recent activity and finding nothing but spiderwebs and dirt. The tunnel had been built with the original structure years ago. The idea had been to fill the tunnel with water so the surrounding groves would have water in the dry seasons. Endgame had taken advantage of the existing tunnel and created an escape route by blocking the exterior water access. They had also shored up the tunnel with wood planks.

King stood, grabbed the backpack, and held it out for her. "Strap this on."

She didn't hesitate, but she was trembling. He couldn't stand the thought of her fear.

"They're coming, but it will take an act of God or some serious luck for them to get in before we're long gone," he said calmly.

She glanced up, her gaze skewering him to the spot. Damn, what she did to him with those eyes.

"See that?" He pointed to the hole in the floor.

She nodded.

"That's how we're leaving."

"Of course it is," she mused as she glanced down. "A dark hole in the ground with creepy, crawly animals and—" She looked up at him again. "Who *are* you?"

A loud bang sounded from beyond the door, and adrenaline pounded through his bloodstream. He took his backup piece from her, strapped it in his thigh holster, and handed her the SIG.

"No time for chitchat. Safety's on. Put this in your waistband. I need you to get down that ladder and move to the side," he ordered.

She stood there, staring at him, lip trembling and calling to everything protective inside him. He did not need this. Not right now. Hell, not ever.

Another *bang* rocked the small house, followed by the sound of something large battering the door.

"Need to move now, Allie. We gotta get gone," he informed her as he bolted the door to the war room and set the timer on the explosives under the floors of every room in the house.

"What's that?" she asked.

"No time. Get in the hole."

Finally, thank Christ, she started down the ladder.

"There're spiders and...*stuff* down here."

"Stop being a baby and move, woman!"

She cursed—a really raunchy one that had his lips tugging up. He set his watch, pulled his headlamp down, sealed the trapdoor, and started after her.

"We have about two minutes before this entire tunnel is blown to hell and back. A hundred meters in front of us is a steel door. We need to be beyond that point before everything goes bang."

He grabbed her hand and pulled her with him. She kept up, and he was grateful she did when his watch beeped. They had ten seconds to get beyond the door that was finally in sight. "Move your ass, Allie," he urged.

He tugged her through the small doorway, pushed her to continue running, and bolted the steel door.

The concussion of the bomb exploding knocked King off his feet. He heard her coughing as dust flew. Clumps of dirt fell between the wooden beams above them, and smoke poured in past the door. "Run!"

In the light from his lamp, he saw her get to her feet and take off like a rocket. They had another hundred meters to go. He overtook her, once again grabbing her hand and pulling her behind him. She didn't fall, didn't falter, and basically held her own until he came to a set of wooden steps.

King handed her the rucksack and shrugged off his backpack as he took his Kimber from his waistband. "Stay here," he told her as he started up the steps.

The door opened into a plantain grove, but there was no telling how much cover they'd have once they exited. Water leaked from the slats of the door above them, forming puddles over the dirt floor. Some drops clung to the thick mat of webs hanging in the corners. In the light of his headlamp, they reminded King of shiny diamonds. He flicked off the light, not wanting any hint of their presence to disturb the field above them. Darkness fell like a hot, smothering blanket.

He hoped the men following them wouldn't see them fleeing. Maybe he'd get lucky and they'd be too busy dealing with the aftermath of the explosion. It wouldn't stop the bastards, but it'd sure as hell slow them down.

He stopped and turned to her. "You ready?"

He couldn't see her in the darkness, but knew she nodded. There was that scent again—wildflowers and some indefinable essence that King recognized was all Allie. He licked his lips, her taste a memory there but also a growing need in his blood.

"Cat got your tongue?"

She made a choking sound, and he didn't know if she was laughing or crying.

"Better let him keep it," he mused.

He continued up the stairs, made it to the top, and started to push open the door, but her voice stopped him. "Why's that?" she asked, and her husky tone made his knees weak.

"Why's what?"

"Better let the cat keep my tongue…"

He couldn't see her in the darkness, which was probably a good thing. "Well now, darlin', better the cat than me," he teased before he pushed the door open to freedom.

Chapter 5

RAIN PELTED ALLIE FROM THE PITCH-BLACK SKY. SHE drew in a deep breath and glanced up out of the hole. Night fell quickly in Africa. There were no sprawling cities spreading their fake yellow light in the darkness of Cameroon. Never had she been more grateful for that than right now. They could hide in the dark.

She took two of the steps and raised her head to let the weeping sky take the dirt from her face. She was suddenly very, very tired. And in her gut, she knew they were nowhere near done running.

"Allie, let's move," King commanded. His big hand appeared in front of her face and she grabbed for it, using his strength to replace what she'd lost back in that tunnel.

She climbed the remaining steps and slithered out of the hole. She lay on her back beside him before raising her head to see the burning structure they'd fled. She could hear the pop and hiss of burning wood and the occasional static percussion of ammunition discharging, but no shadowy shapes emerged from the flames to chase them.

"It just blew right up, didn't it?" she said more to herself than anyone else.

His strangled laughter made her warm. "On purpose at that."

He shifted beside her, and she mimicked his posture.

This left her on her stomach facing away from the burning house.

"See those trees ahead? We make it to the trees and we're home free. Stay low. Grab my belt and hold on. The earth is pocked, so try to stay out of the holes, okay?"

She nodded. He grunted.

"Cat still got your tongue?" he asked.

"Better him than you," Allie responded.

"She can be taught," he murmured as he easily shoved to his feet and reached for her hand.

It was the third time he'd done that—grabbed her hand. She didn't want to notice how perfectly his palm aligned with hers, didn't want to recognize the flare of awareness that sang up her arm and centered in her chest.

He took off, and before she embarrassed herself by being dragged behind him, she released his hand, notched her finger in one of his belt loops, and followed.

He was dangerous. She had no time for a spec ops soldier with an unknown purpose. He was also a huge smart-ass. But his smile, when it appeared, ripped a hole inside her. Allie knew he didn't smile much—his was too rusty, too new when it appeared. The man had no laugh lines either.

She stepped in one of the holes he'd warned her about and stumbled, releasing his belt loop as she went to a knee but forcing herself to remain calm. She gained her feet and continued on, doing her best not to slow them down.

They finally reached the edge of the trees, and Allie glanced back, struggling to catch her breath. By her guess, they were at least half a mile from the burning house. They were in a copse of towering trees now, hidden by the woods and darkness.

"Good girl," she thought she heard him mumble.

"I'm not a girl," she said around a deep breath.

"No shit," he said in a louder voice. "Girls don't look at a man like you looked at me on that plane."

Her lungs were burning, but she found enough oxygen to respond. "Won't happen again."

He grunted. "You'll not only look at me that way again, Redding, you'll do it while I'm buried inside you, riding us both to release."

Her breath stuttered and lodged in her throat. He had not just said… In the middle of gunshots, explosions, and running for their lives, they were going to talk about…*that*?

"Too soon?" he asked.

His face was blank, but she heard the smile in his voice.

Oh God, he had said that. He so had. She should… Well, she should do something. "What happened to the cat?"

He cocked his head and laughed softly, the sound warming her in places she didn't need to be warmed or even made aware of. Her breath released, and she struggled to drag in another.

"You know what happened to the cat, Allie."

"No, I really don't. And I'm a cat person. I like cats. I'd like the cat back now, please," she begged.

She was in so much trouble.

"Do you have your breath yet?" he asked in a guttural voice as he cinched the straps on her backpack tighter and stepped back.

She nodded.

"We have about a mile to cover through these trees. I need you alert and ready. I need you to move in my footsteps. I can't afford to use the light."

Allie shrugged. "I'm always ready, King McNally,"

she said around deep inhales and exhales. It wasn't that she was in horrible shape—it was the fear.

"It's just King."

"I'll use your whole name, if you don't mind," she replied, making every effort to keep the smile out of her voice.

"Why's that?"

She ignored his question. "Aren't there bad guys on our trail? Why are we standing here talking?" She knew why—he was giving her time to rest, because this next bit would be a sprint. Her stomach did that strange flip-flop at the thought that he was taking care of her.

"Because you're sucking wind?"

And there went that lovin' feeling. She turned on her heel and began walking.

He laughed, that same deep, low chuckle that stroked her eardrums and settled deep in the pit of her stomach. "Allie?"

She stopped right before she smacked into a tree that seemingly rose just then from the ground in front of her. "What?"

"Wrong way," he informed her, a smile in his voice.

"Yeah, yeah, yeah—yuck it up..."

She didn't hear him move, but he was there just then at her back, his warm breath trickling down over the sodden collar of her mud-stained black T-shirt, making her shiver. For a precious second his body relaxed, even curving against hers. Then he whispered, "Follow me."

She sighed again, praying for patience with this man who would be her savior but probably, knowing her luck, had been the cause of all her problems to begin with. He shifted, reaching for her hand and placing it once again on his belt. Then he was staring at her over his shoulder, the meager light from the cloud-shrouded moon making his eyes as dark as the night around them.

"I'm going to follow you, but only so far and so long before you answer some questions," she said, infusing as much determination into her voice as her tired body would allow.

He didn't say a word, just nodded. It was enough for Allie in that moment. His nod was more reassurance than any words he could have spoken. She didn't know why, only that it absolutely was.

He gave her time for one more deep breath, and then he started out at a fast clip, dodging trees and holes the rain had dug into the sodden earth. Before long, they were running full out. King kept his pace slower so she could keep up. She was a short woman, and his long legs had been designed to eat up the ground beneath him.

Allie was in decent shape but discovered her cardio was severely lacking. She'd hiked all over Africa, Cameroon especially, but she was sorely unprepared for this sprint to safety. She did her best, stumbling occasionally, but by the time the trees broke and they came to a dirt road, she was practically wheezing.

The rain was falling harder now, and she slipped as he slowed down and came to a stop. She hit his back and slid to her knees slowly.

He turned suddenly, pushing her belly-down into the mud, shoving her pack to the side, and falling on top of her.

"Men ahead," he whispered.

She lifted her head as far as his smothering body would allow and caught a glimpse of flashlights in the distance.

"Friendly?"

He put his mouth at her ear. "Negative. Nobody is friendly except me right now, Allie. Remember that. I need you to stay here. Do. Not. Move. You clear?"

His voice was hard. The man had several different tones—this was his do-what-I-say-and-you'll-live one.

"Clear," she whispered.

He was a big man, and with him spread over her prone form, she felt safer than she had in years. Ironic that there were people a few meters away who would probably shoot them on sight but she felt…protected.

"You've got the SIG and several rounds in your pack. If I'm not back in five minutes, crawl back to the edge of the woods and wait there. Shoot to kill, because if they take you, that means I'm dead. These men are killers, Allie. Understand?"

His mouth brushed her ear with every word. She shivered before nodding.

"I'll be back," he said, and then he was gone.

Allie was left with darkness and a crying sky. She was soaked, and as she positioned her pack on her back again, she brought up her arm and glanced at her watch. He had four minutes left.

A shot and a grunt to her left had her gathering herself to flee.

Three minutes.

Another dull thump followed by a man's short scream, and Allie felt her eyes burn. Terrible time to bawl, a suck-ass time, really, but the tears threatened

and fell, mixing with the cold rain and leaving her gasping silently for breath.

She searched through her watery eyes and the darkness for a hint of King. He represented safety, and if she
couldn't see him, feel him, she was lost. How quickly
that had happened. She trusted him, and he'd become
her only source for safety. Shivers tore through her
body. Allie recognized shock was setting in but could
do nothing to stop her slow slide into that state.

A sound behind her had Allie reaching under her
body for the gun in her waistband. She pulled it out
slowly, hoping the darkness hid her movement.
Survival instincts kicked in, and everything sharpened.
Her sight cleared, and the raindrops slowed in her
limited field of vision. The clouds thinned, and muted
moonlight filtered through, blanketing the world in a
hazy light.

She was going to have to dance with death.

There was another step in her direction, and the
ground seemed to tremble. The SIG had a round chambered, but the safety was on. She thumbed it off and
grabbed a handful of mud with her other hand.

Her father had taught her to shoot and play dirty when
she'd been a teenager. His lessons had stuck.

Would she get a chance to tell him good-bye?

A foot touched hers as a light flashed, illuminating
the ground in front of her.

"Get up," a man yelled.

Allie turned, slinging the mud in the direction of her
attacker's eyes as she lifted her weapon and fired shot
after shot. Once she started, she couldn't stop, reflex-
ively emptying the clip into the man's body.

The light he held blinded her for a second as he fell toward her, his knee in her gut pushing her back into the mud. Deadweight. She'd killed him. Bile rose and her stomach heaved. She was a killer.

She keened, recognized the sound for what it was. She'd become a wounded animal. Safety. Where was King?

Two more shots were fired at a distance as she scrabbled from underneath the dead man. Sobs racked her throat. They were inhuman, grunting sounds that she tried to quiet but just could not.

"Allison!"

She knew that voice and turned to it. King. He slid to his knees at her feet, checking her with his eyes and hands for injury. "Did he hurt you?"

"I'm good," she forced past her dry lips.

Bucketfuls of water had dropped from the clouds, but her lips were dry.

King stood, took her hand and placed it on his belt loop, and said, "We need to move, Allie. More are coming."

Her only thought as she began to move with him, slipping and sliding in the mud but following his tracks to an SUV, was that she really liked when he called her Allie.

In the darkness, she couldn't tell the color or the make of the SUV, but once King pushed her into the passenger's side, she collapsed against the seat and covered her face.

She was responsible for taking a life when all she'd ever wanted to do was teach people how to live.

King climbed into the driver's seat. The engine coughed and finally turned over. He cursed and reached for her trembling hand, enfolding it in his big, warm mitt as he began to drive.

He squeezed her hand, and she turned to him. His mouth was moving, but it took her a minute to understand the words.

"There are—"

Something pinged through her door and fire streaked across her side, stealing her breath. She pressed her free hand to her side and groaned. That *hurt*.

"Goddamn it, Allie!"

She pushed the black back. His voice carried a note she'd not heard yet—desperation.

"What did *I* do?" she asked, fighting the burning agony in her side.

"Hold on," he bit out as he stepped on the accelerator and the SUV responded, gurgling once before shooting forward.

The pain was vicious. Long, fire-tipped claws ripping into her side. Her hand was wet and warm. This was not good.

"I think the bastards shot me," she whispered.

"How bad is it?" King demanded.

"Well, how would I know?"

"Talk to me, Redding. I've got to know—is it a graze?"

The pain took a backseat. "McNally, I'm a Peace Corps volunteer, not a field medic. It hurts. That's what I know. It fucking hurts. Now stop asking me questions and drive."

"You've got a foul mouth, Ms. Redding," he murmured.

"Have you ever been shot?"

He nodded, releasing his death grip on her hand as the road became treacherous. Allie felt every bump, her breath halting in her lungs as throbbing ripped through her.

"I think I'm losing blood," she said. She had no idea if she really was, but something felt sticky on her side.

"I know, baby. Hold on for me, okay? I can't stop yet. Just keep talking to me," he ordered.

"Don't call me *baby*. And it hurts to talk." It did.

"Talk to me anyway, Allie. That's an order."

She glanced up, watching the lights from the vehicle slice through the rain and night. Everything blurred, a high-pitched noise sounded in her ears, and oblivion threatened.

"Don't you dare pass out on me, Redding. I don't have time for it."

There were pretty, floating things in her periphery, and the pain was fading to a dull pulse. "Pretty floaties are good, right?"

"No! That's not good," he said.

His face in the low lights of the interior was hard. Grooves cut into his cheeks at the corners of his mouth— from frowning, she was sure. The man really needed to laugh more. "I'll do whatever I have to do, Redding, to keep you from wimping out on me here."

"Wimping out? I've been shot!" Well, it burned, but when she moved, it didn't feel that deep. Now that she was thinking a tad more clearly, she recalled the sound of the bullet embedding in the floorboard, glove compartment, or whatever. So at least it wasn't lodged inside her. Although just the thought—or the blood loss—made that familiar darkness creep along her periphery again.

She had a sneaking suspicion that terror was making her pain worse.

"Look at me, Allie! Look. At. Me."

She did as he ordered. She had no choice really. Something in his voice tugged at her mind and refused to let it go. "I don't want to look at you."

"But you will."

"No, I won't."

"You're not going to pass out, are you? Don't. I need you here with me. A few more miles, and I'll pull over and take care of you, okay? Hold on," he commanded.

Several moments of silence passed as she tried to do just that. The pain was there, but somehow her mind was overriding it. Her instincts, the same ones that had allowed her to kill that man minutes ago, demanded she do what King was ordering her to do.

"Seriously," she began, "why King?"

His mouth tugged up, and she became fascinated with the lushness of his lower lip. She was going to blame her predilection with his lips on the pain. Because between the mad dash, the brutal attack, and oh yeah, *getting shot*, the last thing she should be noticing was his LMAO lips. They hit a particularly nasty bump in the road, and she cried out. King cursed.

"Focus on me, baby. Look at me."

The insistence in his voice was too much to ignore, but Allie was wading through drying concrete. Why was he calling her *baby*? It made her want to smile like a moron. "I hurt," she said and winced at the whine in her voice. "Oh, God, I'm totally wimping out."

He grabbed her hand and placed her palm on his cheek. "Focus on me." When she looked at him, he started back up. "You wanna know why they call me King?"

"Yeah," she mumbled, fighting the fear like a damn

prizefighter. The pain wasn't so bad anymore, but she was tired—a bone-deep weariness that made her want to give over to the shock and exhaustion. She'd like to pretend this day had never happened.

He sighed, and for some reason, that had her smiling. She frustrated him. That was a good thing.

"I was bestowed a kingdom."

She snorted, but her lips curved even more. "Of course you were."

"You don't buy that?" he asked.

Another delicate snort and "Not for a second."

He smiled but continued. "My full name is Kingston McNally. It got shortened to King by my master chief in SEAL BUD/S training. He said I was a smart-ass motherfucker, but I ruled my unit like a king on a throne. Said my guys followed me because I talked to 'em with the voice of authority. So the shortened version stuck."

"Huh, who'd a thunk it? Someone else recognizing your imperialistic nature."

Her eyes were getting heavier. It was becoming hard to hold her head up and look at him, no matter how hot he was. She was in shock.

"Just hold on another mile, and I'll check you out. Look at me, Allie. Don't close your eyes. Look at me."

The car stopped moving, and her stomach rebelled. She groaned and slapped a hand over her mouth.

She heard him get out, but her eyes refused to open again. Her door did open though. She felt him probing her side, and then he cursed before pulling her into his arms. She cut off another groan by force of will but cried silent tears that rolled down her face like hot lava.

"Don't cry, baby. Not now. I've got you," he said in a gruff voice as he wiped her face.

She breathed in through her nose and out her mouth as he placed her on the ground where he'd laid some type of tarp over the dirt. "I'm okay."

He grunted. His palms brushed her abdomen as he pulled her shirt up. "Not really the way I envisioned you getting your hands under my shirt," she said to the sky.

"So what you're saying is you've given it some thought. You're admitting you want my hands under your shirt. Why, Ms. Redding, you sure do move fast."

"I admit to nothing."

She felt him lift the shirt farther. "Thank you, God. It's just a flesh wound," he whispered. "You've been caterwauling for miles over a skid mark."

Allie grimaced. "It *hurts*."

"You're a wimp."

She wanted to shrug. Tried, she was sure, but had no idea if she affected the gesture or not. "I'm not a wimp, weenie, whiner, or any other w-word you want to throw at me."

He groaned and then laughed. "You're crazy."

"And you're the king. How deep is it?" she asked.

"I'm going to give you my belt. I want you to bite down because this is going to hurt."

"Like a mother—" she began.

"Ah-ah-ah, watch the potty mouth," he cautioned. Then he shrugged. "But yeah, maybe that bad."

She found the strength to open her eyes once more. He'd turned his headlamp on but had it twisted down and to the side so it wouldn't blind her. "How deep is it?"

He shook his head as he placed his belt in her mouth

and stroked her cheek once before he looked at her hard. "Bite down."

She did, and he went probing, pressing on the wound and cursing. "It's not too deep. It may need a few stitches, I'm not sure. My main worry is fever from any possible infection you might get."

A tear leaked from her eye. She pushed the belt from her mouth with her tongue, gasping for breath and trying to slay the dragon burying its talons in her body. "Can you close it now?"

He shook his head. "I'm going to use some QuikClot to stanch the bleeding completely, and I think I have some antibiotics in my kit. We have another hour and a half before we reach Kribi. Once we're there, I'll work on you."

He bit open a QuikClot packet, poured the crystals over her wound, and pressed some gauze over that.

"Thanks," she mumbled. The pain continued to fade, and she breathed deeply.

He nodded. "You're welcome."

"All I wanted—"

"Yeah, yeah, yeah," he said with a grin. "McDonald's fries and a mani-pedi."

She smiled. He'd heard her back on the plane. She should probably tell him… "None of this is really your fault. I don't think so anyway."

He didn't respond. He put her back in the vehicle, and she felt him swabbing the upper part of her arm. The prick of the needle was nothing compared to the pain in her side. The floaties were back, bright silver and blue, swirling in front of her eyes and taunting her with rest.

"That's the antibiotic. You can rest now, Allie."

She heard the sounds of him putting everything away, and then he settled once more into the vehicle. Several moments passed, but she was too damn tired to open her eyes. Then the heat of his palm aligned with hers, and he said, "I've got you," his deep voice rumbling, soothing.

"It's funny but I absolutely know you do, Kingston McNally," she responded and then between one breath and the next, she huddled under the blanket of darkness, letting it take her down, down, down…

Chapter 6

ALLIE'S WORDS TAUNTED KING. THE SOUND OF THEM replayed over and over in his ears as he laid her seat back and covered her with the warming blanket. It was hotter than four hells outside, even in the rain, but with her wound, she could move farther into a state of shock. Her pulse was fine, and he allowed himself a few moments to linger over the soft skin of her neck and jaw before he pulled away and shut her door.

He gathered up the first aid kit and settled it on the floor of the Rover before getting in and continuing the journey to Kribi.

I absolutely know you do. Yeah, those words put a hole in his gut. She'd been in his care when she was shot. He'd only known her a few hours, and she'd been hurt repeatedly. It was unacceptable.

No matter what her familial ties were, she was King's responsibility.

He took a deep breath, constantly checking the rear-view mirrors for any sign they were being followed. He'd taken a circuitous route around Douala proper but didn't feel the knot at the back of his neck loosen until he had them traveling southwest toward Kribi.

The rain slowed, and fatigue pulled at King. His eyes felt like they had sand in them. Cars were sparse, so he turned on the dash light periodically to check her breathing and to keep himself awake. Her face was pale, the heart-shaped curves no less breathtaking. Her eyelids flinched whenever he turned on the light, so he was quick to assess and cut it back off.

Her hand trembled in his, and he refused to look too deeply into the reason why he wanted to maintain that contact with her.

He needed to get her to safety, was contemplating the best way to do that when his sat phone beeped. King released her hand and pulled it from his pocket.

"Yeah?"

"Dresden and Savidge are making moves, King," Jude Dagan's deadened voice said into his ear.

Jude was one of his best men. King still wondered if he might lose him, because Jude had lost something more precious than the air he breathed—he'd lost his woman. That busted op in Beirut had taken so much from them all, but it had taken Ella from Jude. That she'd been their traitor made his loss even more unimaginable.

Something oily moved in King's gut. "Is Dresden showing his face?"

Endgame had been after Dresden's Lebanese arms pipeline when sugar had gone to shit on that Beirut operation. He'd been on their radar because his shipments of Uzis and AK-47s were finding their way all over the world. He'd become a major player on the worldwide stage, and someone was supplying him, giving him unfettered access to U.S. military installations and putting American M4s and M16s on the market as well. Guns, ammo, rocket launchers—you name it, he was gathering them all up, from all over the world, and selling them to the highest bidder. He'd hit four U.S. bases in the last year. Even with heightened security, he'd gotten in and out with little to no resistance. That reeked of inside help.

Endgame wanted to end Dresden. He had to be stopped. That he'd reached out and touched King's team gave King even more impctus to see the bastard taken down.

"Negative. But there's talk Savidge is making friends with Boko Haram. How's your vacation going?"

And there was confirmation of the Boko Haram link. It explained why the terrorists had wanted Allie. It was a connection that had the queasy feeling back in King's gut. Maybe she'd been used as bait for him. "It doesn't stop raining in this country. Rook headed out for his R & R?"

"Ukraine'll never be the same," came the clipped response. "You need a ride?"

"Nah, we're taking a cruise. I'll handle it. I need intel on my supposed courier," King said in a low voice. "Something better than what you gave me last time."

He glanced at Allie, saw she was still out to the world, and continued watching the road.

"I gave you everything the travel agent had," Jude responded in a near whisper.

"Where are you, JD?" King asked.

"Someplace that looks a lot like hell."

"You need to contact Travelocity and find out the rest of the agenda for my trip. They didn't give me everything I needed."

King refused to say anymore. Their connection was as secure as any satellite connection could be, but discretion had been ingrained in them, hence the talk-around.

"I'll do what I can. Can't make any promises. Gave

you what they sent me before you left. If I find anything I'll get it to you ASAP. I gotta run, Your Highness. Holler at you later."

King winced at the nickname. Before Beirut, it had been a way for his team to poke fun at him. Now, in the post-Beirut times, it was nothing more than a reminder of the team members he'd lost in battle.

King shook his head. He'd given his man what he had—they were taking a ship home, and he needed more information on Allie Redding. If he didn't hear back from Jude, he'd have to tap Rook for more information. Rook's wife, Vivi, was a CIA cyber-spy. She maintained her contacts at Langley while also working for Endgame Ops. She traveled a slippery slope, but her intel was always spot-on. The only valuable, reliable, *honest* spook King had ever met, and he still doubted every word out of her mouth.

Trust, but verify.

King's brain sifted through everything he'd learned. The information was there, waiting to be deciphered, but he was missing vital pieces that would tell him the direction he needed to take. He'd been guided to that plane on the same day the supposed information carrier was to be heading to Paris. Then that same plane had been hijacked. They'd been looking for Allie, no doubt about it. The question was why? Was her father being leveraged?

She denied being a courier, but her father was the director of the CIA. And the CIA was all up in Endgame Ops business. Were they up in Dresden's as well? What was the connection?

One plus one plus one wasn't adding up to three. It was adding up to way more than that.

Speaking of Allie, King needed to pull over and hydrate her. He was flying by the seat of his pants now. She said she wasn't a field medic, and King had the bare minimum training in wounds. He'd stitched his own ass up more times than he'd doctored anyone else. Add in the fact that she'd somehow managed to get under his skin, and it wasn't an ideal situation.

He pulled well off the rough roadway and got out, hurrying to her side of the car. He hadn't passed another car in thirty minutes, but he didn't want anyone stopping. He had just reached for her neck when her eyes opened and she gasped.

Her pupils were blown, fear making the blue bleed to black as they dilated.

"It's me, Allie," he murmured.

She grabbed his hand and made a pathetic attempt at fending him off.

"I'm not going to hurt you, baby." King wanted to curse. *Baby? Really, King?* The endearments were falling from his mouth like money from a rich man's pockets.

"Please," she whispered.

"It's okay. I need you to drink some water, okay?" King rummaged through the sack at her feet and located a bottle. He unscrewed the cap and held it to her lips. Water dribbled from the sides of her mouth, and she pushed at him again.

The sight of the dried blood on her hands had fury moving through King. Flesh wound or not, he'd find the fucker who shot her if it was the last thing he did. They'd hurt her. They'd pay.

Find them and do what, McNally? He had another, far more preemptive mission. What he needed to focus on was getting her home. Revenge led to bad things—things you couldn't undo. He had firsthand experience with that one.

"Drink, Allie," he demanded. Fire lit her eyes as the blue struggled to gain a foothold. "Yeah, baby, that's it. Get mad."

"Drowning me," she murmured.

"Drink and you won't drown," he told her, keeping his voice even.

She did, drinking several long sips before she pushed him away and closed her eyes.

"That's my girl," he said.

Her eyes opened again and narrowed. He chuckled as she laid her head gently against the headrest, and then he pulled his hand away, tightening the lid on the water. She licked her lips, and he automatically leaned closer.

Allie yawned, and her head lopped to the side. "Don't think about kissing me."

He lifted her head, wedging his hoodie between it and the seat so it wouldn't happen again. Kissing was exactly what he'd been thinking of. "I won't kiss you *right now*. Can't promise about the future."

He'd never responded to a woman the way he had with her. Her kiss had rocked his world. It was insanity and yet another reason he had to get her far away. He damn well wanted to kiss her again.

He was starting to close her door when she reached out. He leaned back down.

"We're headed toward Kribi. When we get there, I know some people who can help us. Head to Max's bar. It's on the main strip, easy to find," Allie directed him.

"Who's Max?" He didn't like the shaft of jealousy that

streaked through him. A handful of hours they'd been together, and he was jealous over her already? Crazy.

She licked her lips, and King stifled his groan. "Safety. Trust me, King McNally."

She was asking the impossible. Trust was earned, and he hadn't known her long enough for that to happen. She'd followed him when he'd demanded it. She'd given herself into his keeping while giving him nothing more than a bit of sass. She obviously trusted him. Could he do the same? He refused to confuse lust with trust, but the lines were blurring dangerously.

He straightened and watched her slide back into sleep. Confusion cramped his brain. Why would this woman have a contact that ensured safety? Maybe her father had a network for her just in case she ran into trouble? King trusted no one with Allie now. Everyone could be compromised. He would get her to safety his own way.

He closed her door and walked back around, getting in and starting the Rover. King pulled her sat phone from her pants pocket and scrolled through it until he found what he was looking for—Daddy.

He waited there for long moments contemplating the move he was about to make, wondering if he'd lost his mind. The last thing he needed was another agency full-out hunting his ass. On the other hand, while he may hate the CIA with everything in him, having a favor owed to him by the director could be worth a life in the future.

King let his thumb hover over the call button, conflicted, because at the root of the fiasco in Beirut there'd been a mole—a true traitor—and as much as King wanted to forget it, the fingerprint of that betrayal had CIA written all over it.

The sounds of the helo taking fire, the flames as the fuel tank took a direct hit, and the absence of noise as the rotors stopped and the bird fell from the sky—the memories were a riot in King's mind.

He hit Send. It rang only once.

"Allie?"

King grunted. "No, sir, but your daughter is safe."

"Who is this? Why do you have my daughter's phone?"

"King McNally, and I have her phone because she's asleep." He waited and received nothing. "Allie is safe, Director, but there'll be a delay getting her home."

Silence stretched taut along the connection.

"Why does Endgame have my daughter?" His desperation was harsh over the line. For a brief second, King felt the man's pain.

"A better question," King began. "Why is your daughter traveling alone in a compromised area of the world?"

"You don't ask the questions here, McNally. That's my daughter you have. I want her home immediately."

"I'll bring her home, but I'm going to need a favor," King told him.

"I don't bargain with terrorists," Gray Broemig said firmly.

And there was the CIA that King knew and hated. "We aren't terrorists, not even close, and you know this, don't you, Director? Tell you what, let's call it a chit instead of a favor. We can even call it a lifer chit if you want. After all, I technically saved your daughter's life earlier today. So you owe me. Does that make it more palatable, Director Broemig?"

"If she's hurt, I'll kill you."

King rifled through his memory for what he knew of Gray Broemig. Decorated Vietnam vet. Check. Married to his high school sweetheart after he returned from the war. Check. Broemig's wife died in an embassy bombing over twenty years ago, but there'd never been mention of a daughter. A daughter Broemig allowed to traipse abroad unprotected doing work with a volunteer organization? Negative. King hadn't known that one.

Fucking spooks—they all lied, even when the truth sounded better. They buried their lives under layer upon layer of dirt, hoping no one would be smart enough to dig it up. King knew there were motivated people in the world now. He was one of them.

"You could probably do exactly what you've said, but I've got your daughter and if you want her back"— the threat made King's stomach churn—"you'll give me what I want." He'd never hurt Allie, but the threat had to sound real, and if King could do anything, it was make a threat sound real.

"Name it," Broemig demanded in a tone that promised hell had frozen over.

King chuckled. He knew where Allie got her temper. "Just agree to the chit, Director. I'm not quite ready to collect. When I am, you'll owe me."

"I'm bent over a barrel. The chit is yours," Broemig returned. "Now, what's your plan?"

Broemig had taken over the CIA twenty years ago but had been entrenched in the spy world long before then. He was rarely seen and ruled his operatives with an iron fist. Some likened his tactics to those of the KGB. That had never bothered King. He'd always said whatever it took to get the job done was what had to happen. He'd worked with CIA liaisons on several missions over the years—they were well-trained, efficient, cold killers.

"I'm still figuring things out. We'll talk later, Director. But you've got a leak the size of Texas in your organization. Perhaps you should concentrate on that. That tracer on her phone wasn't smart. Somebody has either hacked you, or they followed her movement via that tracer. Either way she's in play now." King disconnected and turned the phone off.

Having the director of the CIA owe you a chit was worth gold. They may lie, steal, and cheat, but they came through on their promises…most of the time. And surely, even though most would sell their soul to accomplish a mission, the director loved his daughter.

"I don't like being used as a pawn."

Allie's voice rippled through him, the husky notes full of pain and anger. He could really get behind a woman who had no problem showing her anger. He could probably get in front, under, and on top of her too.

King sighed. "Then you should have gotten in a different line when they were handing out parents. Games and pawns and aggressive moves are all people like your dad understand. He made the rules."

"That's pretty black and white for a spec ops boy who does his fair share of playing games," she returned.

"The world is black and white until you meet the gray—then everything changes and you have to blend in."

She laughed, but it was a sound without humor. "Pot, I'd like to introduce you to Kettle."

He glanced at her, looking away quickly lest he get sucked into her gaze. Something about her screamed at him to trust her. The circumstances were too unfamiliar though. "I'll get you home safely."

She hissed in a short breath as she shifted on the seat. "I'm not a kid, McNally. I don't like operating blind. I don't like the games either."

"I thought you were a simple Peace Corps volunteer, yet now you talk about 'operating.' Tell me, Allie, who are *you*?"

"Figure of speech, and you're evading my question," she said in a low voice.

Allie stared straight ahead into the darkness. Her stillness unnerved King for some reason. The way she looked directly at him, and what he saw there had his breath catching.

"During our short association my plane has been hijacked, I've been shot at, forced to flee from terrorists, kissed, oh, and the pièce de résistance? I've been grazed by a bullet. None of these things happened until you showed up in my life. You'll have to give me something here, McNally. Something that allows me to trust you with *my* secrets."

A cold, bitter wind rushed through his mind. He'd thought her different, but now she told him she had secrets. What had he expected? So what if her eyes pulled at his soul? She was messing with his mind. King was well aware that everybody had secrets.

But not everybody is the daughter of the CIA director, his gut whispered.

So now he was left with a huge issue—trusting her with a truth of his to find out what she was hiding, or continuing to argue with her and make it much more difficult on them both. He was used to making split-second decisions. This one had him in knots. His gut whispered he could trust her. His mind screamed *oh hell no*.

"Never mind, McNally. I can see I've asked too much," she said with a small, deprecating laugh.

King took a deep breath and eyed her before turning his gaze back to the desolate road in front of them. "What do you want from me?"

She stayed quiet for long moments, finally sighed, and said, "A simple truth. One thing that leaves you vulnerable so I can feel safe enough to be the same."

"Then it isn't such a simple truth, is it?"

Frustration pierced him. The woman was entirely too trusting. How would she know whether or not he was lying? What if he'd been another man, someone really out to get her? Would she have trusted that man as easily as she was offering to trust him?

He was close to shutting down, but something about this woman forced him to give her what she wanted. King fought with himself for a while before he blew out a rough breath. "One thing?" he asked, staring at her intently.

"Just one," Allie replied softly.

"When I was sixteen, I beat my father to death and went to juvenile prison. No matter that I'd endured years of abuse; the system found me guilty. I'd finally grown big enough to give back what he was gifting me with, and the courts sent me away. When I got out at the age of eighteen, I changed my name to Kingston McNally. It was my maternal great-grandfather's name and much better than Thomas Sacco Jr." He dropped it into the chasm of silence between them. "You're one of a very select few who know that information."

Her nostrils flared, and she breathed out slowly. "Wow. You went all in with that one, didn't you?"

He grunted, waiting.

"Not so sure that makes me feel any safer but okay— one good turn deserves another." Allie bit her lip and winced. "When I was six, I snuck into my father's office at our house and called my mother from his blue phone. The blue phone was off limits unless it was an emergency. Those were the rules. But I missed my mother— she was a UNICEF ambassador and had been out of the country for two weeks, promoting an educational program at the Syrian embassy. I managed to evade my sitter and tutor long enough to call her. I told her I was scared and that bad men were in the house all because I wanted to talk to her." Allie swallowed thickly, torment edging her tone. "She walked outside to get better reception, and as she stepped to the gate, a car bomb exploded, killing her instantly. When I was six, I killed my mom."

King's heart stopped, then began to beat in a hard rhythm. He reached for her hand, enfolding it in his before he squeezed. In the meager light thrown by the dashboard display, he saw the blood crusted on her hands. He heard the pain in her voice and saw the lines of it drawn on her face.

She was his responsibility now, and there was no way he was leaving her in anyone else's hands. Returning her to her father earned King a chit. And even as he assured himself her safety was more important, another dangerous idea had formed. Perhaps this woman could be used to get at Savidge. Eliminating his right-hand man would seriously jeopardize Dresden's operation, making him weak.

Someone had put her into play, and turning the tables on them was almost irresistible. He had a really foul suspicion that it was someone close to Savidge who, if King was correct, had a foot in the CIA. The coincidence was too much. King could protect her from further harm. His confidence in that was solid. But could he pass up an opportunity to get at Savidge?

No. But he'd damn well protect her while he did it.

"I'm going to get you home, Allie Redding."

She gazed at him, and in her eyes was something King had never seen before—complete and total trust. He didn't deserve it. She was loony if she thought he wasn't going to use her to get information for his primary objective.

Her eyes were dark, hinting at things King didn't want to know or see about this woman. But the truth was that he did want. And he couldn't help it.

"I believe you, King McNally."

Second time she'd voiced her faith in him. And with that, he lost another piece of himself to her.

Chapter 7

ALLIE DRIFTED IN AND OUT OF SLEEP UNTIL THE SOUNDS of the tires over the road finally stopped. Her side ached, not with the fiery hotness from earlier, but with a dull, throbbing sting.

"I need to get us a room." King's deep, raspy voice whispered in her ears, sinking into her mind and making her yearn for things she'd never known she wanted.

"Hey now, I let you get to second base, but getting a room is moving a little fast." She sat up a little straighter and let out a groan as her muscles tensed and pulled. "Aren't we going to Max's?"

King shrugged his broad shoulders.

"If you'll take me to Max's, you can be free of me," she told him matter-of-factly.

He shook his head. "Not going to happen."

"Arrrrgh!" She let her frustration bubble up her throat and flavor her words. Had they not had a small trust-building convo before she'd drifted back to sleep? "I am not your information carrier-slash-courier-slash-spook. Whoever you were looking for, I am not that person. I help people get clean water and grow crops. I teach school when necessary. I find doctors to come into villages and treat the sick and infirm. I don't carry classified information between agents. I don't do anything illegal—except sometimes I double-park or forget to put money in the parking meter. Yes, my father is

Gray Broemig, but I am not involved in your clandestine games."

"You finished?" he asked in a quiet voice.

Her mouth fell open and outrage threatened to pour forth, but she snapped it shut. "Yeah, I guess I am."

"Good. Now I'll tell you why I'm not going to this Max's. You listening?"

His brown hair had dried and waved deliciously. The longish strands touched the collar of his black T-shirt. Her hands itched to be buried in it.

"Hello?"

His mouth moved, that full lower lip taunting her. Where was the pain from her gunshot wound now? It's like he'd been created to tempt her. Tall, broad, and delicious. He was fine enough to make her forget her pain. And he was taking care of her.

Damn it.

Allie finally snapped out of her reverie and looked at him from beneath her lashes.

"You there?" King asked.

"Just say what you've got to say already. I'm hurting," she said softly. The pain was nowhere near as bad as when she'd first received the wound. It was a dull ache now, but she wasn't above using the presence of that pain to hurry things along.

His hand clenched on his lap. He didn't like that she was hurting. A plus in his favor. She'd have to start keeping track of the pros and cons of Mr. King McNally. Otherwise, she'd fall so far that when he walked away, she'd be lost.

Suck that right up, Allison Elizabeth Redding. Ain't nobody got time for falling right now.

Her inner musing had her smiling.

King ignored her.

"I don't know Max or anybody else in this country. I understand you may, or may not, be the person I was searching for on that plane. But you're in my care now, and I've promised to get you back home. You've already been winged by a bullet on my watch. Did I mention I don't know Max or anyone else in this country?"

She nodded.

"Good, because what that means is that I have no reason to trust anyone. You're in my care. We'll do shit my way, and my way means not going to meet up with Max or any-fucking-body else. We clear?"

She felt anger simmer in her belly. She was trying to help them both! "Jerkface," she pushed out.

"Yes, well, we've already established that. Now sit here. I'm going into that resort and getting us a room, and you'll keep your happy ass right here until I get back."

"I'm so fucking sick of you telling me what to do," she said on a heavy breath. Her frustration bounced back to her, a clanging in her head.

His eyes narrowed. "The sound of that word out of your mouth bothers me."

"Why is that? You toss it around pretty easily."

His hand tightened over hers. "Let's make a deal, yeah? You don't say *fuck* unless that's what you want me to do to you. Deal?"

"Oh-ho! So then it'll be okay to say the dreaded f-word. What's up with that? It won't bother you then?"

He smiled and her stomach somersaulted. "Then it has a different connotation, so it's perfectly acceptable."

"You're such a dude."

"I promise you that before this all over, Allie, you'll find out just how much."

"Fu—"

He placed his hand over her mouth cutting her off. "Remember what I said about that word, Allie."

She didn't need help finding Max's bar. She'd been to Kribi before. She could find it on her own. She might trust King McNally, but that didn't mean she wouldn't do her best to save herself. Max's meant Lo-Lo. Lo-Lo meant CIA. CIA meant a way home without endangering King any more than she already had.

When had *he* become her primary concern? *Remember, Redding, no time for falling…*

Her gaze locked with his. "Okay," she mumbled behind his hand.

"The SIG is under your leg. Safety is on. Use it if you have to, but I won't be long," he said, and before she could blink, he was gone.

Allie waited a single minute, counting each second off in her head. She pulled the SIG out, undid the seat belt, and opened the door. Her right side was numb, and for a second, everything wavered in her vision. Had to be exhaustion. She slid her legs over the side of the seat and very carefully lowered herself to the ground. It took a few seconds to get her feet under her.

But she managed. The wind from the ocean blew roughly, and the tang of salt water rode the gusts. She shivered and pulled the silver blanket King had thrown over her back around her shoulders.

Then she started walking. She began to count her steps, anything to focus and get her mind off the burgeoning sting in her side.

King had brought them closer than he'd realized. Allie only had to go two blocks south, and she was at Max's. She'd almost made it to the door when suddenly it opened. Allie held up a hand to block the bright light from blinding her.

"Allie?"

"Lo-Lo?"

"What the hell happened to you, girl? Why are you here? You're supposed to be in DC. You didn't tell me you were coming here," Lo-Lo accused.

"There wasn't much time. I—"

"Allie," a deep voice from several feet behind her called out.

"I need help, Lo-Lo," she whispered before the fear and pain dug in deep.

"Come in here, girl. Who is that fine piece of man... Oh shit, Allie. What have you gotten yourself tangled up in?" Lo-Lo asked, reaching for Allie.

Allie heard her longtime friend's words, but confusion was a blanket on her mind. That sounded like King's voice. But surely he was still trying to get them a room.

"Goddamn it, Allie!"

Yep, it was King. Allie turned slowly, Lo-Lo's arms wrapping around her middle. When the woman's hand came to rest on her side, Allie hissed.

"King?" her friend queried.

"Son of a... Loretta Bernstein? Been a long time, yeah?"

"Not long enough. What are you doing here?" Lo-Lo asked.

"Me," Allie whispered. "He's here with me."

"Sure he is, baby girl. Tell you what, you look like something my cat dragged in. Let's get you upstairs and—"

King stepped forward. "No. She's staying with me."

Lo-Lo held on to Allie, and she was grateful. Her lease on the ability to stand had expired.

"No, she isn't. You're trouble," Lo-Lo said loudly.

How the hell did Lo-Lo know that? Did they know each other?

"She's going with me, Loretta," King told her. His tone brooked no argument. Allie winced.

"I'm hurting again, King McNally." Allie moaned softly to give her words effect. This whole scene was bizarre, to say the least.

Lo-Lo pulled her in tighter against her body, but neither she nor King turned to look at her. They just continued to stare each other down.

"I'm hurting, King," Allie repeated.

Lo-Lo lowered her to a chair and turned, poking her finger at King's chest. For some reason, the sight of the beautiful, stacked redhead that close to King bothered Allie. A lot.

King pushed Lo-Lo's finger away and bent until his face was even with hers. Yelling—they were both yelling.

"You shot my dog, Loretta," King complained.

To which Loretta replied, "I should have shot you!"

Allie pressed a hand to her side and watched. Her fingers were sticky again. She was probably bleeding through the QuikClot. She had no strength left. Weakness was creeping in, and the pain was sharp.

"I'm hurting," she said once more, louder.

They continued to yell at each other.

"You and your men left me in Shanghai," Lo-Lo wheezed out.

To which King replied, "Yeah—well, you deserved it after telling Chen where to find me and my team, you crazy bitch. Oh, and you *shot my dog*!"

On and on it went for what felt like hours. Realistically, Allie knew it was a minute at most, and she seriously doubted she'd bleed out from... What had King called it? A skid mark. She'd give it another try, and after that, she was going to pull herself up, make her way to the bar, and make damn sure she was at least shit-faced while she suffered.

"I'm. Bleeding!"

Silence.

Blessed, blessed silence.

Then King was there, scooping her up in his arms and walking—to where, Allie had no idea and even less desire to find out.

"I've got you," he whispered, strong arms and big hands holding her securely against his chest.

"No, King. She stays here," Lo-Lo said firmly.

Allie gave up. She'd had enough. He was holding her. Possession was nine-tenths of the law. He'd won. "I'm going with him. But I could use a visit from Akiiki, Lo-Lo."

King headed back toward the front entrance of the resort, then down a path that led who knew where.

"I'll get him. What hut, King?" Lo-Lo asked.

King ignored the question and picked up his pace. To Allie he said, "Only you would have a link to Loretta Bernstein. Damn, woman. You are trouble." He lifted her higher in his arms, securing her tighter against his chest. "I don't want anyone knowing where we are. I don't trust Loretta. And who is Akiiki?"

"Local doctor," Allie murmured. "So tired…"

King hugged her closer. "I know you are."

Had she said that out loud? Geesh. Tired wasn't a sufficient descriptor for her current state.

He slowed and then stopped. Allie raised her face and watched him glare over his shoulder. "Hurry up," he said. "She's been grazed by a bullet."

"Akiiki is safe, okay? Don't shoot him," Allie warned.

He grunted and she was assured.

"I don't know what I did to get tossed into this shit with you, King. But you better not let me die because I'll kill you."

Then she gave over to the blackness again. It was a familiar ride so she took it down once more…down, down, down…

Chapter 8

THE DOCTOR, AKIIKI, HAD COME AND GONE. KING HAD held her hand while the doctor used Steri-Strips to close her wound. It had been ragged and had dirt in the graze but did not require stitches. The doctor cleaned her up and then bandaged her side. She lay quietly through it all, her face marking the pain.

King wanted to take her pain and destroy it. He'd found the bullet that grazed her embedded in the glove box and pried it out before shoving it in his pocket. He didn't question his actions. The bullet had hurt her, and now it couldn't. End of discussion.

She lay still and quiet now, and it seemed wrong to disturb her stillness. There was no life on her face, and no barbed comments came flying from between those suc-culent bow lips. He shook his head and rubbed his chest.

It was crazy how she'd crawled inside him so fast. More and more, he was questioning whether his little head or the big one on his shoulders was doing the thinking.

King rubbed a hand down his face and glanced at the tiny woman lying motionless except for the rise and fall of her chest. The bed swallowed her whole. They'd come to the last resort in Kribi, the one farthest down the beach, and been lucky enough to find it relatively tourist free.

He'd grabbed the last hut on the beach, paid in cash

for several days, and here they were. King could hear the sea beyond the front door of the immaculate hut and was reminded again of how quiet things were without her mouth running.

He let a smile crease his face and wanted to cuss. He'd known her less than half a day, and already she'd changed him. He hadn't thought a person existed who could—and if he'd admitted one might be out there somewhere, he certainly wouldn't have thought they'd manage the feat so quickly.

She'd bravely followed him, never once breaking. Maybe his angst stemmed from disbelief. How many women could go through what she had and not bitch about breaking a nail?

Hell, he'd seen grown men, battle-hardened soldiers no less, cry like a baby while bullet wounds were being fixed up. But not Allie Redding, no sirree.

"How the hell did she get shot?"

He glanced at Loretta and sighed. "See, it's like this. Somebody lifted a rifle and fired. The bullet traveled at a high rate of speed, punctured the door of the SUV, and dug a path along her side."

Loretta stared at him. "I'm not up for your shit tonight, King. That's an innocent girl you've mixed up in Endgame Ops business."

King raised his head to dispute and then shrugged.

"Yeah, no reason to deny it," she said in a low voice. "How many people you gonna get killed before you just let things go?"

He stood so fast his chair hit the wall and bounced off. He was in her face that quick. "You have no idea what you're talking about."

She smiled. "You aren't responsible for what happened in Beirut, but Ella was on *you*, McNally. I don't give a shit what Jude says, and I know he doesn't blame you—crazy man acts like you're the second coming of Christ—but she was on you. You and your Piper let her through the doors, and you all paid for it. Nina was due on that last mission, and she got sick. Ella had you all fooled. I warned your ass, and you let it go. Where's Nina now? Still wrapped up in Endgame drama?"

"I've never trusted spooks, and there is no more Endgame." He could deny with the best of them. He took another step, completely invading her space. Loretta's smile disappeared.

"Step back, McNally. You got my girl over there hurt when you should have been protecting her. You'll tell me what's going on, or I'll make Shanghai look like a paper cut."

King stepped away, letting her words flow over and off him. "How is she *your* girl, Loretta?"

"You know I was Company. I taught that girl how to fight when she was little more than a toddler. I owed her father at first. Then her mama died, and my heart broke for her. She's mine and now she's hurt. If you're involved, it's nothing but Endgame business. Everybody knows you're gunning for Dresden, and I don't want my girl taking the ride with you."

There was some note in her voice that put King's radar up. The subterfuge was there, hell she was CIA, but there was something else. Something deeper that made King's skin prickle.

"I don't believe a word that comes out of your mouth,

Loretta." Because he'd trusted the redheaded harpy once seven years ago, and she'd made him pay for it.

In the end, he'd chosen his own ass over the woman who tried to kill him. No-brainer, really. He'd discovered shortly after that she was the equivalent of quality control for her boss. She hunted down rogues and traitor operatives. On that op in Shanghai, his SEAL team's CIA liaison had been playing both sides of the fence. It had been Loretta's job to bring the liaison in for processing.

"You didn't answer me about Nina," she reminded him.

"Nina is dead."

When the Piper had instructed King that he was adding two CIA liaisons to Endgame's roll, King had been hesitant. His experience with the CIA wasn't good. Over time, Nina and Ella had both integrated into the team. They'd become family. Now they were both dead.

"People just fall dead left and right around you Endgame boys, don't they? Nina was good people. Who killed her? I'd like to visit them."

"You better get a backhoe because they're six feet under," King retorted.

"You got them?"

"Didn't have to. They caught themselves."

Loretta nodded, then cocked her head. "Well done, then. I wondered if you had it in you to work on behalf of the good guys anymore. After Beirut, you had everybody taking bets you were in Dresden's pocket. Word was you sabotaged your team for him."

King cut the overhead lights, making sure a single lamp beside the bed burned. He didn't want Allie to wake to darkness. "I hated that bastard from the moment I found out he was giving decommissioned weapons to young Somali boys so they could kill their parents and join up with warlords. The same warlords who paid top dollar for his illegal arms. He killed my people. I wanted to destroy his pockets, not crawl inside them."

"Too bad you couldn't prove it. Too bad there's a history between you and Dresden. That didn't help your cause either," she murmured before she pulled out a cigarette and lit it, taking a deep drag and blowing smoke up in the air.

"Ella was his contact. You asked who was responsible for Nina—it was her. Once Dresden put a bullet in her head in Beirut, my ability to prove it was nearly decimated." He decided to let the dig about the history between him and Dresden slide. They'd been teammates in SEALs, but when Dresden went AWOL and then mercenary killer slash gunrunner, he'd become King's enemy. King wouldn't let it be anything other than end of story.

Loretta chuckled and shook her head. "Where have you and your team been the last year, McNally?"

"Does it matter?"

"Ella's not dead."

It was as if a bomb exploded in King's brain leaving cotton in its wake. "Her head was blown to smithereens by Dresden. I watched it happen, Loretta. The helo went dead in the air and fell to the earth, and we scattered. He put her on her knees beside Madoc and Samson and blew her away."

"I think you're a born leader, McNally. But you've never been very good at seeing through the smoke to the fire. You've wallowed in the muck of the dark side too long."

There was that note again—hidden meanings, a lie trying to make itself known in her speech patterns and tone. Desperation rode her tone, which bothered King because Allie was involved with this woman. There was a connection, and he simply was not willing to trust her where his brand-new burden was involved. For that matter, what the hell was Loretta doing in Cameroon? And only a stone's throw from Allie this whole time.

He turned on Loretta, stalking back and hovering over her, silently demanding to know what the hell she was talking about.

"She isn't dead," Loretta said with another long drag on her cigarette.

"I watched her fall. We all watched her fall. Unless she was goddamn Superwoman, there's no way she could have survived a bullet to the head," King said harshly.

The memories were violent, tearing through his mind in a tsunami of blood, bullets, and fire. Normally he only remembered in his sleep, but right now, the sights, smells, and sounds were in the forefront of his mind, a movie playing behind his eyelids.

"I've seen the video of that helo crash. I've watched you and your men escape, and I watched Ella give herself over to Dresden. I watched him kiss her on the cheek, then shoot her, and I watched two of his men drag her away before Savidge stepped up and shot Madoc and Samson. She was breathing. Still is. She didn't betray you. She was the sacrificial lamb to the slaughter. And while you Endgame boys are chasing your ass looking for Dresden and his patsy Savidge, well, Ella's out there on her own, playing Russian roulette with her life."

She'd seen video? Goddamn, so the CIA *had* been all over an Endgame op, hadn't they? "She was our CIA liaison, Loretta. You'll defend your fellow spook to the grave." He got in her face again and she backed up, eyes going wide. "Or maybe she was your objective. Is that it? I know you're cleanup for the director. Ella went rogue, and you had to go in and handle business—but Dresden got her first." King almost punched the wall, but relaxed his shoulders and reined in his temper.

"She betrayed us. Gave away our location, our mission specs, our team members, and our strategy. She had Dresden waiting in ambush for us. She's responsible for the loss of Nina, Samson, and Madoc. And regardless of the whys and wherefores, all I want are the whos. Who is paying Dresden to kill my teammates? Who is determined to destroy Endgame Ops?"

"I'm not CIA anymore, McNally. My life is my own now, so watch what you say to me. Accusations can get you gutted quickly. Ella was a victim as much as the rest of Endgame that day, and I don't have the answers you're seeking," Loretta said in a low voice.

"Don't you goddamn defend her to me!"

Loretta raised her hands and stood, backing away. "I've already said too much. But when you're damning an innocent woman to hell, remember that I warned you there were bigger things in play than just Endgame. You weren't the only ones to suffer that day," she bit out before she walked to the bed.

King wanted to fight. Wanted to demand she answer all his questions. But she was the least trustworthy of all entities—C. I. Motherfucking A. Or she had been. It was news to him that she was out of the game.

"Why did you settle here?" he asked, the unknown biting at him.

Loretta stared at him and ignored his question. "Does Broemig know you have her?"

"He knows I have her."

"Does he know who you are?"

"He knows I have her," King repeated.

"That's not what I'm asking, and you know it, McNally. Does he know it's *you*? Never mind, I'm sure he knows. Never doubt his reach. If he doesn't, you should be afraid I'm going to tell him," she said slowly.

He narrowed his gaze on her. "You won't."

Loretta nodded and her lips twisted. "I won't. But only because I don't want anyone else knowing you have her. That would be a death sentence."

King crossed his arms over his chest. "You won't tell him because you just told me Company business. Your boss is a lot of things, tolerant ain't one of 'em."

"Your southern is showing, McNally. I know how hard you've worked to get rid of your past. Might want to watch that," Loretta warned.

"Yeah, Loretta? Why?" She was threatening him. Did she know about him? Where he came from? What he'd done? Did it even fucking matter anymore? He'd told the woman lying on the bed more than he'd willingly told another soul. Ever. Did it really matter if the entire world knew he was a killer?

He'd become something else after he'd signed on with the Navy—not necessarily good, but a man who lived by an honorable code. His father had taken all the good from King so he'd returned the favor. SEALs had offered him a chance to atone. But there'd never been enough expiation. King didn't know if there ever could be. Then he'd been forced to up that ante again with the Piper. Forced to lie again to hide the truth about another lie. Goddamn, his entire life had been about hiding the truth, and he was sick of it.

"I'm not Company anymore, McNally. I won't tell you again," Loretta said in a low voice. "But I still have my resources. Something else you should remember."

She was telling him something, the subterfuge in her words so thick that it raked over his eardrums. Her threats didn't concern him. If his number was up to be punched, that was what it was. He'd go down fighting, but he'd played this game long enough to know Loretta was hiding a lot of information. On top of that, he didn't believe for two seconds that she wasn't CIA anymore. Agents *never* left the CIA unless it was in a body bag.

A groan from the bed had King turning. Loretta went to her side and King followed.

Loretta wiped a hand down her face. "How did she end up with you?"

"I was given information that a courier for Savidge was flying Air France from Cameroon to Paris. Lots of terrorists setting up shop in this country, Loretta. Makes a man wonder why you're here."

Loretta stared limpidly at him.

"She was the only American on the plane's passenger manifest. Then Boko Haram terrorists stormed the plane, hijacking it and threatening to kill her if she didn't tell them who her father was."

Loretta bit her lip. "Oh damn—that's not good."

"She knocked the lead terrorist out with a head-butt, and I had no choice but to get her out of there."

"You took her to one of Endgame's safe houses?"

He nodded.

"Stupid move, McNally," she said with venom.

"You know, I'm thinking for someone out of the game, you know way too much about Endgame's operations, Loretta. Why is that?"

"I thought there was no more Endgame?" she told him bluntly.

"Stop arguing," Allie commanded.

Her voice was weak but no less effective.

"We aren't arguing," he and Loretta said at the same time.

"Good," Allie said on a deep breath.

She was back out just that fast.

"You involved her in your shit. She is the farthest thing from a courier you've ever known. Sweet girl, killer right hook and a mean shot, but so far removed from her father's machinations that they aren't even on the same continent more than a few times every other year or so. If Dresden or, God forbid, Savidge, gets to her, they'll use her. Could be why she was put on the playing field to begin with. These men will not stop. They don't care about guilt or innocence, only whether someone has use to them. Get her home fast and safely, McNally," Loretta demanded in a low voice.

King sighed. "I need everything you know. If we've been chasing our own ass, I need to know. Point me in the right direction, Loretta."

"You're heading in the right direction, McNally.

That's all I can say. Remember to look through the smoke to the fire," she said in a low voice.

Her words sent chills dancing along his skin. King was missing so many pieces that it was hard to form even a partial picture of the situation. He despised that feeling of impotence.

Loretta leaned over, placed a motherly kiss on Allie's head, and shot him a warning look. "I've got recon to do. The locals have probably noticed your presence here, so I need to run interference. How you getting out of here? Where you taking her?"

"Unh-unh, not telling," King told her matter-of-factly.

"If you need me, she knows how to reach me," Loretta said as she stepped to the door. She glanced back at him, face drawn in a fierce frown. "You hurt her, it'll be the last thing you do. That girl right there is worth her weight in gold. And you better keep who she is to yourself. She's not a courier—vowed a long time ago never to get mixed up in her daddy's shit. He wouldn't have let her anyway. Remember that, King. She's an innocent."

King shrugged. "Somebody's dangling her like a carrot, and look what they caught? Little ol' me."

Loretta seemed to stare through him, and then she turned to leave.

King watched her. The silence stretched like a wide, yawning chasm, and weariness rode his shoulders like a fiend. He waited several minutes, giving Loretta ample time to vacate the premises before he followed her out the door and made sure their immediate area was clear.

He reentered the hut, set homemade alarms at each of the windows and the door, and grabbed a bottle of water. King took a deep breath, gulped down the contents of the bottle, and picked up the chair he'd knocked down earlier.

The hut was a single-room dwelling with a bathroom off the back and a full kitchen. Kribi was a resort town. The beaches and waters surrounding them were pristine. People from all over the world and the upper echelon within Cameroon considered this a paradise and vacationed here all year long.

To King it was a pit stop, a place to rest and allow Allie to recover. But it was too open, too impossible to defend for his tastes. Their hut nestled in palms that butted up against the dunes before the sand gave way to the ocean. Someone could come up on them from any direction. Yes, it was the last hut in a line of about ten, but it was too open.

Nothing to be done about it. His passenger on this ride had been injured, and he'd have to let it play out as it would until she was better and he could move her to safety.

When had that become his primary objective? Hours ago, he'd been telling himself that finding the person who would lead him to Savidge and Dresden was the only important thing. That avenging the deaths of his men and proving the remaining members of Endgame innocent was his top priority.

Now?

It was different.

And he'd realized over the course of the last hours there was no way he could use her as bait. No fucking way.

It was her damn eyes. And her gold, silk-spun hair. And her bow lips and her apple-shaped ass and…the list went on and on. What he liked most about her?

Her spunk.

King had no business liking anything about her. Damn.

He sighed wearily and sat down, untying, then toeing off his boots. He needed some rest. She'd be out for a while, and King needed sleep. He tossed the empty water bottle in a trash can beside the bed and folded his hands over his stomach.

What the hell was he involved in now?

He closed his eyes, knocked his head gently against the wall, and tried to dispel the scent of wildflowers in his nose, the taste of her kiss in his memory.

He had a scary feeling it was going to be impossible.

Chapter 9

ALLIE FLOATED UP FROM SLEEP, RIDING A WAVE OF CLOUDY awareness. Fire licked up her side. She was so damn hot. She needed to push the covers off. Normally she only slept with a light blanket, so why had she gone to bed with a quilt?

She didn't open her eyes immediately; rather she continued to lie still, taking stock of her surroundings. Fear was a rush in her bloodstream and a hard beat in her chest. Fear wasn't bad. It was how you reacted to it that made you weak.

Her father's words echoed in her ears. But they made no sense right now.

She strained to listen. Why couldn't she open her eyes?

"Hello?" she called out.

Silence.

Was she alone? Why had he left her alone? He'd gotten her into this. He should be here, talking her through this.

"Kingston McNally…need you," she mumbled.

More silence. She must be dreaming.

She opened her eyes and met the darkness. Someone was lying beside her. Someone large and warm, like a furnace blazing bright. There was something she was missing—where she was, why she was here, wherever here was.

Allie shifted, and the pain made itself known. A dull

ache along her side. A breath hissed in, and with it came a little more lucidity. She reached out tentatively, finding an arm beside hers.

She took another deep breath, trying to control the pain. Evergreen and mint met her nose.

King.

"McNally, for some reason I like you," she told him. She could gift herself with the admission because she was dreaming.

He said nothing in return, and she wasn't sure he'd heard her. Was that even him?

Oh well, the black had crept back to grab her up and take her back under. This time she'd go willingly.

"I like you too, Allie," he said at her ear.

His voice reverberated through her mind. Like a gong set off inside her, it was loud. Too loud. "Stop yelling," she reprimanded him but smiled to soften it. This was shaping up into a very nice dream.

Where was he?

Silence.

She needed him. She reached for the arm, following the strength of the limb before grabbing his hand and twining her fingers with his.

"I'm going to sleep now," she told him.

"I've got you," he said, softer now.

And she was eased.

Chapter 10

KING OPENED THE DOOR OF THE HUT AND STEPPED IN lightly. He lowered his rifle as he noticed Allie still slept. He took a moment to track her breathing, and it was clear to him that her fever had broken.

Her breathing was slow, deep, and even, not the shallower fever-induced sleep of the past twenty-four hours. King had been there the entire time, struggling to keep her from giving in to the infection.

He'd forced her to drink when she rose from the sleep; then he'd given her antibiotic shots as the doctor had instructed him.

She turned to him instinctively for protection and care. Somewhere over the past day, he'd lost a bit more of himself to her. She'd talked in her delirium, ranting soliloquies about her love for her father and her job, and her conflicting feelings for…King.

Now she seemed to be on the mend. Her wound was healing rapidly, and he could only thank whatever divine entity was watching over them that it was.

King placed his rifle in the corner, walked to the bed, leaned down, and checked her pulse and respiration again. When he felt safe that she was sleeping normally, he headed to the small bath and showered.

He'd just put his clothes on when her voice rang out. "Hello?"

He rubbed his chest, barely checking the action.

Small, lost...vulnerable. She reminded him of a child in that second.

It made the other thoughts running through his mind feel dirty.

"King?"

He closed his eyes, pulled on his T-shirt, and walked to her.

"I'm here. You decided to wake up, huh?"

Her gaze met his, and her relief was palpable. She smiled weakly and tried to sit up.

"Here, let me help you," he said as he came over her. "You've only got Steri-Strips closing that wound, so let's be careful, yeah?"

She stared up at him, confusion carving a path across her face before her lips pulled down. He didn't like that look on her.

King traced her lips, meeting her gaze. "You thirsty?"

She continued to gaze up at him and finally nodded.

He snagged a bottle of water and returned to her, holding it up to her lips.

"You tried to drown me last time, if I remember correctly," she mumbled before she took the bottle in shaking hands and drank long and deep.

King almost moaned when she pulled the water away and licked her lower lip. She was a mess, hair all over the place where it wasn't stuck to her face and skin, and she didn't smell all that heavenly, but underneath the sweat, there was something that was quintessentially Allie.

"I didn't try to drown you," he said quietly. "I've got bigger plans for you."

Her pale cheeks colored, and he didn't know if it was with anger or intrigue, but he wanted to find out.

"How long?" she asked.

"You've been down a day. How are you feeling?"

She winced as she tried again to push up. "A little sore. Nothing too bad. Like you said, a skid mark."

He chuckled, but he leaned down to lift her gently. This put her face in his neck, and her warm breath slid under his shirt. He shivered.

King never shivered, yet he refused to look too deeply into it. Now wasn't the time.

Once she was settled, he lifted away and walked back to the refrigerator to grab another bottle of water.

He placed it on the small table beside the bed and then walked to the other side of the hut, staring out a window into the night.

"Thank you," she whispered.

He shrugged. He'd resolved to feel nothing for her as she lay there recovering. King rubbed his eyes with one hand and twisted the bullet in his pocket with the other. It was a hard realization that no matter how much he fought to feel nothing for her, it was a losing battle.

"King?"

He refused to look at her. "Yeah?"

"I think you should just let me go with Lo-Lo. She can get me—"

He whirled around and held up a hand. "No." No way in hell. Loretta stank of subterfuge. While Allie was in his care, she'd not go near Loretta Bernstein.

"But—"

"I said no."

Her mouth fell open, and her gaze narrowed. Frail but no less powerful, she was gorgeous in her pique. "I have rights, damn it."

"Yeah—*right* here, *right* now, you're under my rule and I'm a dictator, baby. Time to man up. I'm in charge and where I go, you go, until I take you back to Daddy." King intentionally kept his voice low.

She didn't respond, and King was grateful for that.

Time for playing was over. She'd been shot, and he was in the midst of something much bigger than he'd realized.

Over the course of the last day, while she'd lain there dead to the world, he'd been ferreting out some truths. Loretta had been a reluctant font of information. She'd visited once more and brought information King would rather not have had.

Someone had placed Allie Redding directly in his path, and they'd done it intentionally. Some murky source had dropped her in Endgame's lap, knowing her connection to Gray Broemig and knowing King would be the one in Cameroon to meet up with the mythical courier. As far as King knew, that source could be Loretta. He had Jude working on that angle, though he hadn't heard back from him yet. If she'd been the one, she was in deep with Dresden. The biggest fear King had now was that Dresden's men were gunning to take out Allie, himself, or both of them.

He'd been unable to contact Jude again. His man had gone completely off-grid, which while not worrisome to King, wasn't the best thing for all parties involved. Especially now that King had irrefutable proof that Ella Banning was alive. Loretta had shown him the video while Allie had been out, and it was clear that Ella had left that site in Beirut hurt but very much alive. King didn't necessarily believe Loretta's assertion that Ella was a pawn. He'd seen the look of loss on her face as she stared at the downed chopper, but he'd also witnessed her look of betrayal when Dresden shot her.

But she had definitely left alive. And if she was alive maybe, just maybe she knew who the hell was gunning for Endgame Ops. The trick now would be finding her. How would Jude react when he found out? How would King tell Jude that the woman he'd loved so deeply might never have been on their side at all?

Ella, Ella, Ella… A lot of roads led back to the woman who'd seemingly betrayed them all.

"What's going on, King?" Allie asked.

His neck tightened as he played with the bullet in his pocket. He should share some truths. Maybe then she'd realize the danger she was in and be more agreeable to following his lead. He almost snorted. The woman could teach stubborn to a mule. "I want you to call your father."

"Okay," she responded hesitantly. "Can you tell me what's going on first?"

He crossed back to the bed and lowered himself onto the same chair where he'd slept for two nights, except when he'd wrapped himself around her. Comfort, he'd told himself. Purely for comfort and to keep her from thrashing about and opening her wound. "I'm not sure where to start, and before I begin, I need you to call your father."

"Why?"

"Because I said so, Allie. You have to learn now that if you're going to make it out of this shit alive, you have to do what I say, when I say to do it."

She cocked her head. "Okay."

A single word of accession, and his anger evaporated. "Do you feel like a shower first?"

She smiled slightly, nose wrinkling, the lines of her mouth shaking for a moment before she straightened her face and nodded. "I can smell myself. A shower might be heaven."

"Let's get you into one then." He helped her up, her already-tiny frame made more so by nearly two days without solid food.

She sagged against him once she made it to her feet. King closed his eyes and took a deep, controlling breath. Having her curves pressed against him felt too good. Way too good.

He put his hands on her shoulder and pulled away slightly. "I changed your bandage earlier, but we need to wrap some plastic around your middle so the Steri-Strips don't get wet."

She nodded.

He moved with her slowly to the bathroom. Her legs were shaky at first, but with each step, she grew in strength. One step up into the bathroom, and she groaned. The sound was a knife in his heart.

He should have killed all those men back at the safe house. And then run over their carcasses with the Rover.

"Sit down," he ordered her as he lowered the toilet seat. She did, and he pulled the plastic wrap Loretta had brought him from the bag beside the sink. "Lift your shirt for me."

Her cheeks pinkened, making him want to trace that color all the way down to her chest and farther. She did as he asked though.

"Looks like my hands are going back under your shirt, Miz Redding," he teased.

Her lips quirked. "Ha, ha, ha, very funny. Still not the way I envisioned it."

"Me either," he murmured.

Her smooth, ivory flesh called to him. Every time he changed her bandages, he forced himself to be quick lest her curves tempt him more. She was awake now though, and if his gaze roved over the bottom curve of her breast, across her ribs, and lower to the enticing slope of her hips, well, he was only human. Emphasis on *man*.

He pulled long pieces of wrap off and wound them around her torso until he was satisfied no water could saturate the bandage beneath.

A lingering touch at the top of her hipbone, right above the string of her bikini underwear (Loretta had brought her killer panties), and he was satisfied for the moment. He lowered her shirt and let his gaze rise to meet hers.

She knew what he'd done. Her breathing was shallow again, and his heart stopped. It was there in her eyes…need.

She unraveled him. He was discovering he only had so much control around her.

It was unacceptable.

He rose quickly and stepped back. "Towels are right there, soap and shampoo are in the shower. I'll be right out in the hall if you need me."

She nodded and licked her lips.

King made it to the hallway before he adjusted his hard dick. His cargoes were comfortable but not with a brickbat in them.

It took her a while, and his ears catalogued every sound she made. He realized she was a proud woman who didn't want to call for help. Or maybe she didn't want him seeing her completely naked.

He wondered if the sight of Allie's naked body would eclipse his fantasies. He heard the water falling and wondered what she'd look like bathed in moonlight. How he envied the water. How he wanted to sip it from her flesh!

Jesus, he was in trouble.

He needed to find a woman before they left here. As soon as the thought formed, he rejected it. For some reason, the thought of slaking this crazy need with another woman felt wrong.

But he couldn't have her. She was too good for a killer. She was too good for Kingston McNally.

The shower cut off, and he heard her drying off slowly. God, it was torture listening to the sound of her dressing.

"King?" she called.

He stepped to the doorway immediately. "Yeah?"

"I'm hungry," she said with a grin.

She'd pulled her wet hair into a ponytail. Her face was brighter than he'd seen it, and the smile curving her lips made him lick his own.

Her gaze arrowed to the action, and her eyes darkened. "Stop," she whispered.

"Stop what?"

"That," she said as she pointed to his lips.

He let it hang there between them—the want. It was an impossible thing. Nothing could happen. This lust was a result of their circumstances and adrenaline. He was going to tell himself that until he believed it.

She cleared her throat, and his mind focused with the sound. He grunted as he offered her his arm. "So the lady says she's hungry."

She tentatively placed her hand on his arm, and he hissed in a breath at the contact.

"I am indeed," she said with a small laugh.

He led her to a small table and placed the makings for a sandwich, along with some chips and a Coke, in front of her.

She raised an eyebrow. "Seriously?"

"What?"

"Isn't this a resort?"

He crossed his arms over his chest.

"Don't do that," she murmured.

Confusion swam through him. "Do what?"

"Never mind," she responded in a long-suffering tone.

He shook it off. "Yes, it's a resort, but I've warned everyone away from this hut."

"Ahhh, yes, the games haven't stopped just because I was grazed by an enemy bullet, right?"

He nodded and took the seat opposite her. King watched her eat, waiting patiently for her to finish. It didn't take her long. A few bites, some chips, an entire Coca-Cola, and she was done.

"You've gotta eat more than that," he admonished.

She rubbed her belly, careful to stay away from her side. "Can't. Speaking of enemies, how about you tell me what's going on."

He pulled out her sat phone and slid it across the table to her. "Call your dad."

"I really hate it when you do that," she bit out.

"Just call your dad."

She picked up the phone, punched a single number, and held the phone up, all while glaring at him.

He smiled.

She frowned.

He thought it a microcosm of their entire association so far.

Her face cleared just then, and the smile that lit her face had his mouth falling open. Goddamn, she was beautiful. He suddenly wanted her to smile like that for him.

"Dad?"

Chapter 11

"DAMN IT, ALLIE, WHAT THE HELL HAVE YOU GOTTEN yourself into?" Gray Broemig growled into the phone.

Allie closed her eyes and sighed. "I didn't get myself into anything. I was headed home, and the damn plane was hijacked."

A rough breath sounded in her ear, and her heart melted. Her father was a worrier by nature. A big, tough-assed worrier. Would he have been the same if her mother hadn't been killed?

Probably.

"I need you to listen to me, Allie. Pay attention," her father demanded.

"I'm listening," she said and couldn't keep the frustration from her voice.

"No sass, young lady," he said.

"I'm twenty-seven, Dad, not six." Allie winced when she said it. She'd been six when her mother died. Because of Allie.

The man across the table from her sat stoically, like an immovable mountain, listening to every word she said.

"The man who has you, has he mistreated you in any way?"

She glanced up at King. Been a pain in her ass? Yes. Kissed the breath out of her? Definitely. Made her forget McDonald's fries? That's a check. Mistreated her? "No."

King smirked and she looked at him quizzically. The

muscles of his arms flexed, almost as if he was holding himself back.

"Allie, his name is Kingston McNally. He's a former SEAL who decommissioned to work for a private entity that is involved in some rough stuff. He's dangerous."

"I figured that out, Dad. The dangerous part anyway," she told her dad as she locked gazes with King.

He inclined his head as if to say, *Go ahead and find out the truth. I'll still be me.*

And she knew irrevocably he would. Because underneath that dangerous exterior lay a core of honor. She'd recognized it from the moment he'd pushed her head down on the plane.

"Allie, he and his group are fugitives of American justice. In the eyes of the law they're no better than criminals. They embroiled their country in an international incident with Lebanon. But he's my only hope of getting you home. I need you to listen to him and do exactly as he says, you understand?"

She nodded, still looking at King.

"Allie, do you understand?" her father asked impatiently.

"Yes, sir."

King's eyes flared at that. Huh, he liked hearing her say *sir*. Kinky bastard. He didn't give her much, but she was learning to read him. He wouldn't appreciate knowing that.

"I'm making everything at my disposal available to him. This is serious, Allie. I don't know that he's a good man, but he's the man for this job."

Her dad had just gone from warning her about King to giving him the all clear for making sure she stayed alive. Her head spun, but she said, "I hear you. I'll make his job as easy as possible."

"Get home to me, Allie," her father said brokenly.

She would have spared him this if she could. But how could she have known terrorists would be gunning for her? "I will."

"Give the phone to him."

Allie handed the phone to King. He said two words, "Will do," and then disconnected and handed her the phone.

Allie placed it back on the table.

King took the phone, dropped it on the floor and, with a quick stomp, decimated it. Her heart stuttered. That phone had been her last contact with her dad.

"I've got you, Allie," King said in a hard voice.

She nodded and breathed in deeply.

"It's time for answers now," she said in an equally hard tone.

"What do you want to know?"

She narrowed her gaze on him, taking in the wide breadth of his shoulders, the muscles of his arms, the firm cut of his jaw. "I heard Dad's version… Care to share yours?"

"Not particularly."

She slammed a hand on the table, trying to control the anger rushing through her but finding herself incapable of it. The action hurt, but she pushed through it.

King looked impressed before his face blanked. "Okay, I'm a SEAL who decommissioned from active duty to join a private security agency. We worked for the good guys—hell, we are the good guys—but we were betrayed. As a result, my team and I are doing our best to take down the entity responsible."

She stared at him, assessing his tone and the look on his face. Her gut said he wasn't lying. His actions spoke of a man used to protecting.

"Go ahead," he told her. "Ask."

"I don't have to," she returned evenly.

"You'd be the only one, and I'm starting to doubt your sanity. Do you normally trust every Tom, Dick, and Harry that pops into your life?"

She cocked her head and fisted her hands on the table. "I don't actually, which makes my instinctive trust in you an aberration."

That shut him right up and lightened her mood dramatically.

"So I'll ask again—*who* are you?"

He pushed away from the table and stalked to the window. She could sense the demons riding him. But this was important. Her father wanted her to blindly trust this man who'd admitted to killing his father and being a criminal in the eyes of the American justice system. And the truth was, she already did. That did not mean she liked the thought of being used as a pawn in whatever war King was waging. She wanted to make sure her eyes were wide open, and that meant knowing his motivations.

"I'm a hunter. A killer."

Oh, he took her heart with those words and fisted it tight in his hands. "Aren't we all to some degree?" she countered.

His head swiveled, and his green gaze was bright in the low light of the hut. He didn't say a word but stared into her eyes. She had the uncanny feeling he was trying to read her thoughts, see deep into her soul, so he could determine whether she was telling the truth or playing him.

Finally, he turned back to stare out the window. "In some form or fashion, yes, we are all hunters and killers. None more so than me. It's what I was raised to be."

She shivered, and he must have sensed the movement because he walked to the bed and brought a blanket back. Always, he was taking care of her. From the moment she'd jumped into his arms from the plane until right now—it was as if he refused to allow anything to hurt her.

Her heart cracked. She didn't want to break the silence because she sensed he was about to tell her more, so Allie folded her hands in her lap and waited.

"I'm on a mission to destroy the people responsible for the deaths of several members of my team."

"I'm going out on a limb here because I know jack about your past, but surely, if they were soldiers like you, they knew the danger. Who were you working for?"

"Endgame Ops." He spit the words out, as if the taste of them in his mouth was abhorrent.

Something niggled at the back of Allie's mind. It wasn't the first time she'd heard that name, but damn if she could remember where or in what context. "Sanctioned?" she asked.

He shook his head. That wasn't good. Allie was her father's daughter and had always had an ability to ferret out secrets and angles. She wished she had a secure Internet connection and a way to access it so she could do her own searching. Because something about Endgame Ops rocked her foundations.

"You have to realize that on paper, Endgame offers

protective services. We work for organizations rebuilding war-torn countries. We keep their people safe. In reality, that's a cover. We operate in the black, taking missions our own government won't. None of our missions were sanctioned. That allowed us to act with anonymity, and we were able to deny our government's culpability in any of our actions. I trained men and women to be the best soldiers they could be, and I led them into the darkness of covert ops. I was a killer by birth and a leader by design."

Of course he was a leader. She'd recognized that the moment she'd seen him. Okay, maybe that had come later—after the mink-brown hair, the high-and-tight ass, and that chest. Good Lord, she wanted to fan herself right now. The man had a way with her hormones.

"So what happened?"

"I really shouldn't tell you this," he muttered.

"But you will," she singsonged. "Because you trust me."

"I don't trust anyone. You'd do well to remember that," he replied through clenched teeth.

That hurt, but she refused to be cowed so she waited. She'd change his mind.

His shoulders tightened, but he didn't look at her. "We ran an op in Beirut a year ago, an incursion operation. It went belly up. Our helo crashed, and several members of my team were caught and murdered. Endgame Ops almost came to an end."

"God, you are so stingy with information." She sighed loudly before she followed with, "And?"

"And I've spent the last year trying to hunt down the ones responsible."

"Why?" she asked softly.

"To destroy them."

"Yeah, you mentioned that." Well, wasn't that simple then? She snorted and he turned to her, disbelief on his face. "Are you a one-man army now? Or do you have help?"

His lip quirked at the corner, and her heart thudded heavily. What this man did to her with the tiniest of movements was a hazard all its own.

"I have help."

"That's good then," she responded with a grunt of her own.

"Why would you care?" he asked silkily.

"It isn't your turn to pump me for information, buddy."

He came back and sat across from her. His seriousness conveyed itself startlingly well. His face went hard, and his intent stroked her skin. "You were on that plane. Why?"

She rested her jaw on her fist. "I told you I was headed home. I've been in this country for two years. I missed home. Plus, things were heating up here. As you can tell, Boko Haram is becoming entrenched in Cameroon. Nigeria is fighting a constant war with them, and they've spread their wings."

"Did anyone know you were heading home?"

"If you're turning this into an inquisition, can you at least grab me a bottle of water? I'm dry as the Sahara," she groused.

He did as she asked, and as he bent to retrieve the bottle from the bowels of the fridge, Allie looked her fill, almost groaning at how his khakis stretched over that amazing rear end.

"I know you're looking at my ass," he said. She could hear the smile in his voice.

"I so am. When I'm better, I'll turn around often so you can do the same. I'm totally willing to return the favor."

He snorted. "What if I don't want to look at your ass?"

"You don't want to go there with me."

"No?"

She cleared her throat and lowered her voice as deep as she could. "'You'll not only look at me that way again, Redding, you'll do it while I'm buried inside you, riding us both to release.'"

He stilled, threw back his head, and laughed. It was one of the most beautiful things she'd ever seen or heard.

Then his face blanked when he looked at hers. "Don't," he said suddenly, harshly.

She met his gaze, wondering what he was talking about.

"Don't make this harder on me," he repeated roughly.

She glanced away, afraid she'd burn to cinders at the look in his eyes. "Sorry. I don't want to make anything harder than it already is."

He handed her the water. "It's pretty fucking tough. My neck is itching, and it's time to get moving. I'll give you tonight to rest up, but we need to head out soon."

Allie drank the water and breathed heavily. She was sore, but healing fast. She would survive. She'd made it through a bullet's grazing kiss, anything that came after was child's play. Right?

"I didn't tell anyone I was heading home. That's always been the way it is. I buy my tickets and head home—no notice, no nothing. I'm always careful. I've been taught to watch my six and take the unknown into account, but I'm not a soldier. I'm a caregiver. So those things come harder to me. I didn't notice anything unusual. I had one of the villagers drive me to Douala, was a little late arriving, but everything was fine. You know, until the bullets started flying."

He gazed at the table, his index finger making circles in the condensation from his water bottle. "Six people, including me, knew I was in Cameroon, and I was only here because I was expecting to meet a courier."

"Meet, as in kidnap?"

"You say *to-may-toe*…"

Allie raised an eyebrow.

"How long ago did you reserve your flight?" he asked.

"Two weeks. I called my dad from the satellite phone when I arrived—"

The same sat phone with the tracker embedded in it. His head snapped up. "Wait, you said nobody knew, but Loretta knew. I heard her say she thought you'd be gone by now."

There were some things Allie would never doubt. Lo-Lo's loyalty was one of them. Just like she knew Kingston McNally would never willingly harm her. Some things just *were*.

"It's not Lo-Lo. I don't know how anyone found out, but it wasn't from her. Maybe they were tracking my cell phone. You said that was a possibility."

He rubbed a hand down his face. He'd said it before, and it bore saying again—she was too damn trusting. The look on his face spoke of his doubt. His mind tickled with the possibility that Loretta was involved in this somehow. "I told your father I'd get you home, but he's got a leak somewhere. It's the only thing that makes sense. Somebody has put you smack-dab in the middle of this. You say it isn't her. Okay, but I'm not willing to trust her any farther than I can throw her. For shits and giggles, let's say it isn't her. That means someone besides Loretta knows who you are, what you are to him, and they're using you to do one of two things: get to your dad, or get to me."

"I didn't even know you existed until a few days ago. Why would anyone think you'd be swayed by putting me into play?"

"It's not you, it's what you represent" came his hard reply.

Allie clenched her fists tight. She was getting angry, and that wouldn't help anything. "What do I represent?"

"A link to the man I was told you were handling information for, and through him, a link to Horace Dresden."

"And why is that important?"

"Horace Dresden and Vasily Savidge are the ones who killed my teammates in Beirut."

Fear tripped through her. "I have never been a courier. So why would the person setting all this up think you'd keep me so close after you discovered I had no link to Dresden?"

"Because you're also a link to the CIA," he said roughly.

She sighed. "I know I'm a bit slow, but why is that important?"

His gaze was on her, but his mind was somewhere far, far away. "Because it was CIA who betrayed us and gave Dresden the heads-up we were coming in Beirut."

He stopped there, and she could have screamed in frustration.

"And?"

He got up and began pacing, his big body and long legs eating up the tiny hut in a loop. "There is no *and*. The less you know, the better off you are."

Frustration had her gasping for breath. *No sudden moves, Allie. You might hurt yourself. Or him.* "You just said you have no idea what their true motivation is for using me. The thing about that whole statement? They're using me. So I'm all up in this whether you, me, or Gray Broemig likes it or not."

Anger rushed through her and she stood suddenly, the need to move and expel the sudden excess of energy overwhelming. She began to pace.

"Stay in your seat, woman."

"Don't tell me what to do," she returned. "I want the truth, King."

"I work in the black, Allie. I do things other people refuse to do so that in the end, the greater good is met."

"What does that mean? Spell it out," she demanded. Her heart was in her throat. She knew what it meant…

He sighed and rubbed a hand down his face. "They obviously thought I'd be willing to use you to get what I want."

Her disbelief was tempered by her meager knowledge of how black ops worked. "And are they right?"

He looked at her, his green gaze intent. Would he be truthful here and now? There was a lot riding on this. She trusted him, even though she doubted her sanity to do so.

"No. I won't use an innocent to do my dirty work."

Relief poured through her, making her momentarily weak. "Thank you." It was all she could say. His answer meant he believed her—she wasn't an operative and had no idea how she'd been pulled into this mess.

He crossed his arms over his chest and widened his stance. "I can't tell you Endgame business. You know too much as it is now. I won't put you in more harm than you're already in. Trust me, knowing Endgame business gets people killed."

"What about you?" she whispered, stopping in front of him and giving in to the urge to touch him. She stroked a finger down his stubble-roughened cheek.

"I can take care of myself." Their gazes locked, and she heard everything he didn't say. He was constantly in danger. It surrounded him like a mantle. She hadn't noticed that hard edge when she'd first seen him on the plane. Truthfully, she hadn't been able to see past the instant lust.

And she knew then she was getting nothing else from him today. "I'm tired. If we're leaving tomorrow, I need to rest. Can you tell me where we're going?"

"I won't know until we get there," he replied.

Evasion—he was a master at it.

"Nice. Great answer." She was the one crossing her arms over her chest now. "I don't like being kept in the dark."

"You can't tell what you don't know."

Ahh, the flip side of being innocent. Apparently, she wouldn't know plans until they happened. His words made her shiver, but she walked to the bed and lay down gingerly. Soon they'd be on the move. She needed the rest if she wasn't going to slow them down.

"I'll wake you when it's time to go," he told her.

"Can you at least tell me why we can't hit the closest U.S. base and send me home on a military plane?"

He shook his head. "I promised your father I'd deliver you home personally. Until he knows who the leak is, nowhere but with me is safe. The man responsible for my team members' deaths has access to U.S. installations worldwide. I won't risk you by trying to get you home easily."

"And yet you say people are gunning for you and your men," she reminded him.

"I can protect you, Allie. Trust me."

She glanced up, sleep teasing her. "I do."

He turned away, and she thought she heard him murmur, "I'm sorry."

She didn't respond, unsure what he was apologizing for. She breathed in deeply, knowing that for right now she was as safe as she would ever be.

Because she was with him.

Chapter 12

KING'S NECK PRICKLED, AND HE GLANCED OUT THE window he'd been standing beside for hours. Allie had nodded off long ago. He checked her breathing before he grabbed his Kimber off the bedside table and stepped to the door.

Someone was out there. Someone doing their best to avoid detection. Friend or foe? He was about to find out. He began counting his breaths, slowing them until his blood was quiet in his ears.

A slide of boot on sand, the shift of a rock beneath the same boot. Then the knob turned and King struck, throwing open the door, and kicking up and out to push the big man back.

"Goddamn, King. It's me," the man hissed.

"You know better than to sneak up on me, Chase," King said in a low tone.

"Figured your lady might be sleeping," Chase said with a grin. "Didn't want to disturb her."

King shoved with his hand this time, and Chase stumbled back another step. "Fuck you," King replied, adding, "You can come out now, Jude. I know you're there."

He turned and headed back into the hut. Chase followed, and then came Jude, his face rueful as he shut the door softly.

"Nice place, Your Highness," Jude teased.

"I haven't heard from you. Truth be told, I was starting to worry. Why are you two down my way?"

"Jude said you needed help. I brought you me, and Black is close by," Chase said with a grin, holding his arms open wide.

"I told him to contact his source and find out why the hell I was led to her," King returned, pointing to where Allie was lying.

"Apparently his original source is no longer cooperating. But she's the courier. That's what Jude wanted you to know. Said no matter what you thought you knew or heard, she's the one we're looking for."

King shook his head. "Jude can't speak now?"

Jude gave him an impenetrable look. The man was hard. If King was a boulder, Jude Dagan was a frigging mountain. King shook his head. "No way. She's important, but she's not Savidge's contact."

Chase rubbed his chin. "Jude is rarely wrong."

"Yeah, Your Highness, I'm rarely wrong," Jude tossed into the conversation.

As soon as Jude finished his sentence, his mouth twisted. They all knew the truth. Jude had been wrong one time before, and it had cost him his heart. It had cost Endgame three valuable teammates.

King rolled his shoulders. He had just as much, if not more, culpability because he was their leader. He should've known, damn it.

"I can't figure out what Savidge is doing." King ran a hand through his hair and cursed. He noticed that Jude was staring at Allie sleeping peacefully on the bed. He clenched his fists, and King straightened. "Is he using her to get to her dad or us? Or both?"

Chase must have noticed the sudden tension in the room. "Jude, tell him what you know."

Jude sighed. "Savidge is doing Dresden's dirty work, as always. By the way, word is Dresden is back in the States and your boy Savidge has holed back up in Beirut."

Goddamn it. They had a bead on Savidge, and he had the complication of Allie Redding.

"Does Rook know?" King asked. "And the contact inside Dresden's operation—they still providing us with all this information?"

"Rook left the Ukraine the minute he discovered Dresden's location. And yes, the contact is still operational. It's like Christmas every month of the year because all of their intel proves to be true," Jude whispered.

"I want to know who that contact is as soon as possible. Has Black made any headway?"

"None. The contact is adamant they'll provide intel in exchange for future services," Chase explained.

King rubbed his eyes. "They might ask for more than we're willing to provide."

"Anything's possible." The other man glanced at Allie. "She's gotta be a link." It was like Chase was reading King's mind.

"She's Broemig's daughter."

Jude inhaled sharply. "No fucking way that robot has offspring. Though like I said, anything's possible."

King nodded. "He does, and there she lies."

"Best-kept secrets and all that. Hell, I'm just glad it's you and not me." Chase winced, then took a deep breath. "There are several items in the packet Jude has. You can take a cruise or fly—you've got options," Chase informed him.

"Plans have definitely changed."

Chase nodded. "We figured as much."

King pointed at Chase. "I need you to find everything you can while keeping an eye on the situation in Burundi. That warlord is running diamonds and lining Dresden's pockets. We need him as leverage." He sighed and ran a hand through his hair. "Goddamn but there's a lot of balls up in the air. Something smells about all of this. I came here to track Savidge, and I'm being led on a merry chase. It stinks."

"I'm on it." Chase responded.

Jude handed him the packet. "You said to formulate a new itinerary, so I contacted Black and he brought these."

"He just brought them to you, huh? Why is Black on this continent? You know what? Never mind. He's always got another agenda. Worse than a damn spook." King opened the packet and smiled. "It's like you and Black read my mind."

"The king calls, and I must answer," Jude said with a dark laugh. "Someone owed me a favor, and I collected. He'll be waiting for us at the private airport right outside Douala. Your lady's face is all over the telly on this continent. Funny, nobody had a good description of you."

"How reliable is this contact?"

"Only the best for His Majesty."

"Fuck you, Jude."

"You've already said that. As my venerated leader, shouldn't you have a wider vocabulary?"

"How about this? Get Black and meet us in Douala. Since we've got the intel, we may as well strike while the iron's hot. We can stop in Serbia to pick up a few things," King said with a grunt. A *few things* being weapons.

Jude nodded and smiled. It was a mean smile. "New Rover is parked in the lot. Taking a trip, gotta have wheels, right? I'll see you in Douala, Your Highness. I'm out," he said and then disappeared out the door, making no sound. It was eerie how the big man moved so silently.

"Wait, Chase. Have you heard any rumblings about Ella?"

It was infinitesimal but there was a shift in his man's gaze, a darkening that made King's gut burn. Chase was hiding something. King let the silence grow, just stared at Chase until he began to shift from foot to foot.

He recognized the moment Chase gave in to the inevitable. "There are rumors of a black-haired woman riding shotgun with Dresden. Said to have eyes the color of frost and a scar on her temple from his bullet."

"You didn't think to share that with me before now?" King's voice was arctic now. Trust was built on a foundation of truth. Without truth and complete disclosure, trust crumbled. He needed to trust every member of his team. That's the way shit worked.

"I didn't know for sure. Wanted to confirm before I brought it to you. I think that's who Jude is chasing."

"Goddamn it, if he chases her, he could be chasing a ghost."

"I agree, but you know how much he loved her— crazy in love with that woman."

"She killed Nina, poisoned our top intel gatherer like she was trash."

Chase looked right at King then, and what King saw in his gaze had him nervous. "What if it wasn't Ella who killed Nina? What if Ella was a pawn?"

"She was definitely a traitor to Endgame—hell, to her country. But she was too smart to be a pawn."

"I think the Company used her, King. I think Ella may have been an unknowing plant from the beginning. I think she was a sacrificial lamb."

It was the second time in as many days that he'd heard that term used in reference to Ella Banning.

"What was the purpose, Chase? I've thought about all this over the past few days—"

"Yeah, why?"

"Remember Loretta Bernstein?"

Chase smiled fondly. "About five eight, stacked, with long, red hair? Pushing fifty with the body of a twenty-five-year-old? Yeah, I remember Loretta."

"Well, guess who else knows Loretta?"

Chase's gaze moved to the bed. "Loretta is Company."

"As Company as anyone ever was," King spit out. "Told me Ella was alive and walking around on a suicide mission. But let me ask you this: Assuming she's still alive and *if* she was a deeper plant for the CIA, what the fuck was her mission?"

"I have no idea, but she got three of our teammates killed. I'd like a few minutes with her, even if she's innocent in all this."

"I need you to return to Burundi. The situation with the warlord is heating up. And I need you to remember, Chase, that there are varying degrees of innocence," King warned before he turned his back and let his man leave. There weren't many people King would turn his back on. Chase was one of maybe five. He glanced at the blond hair peeking out from the blanket. Possibly six now.

Long minutes of silence took hold while King sat beside the bed. He'd worn a spot on the floor with his pacing, and now the seat beneath him seemed permanently conformed to his ass. He dropped his head in his hands.

He heard her shift on the bed, knew she was awake before she spoke.

"Who's Ella?"

He took a deep, cleansing breath. "One of your dad's spooks. She was a CIA liaison to Endgame over a year ago. She led my team into ambush. That op in Beirut I told you about earlier? Yeah, that one. Three teammates just gone. We thought she had died as well."

"I'm sorry," Allie whispered.

"Not your fault. Your dad's maybe, but not yours. Unless there's something you aren't telling me?"

She shook her head.

"I'm not involved in my dad's business. I won't be a pawn, King," she said firmly. "For anyone."

He glanced up at her, recognizing the ring of truth in her words, knowing he had no choice. "I won't use you," he promised her again.

No way he'd use her. Over the last seventy-two hours, she'd become important to King, and as messed up as the entire situation was, he'd never use her. Someone had led King to Allie Redding. The same someone who knew what the hell they were doing—moving pieces on the fucked-up chessboard that had become his life.

He knew in his gut that he was going to regret his plan, but it was what it was. He needed to get them to the United States, but it was going to be a circuitous route through Belgrade, Serbia.

King had people to visit, plans to set up. It was time to find out what was going on.

Time to kill some bad guys and jot their names in the Book of the Dead.

Hooyah.

Chapter 13

"WE'RE HEADING BACK TO DOUALA?" ALLIE ASKED AND winced when she heard the tremble in her voice.

"Yeah."

Apparently this was his you-get-no-answers-from-me tone. Since she'd woken up this morning, he'd given her nothing but one-word responses. So much for disclosure. He was locked up tight now. No information forthcoming.

Allie wanted to scream. But she didn't. She'd been raised better than that. "So, it's a pretty day, huh?"

"Yeah."

Allie rolled her eyes. "Where are you from?"

"Somewhere."

"Me too!" she enthused sweetly. "My somewhere is Virginia. I was born in a private hospital run by nuns and raised outside DC, to be exact. Hmm, let's see… Have any siblings?"

"No."

His jaw was locked, and there wasn't a glimpse of the man she'd become accustomed to the past two days. This man was straight soldier. This was King.

She glanced out the window and watched the grass-lands speed by. Nobody was chasing them this time, but she'd be interested in finding out how he was going to get them on a plane without any problems.

"When I was little, I traveled a lot with my mom," she said into his silence. "She used to listen to me chat.

I've had a problem since childhood. If there's a void of sound, a lull in conversation, I feel compelled to fill it. If I don't, I hear everything and it drives me a bit mad." She turned her head and pinned him with her gaze. She had no idea why she'd started down this path, but now she couldn't stop. "She'd say, "Allie girl, you talk like a lovely loon. Keep going, please, until I go insane." And we would giggle like crazy people—or at least I would."

"I remember traveling with her to Syria, Greece, South Korea, Iraq, but we never came to Africa, and I always wanted to see the lions on this continent. She told me one day she'd take me, but then a terrorist blew her away. When I finally saw the lions, it hurt to know she wasn't there with me."

The road continued and time passed, animals in the distance ran, kicking up clouds of dust. This land, close to the sea was more desert than anything, and even though it'd been raining until yesterday, the soil soaked up the water fast. Up until three days ago, Allie had resided right outside the lush jungle of the Dja Faunal Reserve. She'd served the people there with a joyful heart, knowing her mother would be proud that Allie was spreading her love and knowledge by working in the Peace Corps. She'd gotten to see her fair share of wildlife, and she'd also gotten to visit the Congo, Ngorongoro Crater, the Serengeti, and Chobe National Park in Botswana. She loved this continent but was ready to leave.

Terrorism had taken over everything. Religious zealots were looking to spread their power base. Children were being taken from the cradle to the grave in a few

short years. This beautiful continent was being threatened by a famine of an entirely different sort. Instead of
starving bodies, they were starving souls.

Allie rubbed the area over her heart.

"What's wrong? Do we need to stop?"

Now he wanted to talk. So she remained silent. Two
could play at his game, and though she hated playing at
anything, she was learning pretty damn quickly.

"Are you okay?" King asked, this time his voice
more demanding, rougher.

"Yeah." She was intentionally mimicking his suc-
cinct answers.

He chuckled. "Think you're funny, don't you?"

"To someone. Somewhere."

"Look, I've got things on my mind. Once I've worked
everything out, I'll let you know the deal. For right now,
we're going to hit a private airport in Douala and take a
little trip to Belgrade."

"Wait—we're traveling by plane? Isn't that kind of
out in the open? And why Belgrade?" She was sick of
asking questions and getting no answers. Last time she'd
been on a plane, people had hijacked it. Flying didn't
sound like the safest form of transportation for her. Not
in this situation.

He lowered his brows and muttered, "Because."

Ugh.

She'd been doing all the talking, so she'd just continue. "*Da li se sećate da je noć u junu na Dunavu?*" she
quoted from memory.

He finally smiled at that. "First, kudos to you for the
Serbian. Second, I've never been on the Danube River
at night in June, so I can't say I recall it. Third, I'm not

sure that's what Charles Hamilton Aide meant in that particular song."

She shrugged. "Yeah, it's one of the only things I remember from my world literature class in college. I had to use one quote from a single poem or song of an obscure writer. I chose that line and learned it in Serbian so I could wow and amaze my teacher."

"How'd you do with that?"

"Oh, easy A. I picked a very obscure writer, learned the entire poem in another language because the Danube River is in Serbia—you know, really went out of my way. Of course, he could've cared less what I said. He was too busy ogling Carla Davenport's legs. She always wore the shortest skirts." Allie stared out the window, trying to hide her laughter.

"Do you wear short skirts?"

"Depends on the occasion," she responded impishly.

"I'll have to come up with something then. I have a feeling Carla Davenport's legs have nothing on yours," he murmured in a low, heat-filled voice.

That voice took her insides and twisted them right up. Chills danced on her skin.

She needed to find safe ground here. "You're a very learned man to be such a…"

He glanced at her, hands tightening on the wheel. "A what?"

"I was going to say jerkface, but decided at the last second that discretion was the better part of valor in that fight."

He nodded. "Wise decision."

Allie saw a sign that read "Douala, ten kilometers," and her palms began to sweat. She wiped them on her skirt.

"You're nervous?" he asked.

"Yep. Last time I tried to leave on a plane from this airport, I ended up hijacked and... Well, you were there, remember?"

"I won't let anything happen to you," he told her.

"Don't know that you can control the entire world, King. Oh, I have a feeling you'll try, but I've got a wound on my side that clearly indicates not everything is under your power."

"Point taken. But this time, I know more about what I'm fighting. And knowledge is the ultimate power, isn't it, Allie?"

"Touché," she said with a smile.

"Set my pack between us," King ordered.

They were back to his do-what-I-say-and-you'll-live tone. She hated that tone. But she did as he asked.

King rifled through the pack as he drove, pulling out a smaller pack and handing it to her.

"You will now be Mrs. Filipovic, first name Dara. We are returning home after a joyful holiday in Kribi. Didn't you have an amazing time?"

Allie giggled and wondered who the hell *that* woman was—the one giggling. "It was glorious. Our hut was absolutely stunning." She pretended to mull for long moments, and then she nodded. "I have to say one of my favorite memories is of our hut."

He laughed, and her stomach did that squirrelly thing. She loved that she was the one to make him laugh.

"I have to say I agree, darling," he said in that deep, husky baritone that made Allie think of rumpled sheets, his big body sliding against hers, and breaths being exchanged in the darkness.

Or maybe she'd need the lights on so she could watch. Her gaze focused on his hands. Such strong hands— capable of killing with ease but equally capable of gentleness. Her gaze slid up to his forearm, the tanned, firm skin covering hard muscles that flexed when he moved. Even the man's elbows were sexy. The rest of his body was as roped with muscle as his arms.

Allie didn't like that she noticed, but notice she did. Didn't like that she wanted him to call her *darling* for real. Oh, who the hell was she kidding? She was dying for him to call her that for real.

King cleared his throat, and her gaze shot up to meet his. There was something in his eyes that called to her, that made her want impossible things with this impossible man.

Why him? He didn't talk unless he had to. By his own admission, he was a dictator. And yet, he was a gentleman. He'd cared for her when others may have left her to her own devices once they found out she wasn't who they thought she was.

Except she was even better than he'd thought she was. The *fucking mother lode*, he'd said.

"You can't look at me like that."

He was a beautiful man—just gorgeous. His square jaw, covered by a short dark-brown beard now, told his story to perfection. Sculpted, hard-core, stubborn male.

"Like what?" she asked him. Wait, was that her sounding breathless?

"Stop."

She threw her hands up in the air. "Okay. I'll stop looking at you," she said around her laughter. Then she turned to once again stare out the window.

The silence became overwhelming, but they were

entering Douala proper so she held her tongue. The *whump-whump-whump* of the wheels over the road might drive her insane, but hey, she'd been there before.

"It's Isaija Filipovic," he said.

She swore that if that slight kick of his lip upward turned into a full-blow smile, she was going to go off on him. "What are you talking about?"

"My name is Isaija Filipovic," he reiterated in a very calm, very deep voice.

"What the—"

"It's Serbian for Isaiah. There wasn't a proper translation for *jerkface*, so I went with a tried and true."

She stared at him. It took a few seconds for his words to sink in. When they did, she started laughing and couldn't stop. The sound rolled out of her, a cathartic wave of mirth that had her gasping for breath and wiping tears from her eyes.

"Feel good?" he asked solemnly.

"I have to say that yes, that felt pretty good."

"We're here," he told her as he pulled up to a tiny airport that boasted a single dust-laden runway. She'd thought they'd be hitting the main airport in Douala.

She should have known. He was the black ops master and would never endanger them that way.

"We just walk right in?"

"Yep. Right now. We get out and walk right in. Let's do it," he said as he parked at the curb.

He pulled his pack with him, and she wondered if he was strapped with weapons. What would happen if they were caught?

"Let's go, woman," he urged as he opened her door and held out his hand.

She grabbed it, and there again was that uncanny feeling of rightness. She stood, ignored the tiny twinge in her side, and stepped next to him. He'd called her *woman*, and her heart had raced. Allie knew his use of the word was for show, but the sound of it, along with the attentive look on his face, made her feel…things. He might be moving to her list permanently.

Mani. Pedi. Fries. Kingston McNally. Definitely not in that order. *You're in big trouble here, Allie.*

He swung his backpack onto his other shoulder and wrapped his arm around her shoulders. Then they were walking through a tiny building. No one glanced at them. Of course the place seemed abandoned. This was how they were getting into Serbia. Private plane.

He'd given her a loose, flowing skirt and a longer, rose-colored top, also loose, along with some Keds this morning. They'd still had the tags on them. He was dressed in khaki cargoes, sneakers, and a T-shirt with a button-down over it. Casual described them to a T.

"Try not to talk. Seriously, let me do the talking if we run into anyone," he said in her ear.

"Got it," she replied.

And with that, they boarded a sleek Jetstream. Two very large men, who King introduced as Jude Dagan and Harrison Black, boarded after them. They were members of Endgame Ops. Allie wondered if maybe their presence was overkill. Then she remembered how many times she'd been shot at since the hijacking and became grateful for having them there.

There were several tense minutes as they waited for the all clear for takeoff when Allie wondered if there'd be a repeat of before, but everything went smoothly.

He'd stuffed her in the window seat, his big body protecting her from everything.

She didn't fully relax until they were airborne.

Allie had no idea what she was heading into. But he'd promised to get her home. If she had to detour with him, well, she was placing her faith and trust in him—even though she didn't know anything about him except that he'd killed his father, changed his name, made a new life as a Navy SEAL, and been screwed over on an undercover operation in Beirut. He had demons—big, snarly, glowing red demons. Oh, he also kissed so well that he made her forget all about McDonald's.

And that was going to have to be enough.

He grabbed her hand, and she twined her fingers with his.

She prayed it was.

Chapter 14

Belgrade, Serbia

KING SAT BACK IN HIS CHAIR AND PROPPED HIS BEER ON HIS stomach, never taking his eyes off the gorgeous woman sleeping peacefully on the bed in front of him. His gaze veered behind her to the bank of windows the bed butted against. Belgrade was chilly this time of year, though things remained green. Fall hadn't quite decided to take hold yet but was making a valiant effort.

The sunsets here were magnificent, the current one no exception. They'd landed around noon after a layover in Athens, Greece. The trip, rental of a vehicle once they'd arrived, and registering into the Hyatt Regency had all been uneventful.

If there was one thing Harrison Black did really well, it was create new identities. When Jude had given King the packet with the fake IDs, he hadn't hesitated to trust them. That had been Black's niche in Endgame Ops. Sure, he was as deadly as the rest of them, but each man brought a different set of skills to the table. That had made them one of the most elite fighting units King had ever known. Not even SEALs operated as well as Endgame had.

His eyes caught on a particularly brilliant shade of orange that blended into the salmon of the falling sun. As the colors slowly faded, the shadows became long, falling over the Sava River and burying the buildings below in darkness. Ten stories above the ground, there was still enough light to see in the room without turning on a lamp.

He took a drag off the beer and sighed. It wasn't raining, which was always a plus.

As Allie shifted on the bed, one of her legs peeked from under the sheet he'd consistently had to cover her with, and his breath stopped. Her leg was long, lean, supple, and an ivory color that made King want to trail her skin with his fingers, maybe leave some sign he'd touched her skin—that she was hi—

Whoaaaa, boy. She wasn't his. Couldn't ever be. He'd made a promise to get her home safely, and until he could do that, she was staying close to him. She was also a bit of an ace in the hole. Keeping her safe in King's shady world would require skill and strategy, but the stakes were too high to fail.

Her toenails were bare, and the sight of them had a smile pulling at his lips. What had she said on the plane? Mani, pedi, french fries. The woman was tough but so damn feminine that his back teeth ached from clenching his jaw so hard. Had he met her at any other time in his life, he would have already had her underneath him, enjoying the rounded breasts that pressed against every shirt the woman wore.

She'd walked into the suite, asked him for a T-shirt, showered, and fallen into bed. She'd slept for twelve hours straight. King had put a Do Not Disturb sign on the door and left to handle business, leaving a note on the nightstand telling her he'd be back with clothes and food. The clothes remained in the bags he'd brought them up in, and the food was long since cold, but she was getting much-needed rest so King hadn't disturbed her.

What he had done was watch her, cataloging every inch of the skin he was blessed enough to steal a glimpse of, along with every mole or freckle that was exposed. Her hair had dried and was a thick, bone-straight, shimmering mess on her pillow. She was lying on her left side, facing him, and the sheet had fallen when her leg shifted restlessly.

King's T-shirt had ridden up and was bunched around her slender, slightly rounded tummy. It was the curve of her hip that caught him, had his breath catching and his heart beating triplicate. It was unmarred by any string or material—just ivory skin that looked so damn soft and fragile he could drown in it.

The woman was commando. His T-shirt had stroked over that rounded ass, nestled against her mound, and, in general, had touched places on her body King could only dream about.

He took yet another pull of his brew, finishing it off as he breathed out roughly and adjusted his hard cock. It was a permanent state around her. There wasn't much he could do about it. So he did his best to ignore it. Truth be told, it was about way more than the physical need he felt for her. Yes, she was beautiful. But her sassy mouth and grit got him there too. And therein lay his problem. He liked her and was quickly adapting to having her in his life. This presented a set of problems he'd never experienced. It made him uncomfortable, both mind and body.

He needed to get up, leave her to rest in peace, or he was going to lose the tenuous hold on his control.

A discreet knock sounded, and King stood, grabbed his gun, and padded to the door.

"Service," a low voice said.

King opened the door, standing behind it as adrenaline kicked in. He pushed it down. A small woman dressed in a hotel uniform held a package. She smiled, handed it to him, and bid him good night.

He'd been expecting this package and placed it in the seat he'd vacated. He'd met with Adam Babic earlier, knowing Jude and Black were close and would keep an eye on the room. Babic was a former Serbian special forces commander who lived a very private life away from the public eye in the crumpled buildings of eastern Belgrade. He was a solid contact for King simply because the proud man would go to his grave trying to pay King back for saving his life during a nasty skirmish in Bosnia years ago. Belgrade had seen its fair share of damaging wars, from WWII to the most recent Serbian conflict. Serbs and Bosnians, Catholics and Muslims had fought for so many years that it was hard to separate the country from the conflicts that had forged it.

King had tapped Adam because the man always had his nose to the ground. Drugs, weapons, people—if it could be trafficked and run through Serbia, Adam knew about it and did his best to dismantle any conglomerates he ran into. Some would call him a crime boss with a stranglehold on Belgrade. Adam called himself an entrepreneur who preferred to keep the riff-raff out of his town.

Jude's intel was supported by Adam. Savidge was definitely back in Beirut, according to Adam, running Dresden's death business with an iron fist. Adam kept tabs on Savidge because Belgrade was the bastard's home turf, and Adam would want to know if he was making incursions. Adam wouldn't tolerate Savidge in Belgrade.

"Vasily Savidge is making moves," Adam had told King earlier. "He's turning up the heat in Africa and making end-run forays into the Ukraine with little to no resistance. Men, women, boys, and girls, AK-47s, heroin—he's expanded his boss's business by leaps and bounds over the past two years, King. If you want to kill that gnat, you damn well better be packing more than a grenade."

"What's his weakness?" King asked his contact.

"Blond women."

King's heart had stuttered at that. Then he'd calmed. Jude and Black were with Allie. No one would get to her past them. And Savidge was in Beirut. King needed the information Adam had, so he took a deep breath and beat back the residual fear. "Any sign of CIA?"

"Those rats are everywhere, King. You know this," Adam admonished him. "But overt moves made by the US of A? No. I think they pulled out their station chief a few weeks ago. Word is, Savidge threatened the man's wife and children who were living here in Belgrade. The chief left that day, and no one has replaced him. At least not in the last twenty-four hours."

King had waited patiently for Adam to supply him with a pack filled with weapons—everything from a dismantled M110 to grenades and a brick of C-4. Pack a cannon, indeed.

He'd left the meeting with Adam with more questions than answers, but he'd also left with Adam's promise to deliver more weapons and money to King and his men the following day.

He'd returned to the hotel and made plans with Black and Jude. The two of them would do recon in Beirut while King took Allie to DC. They'd report on what they found at Savidge's place, and then King would meet with his men and make plans to eliminate the bastard. It was as close to Savidge as King had been in a year. His body ached for action.

On the flip side, he was taking Allie home tomorrow. Jude had set up yet another under-the-radar flight, assuring King he could get into DC and out with minimal fuss. King would contact her father when they landed in the States, and once he'd handed Allie off to Broemig, King would head to Beirut. He didn't know how he felt about not seeing her again. She'd burrowed inside him so easily that a piece of him, a big piece, balked at the thought.

"What's wrong?"

Speak of the devil, and she shall awaken, King thought, a smile tugging at his lips.

"What makes you think something is wrong?" he asked, turning and meeting her gaze.

"You're just standing there, staring out the window," she responded.

"I'm not allowed to do that?"

She sat up carefully, making sure to pull the sheet around her. He mourned the loss of his view of her skin.

"Do what you want," she said, and her voice sent needles of need through his groin. Soft, husky…she'd kill him with it.

Shrugging, he walked to the bar on the wall opposite

the windows. He pulled out the food he'd brought back and threw it in the microwave. After warming it for about thirty seconds, he put it on a plate and walked back to her.

Her eyes widened, and she gasped.

"Is that what I think it is?" she whispered.

He smiled at the awe in her voice. "You were asleep when I brought them back hours ago—but I figure warmed-up fries are better than no fries at all."

Her smile was worth every bad thing he'd ever done that had led him to this place. That smile lit him right the hell up, made his hands clench, and made his cock even harder. She licked her lips, reached reverently for one of the long, slender fries on the plate, and he thought he might need to look away.

"Do I need to give you two a minute?" he asked, barely masking his smile.

Her gaze rose to meet his, and there was the imp that lived beneath the strong shell of the woman he was coming to know. "A minute isn't nearly long enough."

He left the plate in her hands and turned around quickly, putting distance between them before he said to hell with the fries and fucked her six ways from Sunday. She didn't call him back, just dug right into the fries and didn't come up for air until they were all gone.

He wondered if she'd lick the plate before she shot him a glance, and he knew for a fact that's what had been on her mind. Imp. She smiled and put the plate beside the bed before she stood stiffly and walked over to stand directly in front of him.

He watched her warily, unsure what she was going to do.

Then she moved in to him, wrapping her arms around his torso and laying her head over his heavily beating heart before she whispered, "Thank you."

Well and truly fucked. That's what he was in that moment. His arms rose of their own volition, and he gave her a small squeeze before he stepped away and headed to the bathroom.

"I'm going to shower. There are more fries in the microwave," he told her, then sought refuge in the massive bathroom.

He should be a gentleman and let her shower again before he did, but as he looked in the mirror, he recognized he wasn't strong enough for that. He took several deep breaths, trying to control the lust barreling through his body, and as he calmed his racing heart, he gave himself a hard look in the mirror.

He needed a shave, a shower, and a few hours of uninterrupted sleep in that bed. He cursed as he took off his shirt and lathered his face. He couldn't think about the bed with her in such close proximity. His dick would never let him sleep.

King concentrated on removing the beard from his face, then took a long, cold shower. It didn't help. He walked back into the suite to find her staring out the same windows he'd been looking out earlier.

"Shower's free," he said.

Their gazes met in the window, and for a second, it was as if time was suspended. It was just the two of them, alone in a hotel room, a man and woman, each needing the other.

"It's not that simple," he murmured, reading her face so clearly it was like a book with her expressions as the words.

"Nothing with you would be simple, I'm thinking," she said with a small grin.

He was reminded of what he'd said to her three nights ago.

"Would it be worth it though?" she continued. "Oh, I'm sure. You look like you were built to be good at two things, King McNally."

He cocked his head, reveling in their banter. "Only two?"

She chuckled, low and husky, and he was forced to lock his shit down. His cock was beating at him behind his sweats. If she looked down, she'd know he was hard and ready. She looked, and he hissed in a breath.

"Probably way more than two," she said softly. "But two that I'm sure you excel at."

He wanted to sew his mouth shut, but the words tumbled out anyway. "And those two things would be?"

"Come on, McNally. Are we going to play games now?"

"I thought that's what we'd been doing," he told her honestly. But once again, her words were the reminder he needed. This was an op, not some lust-filled jaunt across the world.

"You have. But I'm not a player. I told you that. I am, however, into honesty."

He waved a hand at her, deciding he'd finally lost his mind. "I'm not stopping you."

She turned around, pinning him with a blue gaze so intense he felt the heat under his skin. "Fighting and fucking."

Her gaze fell again, and she took enough steps toward him that they were only a foot or so apart.

He nodded but swallowed hard. She'd said the f-word. "I'm good at both."

"Of course you are." She smiled and pointed at his cock. "I've seen you kill and felt your kiss. Tell me, is sex a weapon for you too?"

"Do you want to find out?"

Please let her say no. He willed it to happen. He was losing control.

"I think…yes. I do want to find out. Will I? Well, that's the question, McNally. There's no doubt I want you desperately. I have from the moment I saw you on the plane. I've never experienced the pull I feel toward you."

Her honesty would unman him. He wanted to sink into her body and not come up for air. He wanted to drown in her.

"Watch what you say, Allie. In fact, don't say another word. What you're feeling is a by-product of adrenaline overload and fear. It happens. What I need you to do is go take a shower and not mention this to me again."

Her gaze fell, and he was left feeling like he'd kicked a puppy. He didn't want to kick her; he wanted to pet her all over with his hands, his tongue, his cock, and anything she'd let him touch her with.

She nodded and started to walk past him. But then she stopped suddenly and looked up. Heated wildflowers. Goddamn, he was done for. She didn't touch him, but she didn't need to. He wanted her, had from the moment she'd stared at him on the plane.

"Adrenaline and fear? What about just plain, old want? What if it's as simple as this woman wants this man? I think you've been in the game too long, McNally. I'll let you chalk it up to the fight and situation we're in, but I won't do the same. I'm not a liar or a coward." She ended her salvo and walked to the bathroom.

The saliva in his mouth dried up. This was really bad. So bad he didn't have a frame of reference for it. The last thing he'd needed was this woman. Any other woman, and he'd have been fine. *Allie Redding* couldn't have happened at a worse time.

King walked to the packet he'd been brought, placed it in his pack, and then headed to the only bed in the room to lie down. His mind raced even as her scent surrounded him. He had to sleep; there was no choice.

So he thought about his mission. He thought about Beirut. He thought about blood, death, and revenge, and when she walked out of the bathroom, he was ready to rest.

"There are clothes in that bag over there." He motioned before he threw his arm over his eyes. "I've got to sleep for a few hours. Don't leave the room," he warned her.

"Yes, Your Highness," she quipped, but there was humor in her tone so he let her sass go. He grunted instead.

"More like it," he murmured and heard her gasp.

He'd won that round then.

Good.

Chapter 15

HIS CHEST ROSE AND FELL EVENLY, LETTING ALLIE KNOW he'd finally gone to sleep, or whatever version spec ops soldiers used. Her father had once told her that true soldiers were always vigilant. They didn't sleep, didn't eat, and didn't shit when they were on ops. Of course he hadn't meant that literally, but every black ops member she'd ever met looked like they met those criteria.

She smiled at her thoughts. The tension in the air abated, and the constant energy that surrounded King dimmed to a low buzz. His cock was semi-hard, slightly tenting his sweats, and Allie licked her lips.

What the hell had she been thinking when she told him she wanted him? She was certifiable at this point. She ran a towel over her hair and watched him sleep.

He'd brought her McDonald's fries, and her heart had melted.

Sure they weren't even half as good heated up, but those had been the best she'd ever tasted, because *he'd remembered*.

King had gone out of his way to give her something she wanted. Allie had known instinctively that he was that type of man. Honorable, giving. No matter that he killed efficiently and without remorse. She'd never judge a soldier for acts of war. And, like her father, King was constantly embroiled in war. Nothing mattered but that he'd made her feel something she'd never felt before.

She refused to put a name to it. Couldn't have if she wanted to. There was no doubt their situation was unique. Did adrenaline and fear play into her need for him? Maybe. She gave it more thought and then decided yes. Was that the entirety of their connection? Absolutely not. Breaking their attraction down to basics was simple—she was a woman attracted to a man, needing him now in that age-old fashion—and not just any man, but the one lying on the bed.

Allie sighed, unwilling to give herself an out. She wanted him. King McNally. Not because he'd saved her life. Not because he'd assured her he'd get her home. But because his body, along with the honor that bled from him, called to her, and she desperately wanted to respond.

Catching a glimpse of herself in the window, she winced. She looked like a broken waif. Before heading to the bathroom, she turned, grabbed the bag he'd gestured to, and pulled out the items one by one. Lancôme lotion, makeup, hair bows and bands, several changes of clothing from jeans and T-shirts to a sequined, floor-length, off-the-shoulder Yves Saint Laurent gown, and shoes—Nikes and a pair of sky-high black Louboutins. What the hell did he have planned that she'd need this dress and those shoes?

She held the dress up, admiring the way the black played against her cream-colored complexion. It wasn't a dress meant for her. The thigh-high slit in the side was meant for a seductress. Allie was just a regular woman. Not one who could pull off that thousands-of-dollars dress.

But for a moment she wanted to be that woman.

She pictured herself dressed in the sequined gown and wearing the Louboutins, which would add several inches to her height, and behind her stood King. Black tux, trimmed mink hair, big body sheltering hers, large, tanned hands on her shoulders. The image was there, imprinted on her mind.

But it would never be. Because he was asleep now, and Allie was about to leave. She reached into the bag and pulled out the final pieces—wispy silk and lace lingerie in black, red, purple, and royal blue. Her breath came faster, and heat spread through her abdomen. Her need was an almost physical ache between her legs. How quickly it had hit her—and under the shittiest circumstances possible.

Had he picked these for her, or had a salesperson done it? Had he touched these bras and panties, cradled them in his big hands, leaving the lace and silk at his mercy? She almost moaned at the thought.

Instead, she pulled on the blue bra and panties. Allie placed a new bandage over her wound, which was starting to itch. She'd always been a quick healer. She still had some residual fatigue from the fever but was doing really well. Now a fever of an entirely different sort was plaguing her.

The jeans and a T-shirt were next, followed by socks and the outrageously colored Nike Air Maxes. She pulled her hair up and secured it with one of the rubber bands he'd brought her.

He'd thought of everything, and the pang in her chest struck her hard. Her mind whirred as she dressed, and ultimately her decision was made.

She had no choice. If she stayed, she would slow him

down, and honestly, he was way too much for her to handle. Allie would run now because he scared her and she didn't want to play his spec ops games. She wasn't a pawn to be placed strategically at other players' whims. He'd said he wouldn't use her, but if she put herself in his place, could she resist?

What happened to the trust, Allie? It was there, but so was grim reality. She had worth, and as the daughter of the head of the CIA, it was a whole helluva lot.

So she was removing herself from the game board. It was better this way. Her mother had been used against her father, and he'd suffered the last twenty years without her. It was Allie's fault her mother was gone, but she'd vowed to never be a part of the subterfuge that surrounded her father. He'd asked her to trust King, and she did, but she'd be a fool to think he wasn't going to use her link to her father in his ploy to find whoever had betrayed Endgame Ops.

So while King had been gone, she'd planned how this would go down. It was simple, really. She was going to walk out of this room, catch a cab to the airport, and leave. She hadn't seen Black or Jude since they checked into the hotel. She'd deal with them when and if she had to. The objective was to not look guilty as she fled. She'd take a random flight first. Then wind her way back home from there.

The only issue was money—and she was going to solve that by *borrowing* King's sat phone. She was going with her first option. She'd contact Lo-Lo, get her to handle the funds, and then be off. By the time King found her, she'd be home in DC, safe behind the walls of her father's home, and King would be safe from anyone searching for her.

No muss, no fuss. She glanced around, longing becoming a sharp, bitter burn in her chest when she took in the dress and heels. Another time, another place, and maybe...

She shook her head and walked at a normal pace into the main part of the suite. If she even hinted at subterfuge, it would no doubt trigger his instincts. So she didn't walk too lightly. Allie spied his sat phone on the bedside table so she headed there, grabbed it up, found a packet containing a large amount of money, and *borrowed* some of it. She put it all in the purse he'd given her before they flew here from Cameroon, and then she looked over at him.

His breathing remained even. His lips were parted slightly, the full lower one calling to her. She licked her own and swore she tasted him there.

Allie stood and looked around the room for the last time, seeing the discarded McDonald's paper bag in the corner trash can and turning away from it all. She opened the door, stepped into the hall, and walked to the elevators.

When the elevator reached the lobby, she stepped out, keeping her gaze lowered. She sat in a seat near the main hotel counter and dialed Lo-Lo. Cool, controlled, collected—she had more of her dad in her than she'd realized.

"King, I don't have time for your bullshit," Lo-Lo bit out into the phone.

"Well, gee, and here I thought you'd make time for me," Allie responded dryly.

"Allie?" Lo-Lo's voice changed, panic weaving into the tones. "Are you okay? Where's King?"

"He's sleeping."

"Are you alone, Allie? That's not good. Get back to the room now," Lo-Lo spit out in rapid-fire succession that hinted at the Company soldier she was.

"I'm leaving," Allie said firmly. "I need you to book me a flight anywhere in the next half hour. Once I arrive at the destination you've set up, I'll need funds wired to me through Western Union. From there, I'll get myself back to DC."

"No, Allie. You get back to King right fucking now," Lo-Lo demanded.

She'd never heard Lo-Lo demand anything of her except to shoot straighter. It was odd that the woman who'd tried to keep her from going with King now wanted her to stay right where she was. The hair at the back of her nape prickled. "I'm not going back. I want to go home, Lo-Lo. You'll either help me, or I'll do it on my own. Are we clear?"

Lo-Lo barked out a laugh into the phone but her silence communicated her tension. Then, "You are a target, Allie. There are people looking for you and McNally right now. If you don't get your ass back up to that room right fucking now, I'll come to Belgrade myself—and it won't be pretty."

It struck Allie as odd that Lo-Lo knew where they were. Had King told her? And now she was demanding that Allie return to King? She knew then that this, whatever this was, had to be huge. If Lo-Lo wouldn't help her get away from King, it must be much larger than King had hinted at.

And still she was going home. If anything, she was even more determined to get off this insane merry-go-round.

"Allie? Allie! Goddamn it, girl, get back up—"

Allie disconnected and sighed. On her own it was, then.

She walked calmly to the desk and handed them the sat phone. "Please have this sent to Room 723 in a few hours. He's sleeping right now, and I don't want him disturbed," she requested.

The hotel clerk nodded, and Allie turned and walked to the entry. Her heart skipped a beat as she saw King's men, Jude and Black, entering the lobby. Quickly turning her back, she pretended to blend in with the family at the desk. She waited with bated breath for King's men to notice her, but by some quirk, she escaped their roving eyes.

She gave it five minutes before she exited the lobby and located a cab idling by the curb. She walked to the driver and asked if he spoke English.

"A little," he replied, but he smiled.

He looked like somebody's grandfather.

"Airport?" she asked.

He nodded and she got in.

Thirty minutes later, she was in the terminal. She walked to the Air France desk, asked for the next available flight, and was told the next one with a vacancy was to Madrid. She checked her funds, saw she had almost five thousand dollars, and booked the flight under her assumed name.

No one looked at her funny; no one stopped her. This was turning out to be much easier than she'd anticipated. She headed to the gate and boarded with no incident. Adrenaline had her shaking. It wasn't until she was in the air that she truly believed she'd accomplished it.

Allie Redding, Peace Corps volunteer, general

do-gooder with not a single subversive bone in her body, had managed to elude the most determined spec ops soldier she'd ever met.

Elation was swiftly followed by a hollow ache in her chest. She shifted in her seat before checking her watch. She'd only been gone an hour and a half—was he awake now? What the hell was she going to do when she got to Madrid? Rest? Grab another flight immediately?

Consulate! She could go to the American embassy and seek shelter. With a plan in place, she laid her head back and took a deep breath.

It was better this way for them all. King could go back to hunting his betrayer with no worry he'd get her hurt, and she could breathe air that wasn't scented with evergreen and mint.

It was better.

It had to be.

Chapter 16

SOMEONE WAS KNOCKING. KING SAT UP IN A RUSH, BREATH leaving him as he took in the silence of the room.

Allie was gone. He grabbed his Kimber and threw open the door. A man was standing there holding King's buzzing sat phone. His heart dropped. *Goddamn it!*

He took the phone and nodded, slamming the door as he answered the ringing summons.

"King."

"She's in the wind, McNally, heading to Madrid," Loretta said in a hard voice. "What did you do to her?"

King rubbed a hand down his face. Madrid—why Madrid? "I haven't done anything…yet. When I get my hands on her though…"

"I've got someone meeting her plane. Go back to your Endgame Ops games. I'll take her from here," Loretta said, acid dripping from her voice.

"Whoever the fuck you've got meeting her, call them off. Tell them she went to another location. I'm not shitting you, Loretta. We can't risk Savidge being all over her. Call your man off now," King bit out.

"You have no idea how close Savidge is to grabbing her. You obviously can't hold her. My man is a good operative. He has no dog in this fight, and he isn't in Savidge's or Dresden's pocket. Back off, McNally," she warned him.

King disconnected. He immediately dialed Jude, got no answer, and then dialed Rook.

"Your Highness," Rook answered drolly.

"I need a contact in Madrid," King said hurriedly into the handset. He pulled out his laptop, booted it up, and put the phone on speaker.

"Knight knows some people. I'll get him on it. Who're we looking for?"

"Allie Redding, but she's probably flying under the assumed name of Dara Filipovic."

"Damn, hoss, you lost her already?"

"Fuck you, Rook." King tapped into the main database for the Belgrade Nikola Tesla Airport. He ran a query on Dara Filipovic and found her outbound flight to Madrid. "She's heading in on flight 904, Air France." It was disturbing that Loretta had that information.

"Give me a few, and I'll let you know what's what. Do you need Vivi on this?" Rook asked.

"Not yet," King bit out and disconnected.

He slammed the laptop closed, shoved it in his backpack, and gathered everything up. She'd left. Son of a bitch, but the woman was a sandwich short of a picnic. What if Savidge had someone watching for her? What if he'd gotten her?

What if he knew where she was headed even now?

King headed for the door between Jude's suite and his, pounding on the thin wood. Harrison Black answered, Jude right behind him.

"She's gone," King bit out.

"What the hell?" Black exclaimed. "How did she get past us?"

"You weren't looking for her to sneak out. Now she's making a beeline for home through Spain," King said on a sigh.

Jude went deathly still. "We still a go for Savidge?"

King really wanted Savidge. Badly. But the taste of desperation in his mouth was all for Allie. "You're still a go. But I've got to find her and get her home. Damn woman will be the death of me."

"Jude and I can keep the original plan. Meanwhile, do your best to find your girl."

His girl. "She's not a girl," King responded automatically, wincing as Allie's words came back to him.

"Well, Your Highness, we definitely noticed that," Jude drawled.

"Fuck you, Jude—now get out and do your jobs. I'm ordering recon only on Savidge's place outside Beirut. Keep tabs on the bastard until I can meet up with you both. I'm going to track down our wayward Ms. Redding, and I'll meet you in Lebanon as soon as I can."

"That's a big ten-four," Jude responded.

"Aye," came Black's affirmation.

King walked into the bathroom and saw the gown he'd purchased for her hanging on the back of the door. Adam had set him up with a woman who worked in the high-end department stores, and she'd personally handled his purchases. He'd seen the gown and wanted to see Allie in it. It'd been an impulse purchase—no rhyme or reason behind it—a purely selfish move.

He threw it and everything else she'd left into the bag, shoved that into his duffel, and headed out the door.

King hadn't known fear since he received his last beating at the age of fourteen from his daddy. He'd hit a growth spurt that summer and grown much taller and broader than his father. He'd just gotten too damn big to hit, and the fear had ended.

Right now, he was as close to the emotion as he ever wanted to venture again. He headed to the lobby and checked out. Appearances were everything. If he'd left without paying, he'd never be able to stay here again, regardless of which fake identity he used. He'd been forced to use one of the credit cards because apparently she was a sneak and a thief. She'd stolen over five thousand dollars.

You should have been honest with her, told her all your plans, his conscience admonished.

She didn't need to hear it all, his mind warred. For some reason, she hadn't trusted him as much as she'd let on.

Either way, she was now on her own, miles away and without protection. He flagged down a cab and answered his nagging sat phone.

"Talk to me, Rook."

"Knight has one of his contacts meeting her. I need you to forward me a pic ASAP. He has to know who to look for when she exits the terminal. He'll be taking her to the Westin Palace. I need to know for sure what name she's traveling under."

"Dara Filipovic, and I'm sending the picture as we speak. Tell your man to be aware that a Company man might give him some shit. Apparently, Allie Redding is great buddies with Loretta Bernstein," King told Rook as he pressed a button on the phone and shot his man a picture he'd snuck of her on the plane.

"Well, shit. If Bernstein's involved, your girl should be fine, right? Hold on, the picture's coming through. Damn, she's hot. Doesn't look like a spook, but neither does her daddy. Listen, let me get this information to Knight, and I'll let you know when she lands."

"The second she does. And Rook, I don't trust anyone in the CIA, least of all Loretta. Tell your man to watch his back."

"Yes, Your Highness," Rook said and hung up.

King rubbed his hand over his eyes. He'd needed sleep, and she'd taken advantage of that. Was she okay? Scared?

Why was he feeling anything other than anger right now?

He made it to the airport only to find the next flight to Madrid didn't leave for another four hours. So he hunkered down in a café and got busy. There were plans to make. He needed to get her on U.S. soil ASAP. The woman was a hazard to herself.

He could coordinate Endgame's next moves from Madrid, but after he dropped Allie back home, he'd need to hustle ass to Beirut. There was no telling how long Savidge would stay in one place. Though Jude's and Adam's intel suggested Savidge was holing up for a long visit, intel sometimes changed rapidly. After they eliminated him, they would begin working in earnest on Dresden. How scared would the bastard be, knowing they'd gotten to his number one man? King relished the thought of it.

Dresden had grown in power over the last two years and was making moves into Russia's underbelly. He'd infiltrated the Russian mob and had them kowtowing to him. Anything for money. Dresden had his hands in every dirty pie in the world, it seemed.

King really hated that son of a bitch. He was a scourge. King owed him for so much, but if Allie was in his sights, there was going to be trouble all the way around. Because King had realized something when he'd woken and found her gone.

She'd become important to him.

He didn't contact Loretta. She was a dead end now. Indeed, she had her own agenda, and while she might care for Allie, care what happened to her, Loretta's and King's objectives didn't align enough for him to keep her in the loop.

He gave a passing thought to contacting Broemig but discarded it as soon as it popped into his head. No doubt Loretta had already been in contact with Allie's dad. Instead, King boarded his plane, stowed his carry-on duffel, and waited for Rook to call him.

An hour into his flight, the call came through. "She's landed. Knight's man has her and is transporting her to the closest hotel. There was a tagalong for a few miles, but they drifted away."

"Tell Knight not to engage," King ordered.

"Already done," Rook said with a sigh. "I know how this game is played, King."

King groaned. "I know you do, Rook, but she's…"

Rook snickered. "She's what? Important?"

"She's what she is. If Knight's man harms her or she's hurt on his watch, I'll gut his ass. Groin to throat. He'll never see me coming. Tell him, Rook. Warn him."

"Never thought I'd see the day King McNally took a nosedive."

"This coming from the man who can't keep his woman in one place."

"Goddamn woman is gonna be the death of me, McNally," Rook said, and his voice rang with both irritation and fondness.

"Savidge is in Beirut. Have you located Dresden?"

"Not yet. But we're close. I'm locked up with Vivi. He makes a move toward my woman, I've got a bullet with his name on it," Rook promised. "Hey, have you talked to Jude or Chase?"

"Chase is back in Burundi following a lead. Jude is working with Black and was just in Serbia with me. We had a helluva lead on Savidge, but then Ms. Redding hit the high road. I made a promise that overrides my desire to have Savidge's head under my gun. But make no mistake, Rook, Jude could go rogue at any minute. He's keeping his eye on Savidge right now, but I'm worried. Word is Ella-Bella didn't kick the bucket when we went boom in Beirut. Heard those rumors?"

"I have. In my bones, I know he's been chasing after her between jobs, Your Highness."

"If Jude has even an inkling she's alive, he'll go in guns blazing and blow this whole thing to smithereens."

Silence stretched between them before Rook asked, "Have you given any thought to using your woman as a pawn?"

King growled. "She isn't my woman, Rook. She's an operation. I thought she was Savidge's courier. Found out she's Broemig's daughter. If you think I hadn't given that some thought, you're stupider than I gave you credit for."

"Yeah, yeah, yeah, I hear you. You might want to give that some *more* thought before you do it. Broemig is a straight-up killer. You'll be on his shit list forever if you use her and it doesn't pan out. Hell, if it works out, you'll still be on his shit list. Could make holidays rough." Rook paused. King rolled his eyes before the man started up again. "Speaking of panning out, Vivi traced back a trail that leads pretty high into the White."

Holidays? King had only recently admitted to himself he *liked* Allie, and Rook was talking about them having holidays together? Oh, who was he kidding? He way more than *liked* her. He pushed those thoughts aside for now.

"Damn," King breathed out. *The White* was code for the White House. "Is she following it?"

"Yeah, man. We ain't stupid. Did you bump your head really hard when we crashed that helo?"

King's lips curved. How many smiles did that make since he'd met Allie? Ten? Twenty? She was changing him. "I'm out. Watch your six, shoot to kill."

Rook laughed then. "Don't be brave, be accurate."

"Hooyah," King said softly before he hung up and leaned his head back. He glanced at his MTM tactical watch and noticed he had another five hours in this flight.

He closed his eyes. Maybe he could get some rest, but chances were slim. Worry had lodged in his gut, and it was churning. He couldn't see her, wasn't there to protect her. It was unacceptable.

Because she'd become something more to him than part of a mission.

And that too was unacceptable.

Chapter 17

THE SUN IN ALLIE'S EYES WOKE HER. SHE DIDN'T REMEMBER falling asleep. The cabbie she'd flagged down outside the Madrid airport had brought her here after telling her the American Embassy was closed and wouldn't reopen until the morning. She knew she could get in—just walk up to the gate and request entrance from the Marines on guard. But there were pieces to this puzzle that didn't add up.

Something in her gut told her to wait. So she'd allowed the cabbie to bring her here after he'd told her it was the best hotel in Madrid and she would love it. He spoke fluent English, but it was flavored with an accent she couldn't place.

He'd been nice though and gotten her to the Westin Palace quickly. She'd checked in with no problems using the Dara Filipovic identity. She'd paid in cash for one night. The less attention she drew to herself, the better off she was. It was only for one night, and she was sure that she could make it to the embassy in the morning. She'd been hurting and tired, so as soon as she'd closed the door and locked it, she'd found the bed, crawled on it, and fallen asleep.

Now, she pushed her heavy hair from her face and groaned. Her side pulled ever so slightly but no longer hurt. She had to pee like a racehorse, and she was hungry. Allie sat up gingerly and slid off the bed, coming to her feet. She padded slowly to the bathroom and handled her business before wetting a rag and washing her face. Once she'd brushed her teeth with the courtesy brush and paste, she returned to the bedroom, walking to the windows and becoming entranced with the gorgeous view of Madrid. It took several moments before a chill swept over her skin. Something was off.

She started to turn around, but an arm around her chest brought her against a hard body. Then she smelled it...evergreen and mint. That smell prevented her from struggling against the man who held her firmly but not so tight he was hurting her.

"You found me," she said on a heavy sigh.

"Looks that way."

"You can't keep me, King. I'm an American citizen. I have rights," she stated even as her body relaxed into the heat of his.

He'd found her. She wanted to smack her head. She'd made it easy by using the Dara Filipovic name. *Bonehead move, Redding.* And he was here now. Part of her was wary, part of her was angry, but the biggest part of Allie was...*relieved.*

His warm breath feathered over her ear, sliding down her neck and making her nipples tighten. "We've had this discussion about your rights. You left me. I followed. For now that's all you need to know." Oh, his voice was wonderful. Deep, gravelly, and stoking a fire inside her that she wasn't prepared for.

"I won't be used, damn it!" Her anger caught her by surprise.

"Nobody said you would be." He was a rock against

her, unmoving, unyielding. "In fact, I specifically told you I wouldn't use you. What happened to the trust?"

His words echoed her thoughts from yesterday, which brought her up short. "I'm not stupid. There's no other reason for you to hold on to me except as a bargaining chip. You'd have had me on the first flight to DC if you had no intentions of using me."

"I'm protecting your ass, and you left the safety of our room like it was nothing. Do you know what that shows me, Allie?"

She shook her head, incapable of speech because she swore he'd just licked the skin under her ear.

"It shows me that you need protecting. If from no one else, then from yourself."

He shoved her away gently, and she took a single step before she turned to him. He'd followed her, broken into her hotel room, and was now saying she couldn't take care of herself? She'd been chased, shot at, winged by a bullet, and now she was running for her life. She went after the only one she could…King. She punched his chest, and both her side and her hand paid for it. He stood there and took it. "Fight me back, damn it," she yelled with a grunt.

He shook his head and opened his arms. Her fight disappeared then, leaving her drained and weary.

"I can't fight you. You're already hurt," he said quietly.

Her brows lowered, and she growled.

"Stop growling, and don't look at me like that," he told her in a dark, guttural voice.

Her head snapped up, and she met his glittering green gaze. Lust, need, and anger were written on his face—a potent combination creating a spell that she was falling under.

"Take a shower. We need to relocate," he murmured. Then he turned and walked to stand by the front door.

She lost her mind then. Her gaze became hazed with red. Rage moved through her in a white-hot wave. She growled again and felt animalistic doing so. It was quite the stress reliever.

He went completely still, face blanking, but oh how his green eyes glowed. "That's it," he said, determination riding his features.

Then he was there, picking her up and walking her backward until her back hit the wall. He leaned down until their gazes were level. "You pushed me. Remember that when we're done here."

He used his fingers on her jaw to hold her mouth open, the threat implicit. If she didn't grant him access, he would damn well take her mouth anyway. Her gaze locked with his, and something intense and beautiful shimmered between them.

It was lust but so much more. Her breath locked in her throat. Then his mouth was on hers, teeth gnashing, lips locking, and he was breathing for her, taking her in a way she'd never been taken before.

The man was a master. His mouth on hers did things to her body she'd never imagined. Heat built as her body unfurled for him, a flower blooming amid the fire. His hips held her against the wall as he devoured her lust.

He pressed his hips into the cradle of hers. He took her mouth again, and there was no more thought, only pleasure.

Her hands settled on his shoulders and moved into the silky hair at his nape. He bit her lower lip and then laved it with his tongue. She hissed and pulled his hair. "So good," she keened.

"Yes," he murmured, his lips now at her neck and moving lower. He nipped her collarbone, and she groaned.

"Your mouth," she pleaded, and he was back, inhaling her, teasing her with deep strokes and small licks.

His hands under her ass held her firmly in place. He was reaching for a place inside her she didn't want to relinquish, yet she didn't want him to stop. He took two steps and had her on the bed, his hips nestled once again within the cradle of hers, his hard length pressing right where she needed him.

"You're a fire in my blood," he said roughly.

His hands framed her face, thumbs stroking her cheeks. A thrill moved through her, and her hips flexed. There was a twinge in her side, but she ignored it. She'd done that to him, made him flushed with passion, made him hard with lust. For her.

She traced his lips, and he sucked her finger into his mouth, teasing the tip with his tongue. Her vision wavered, and her pussy clenched. She felt empty.

"I need you," she whispered. "I don't know why, but I need you."

His brows lowered, and his mouth flattened. "You ran from me." He flexed his hips, and her eyes crossed. Any more of that, and she'd orgasm in his arms while they were still fully dressed.

"No more running," he said in a hard voice. "Tell me you won't run anymore."

"I won't run anymore," she parroted.

His thumb traced her lips, and it was her turn to taunt him. She flicked her tongue, tasting him. He pushed his thumb against her lips, and she opened them, taking him inside and sucking him hard.

His green eyes narrowed and went black. His body stilled completely as he raised his head and cocked it.

Then her world exploded.

Literally.

A loud boom ripped through the room, leaving behind a rushing *whoosh* that brought flames and glass raining down on them. He rolled off the bed, taking her with him before he pushed her down and covered her with the comforter. She saw his lips moving, but her hearing had been decimated by the explosion. All she heard was a ringing in her ears, loud and insistent.

She watched him move through the smoke, gathering his duffel and reaching for her. Someone rose out of the gray behind King and hit him hard with some sort of metal pipe. The blow glanced off his back, but King went down, rolling and taking the man's legs out.

Allie stilled, a scream dying in her throat as she watched King engage the man. He began blocking the blows, fighting like a demon, catching the man with a short right punch to the solar plexus and then following it with an elbow to the face. Another man entered the room, and Allie knew he was there for her.

Her hearing rushed back then with the sound of burning wood, fire alarms, and people screaming racing through her head. Her gaze centered on the man aiming his laser-sighted pistol at her.

King called her name, and she glanced up as the man who'd originally attacked him struck again, hitting King in his side with the piece of metal. King blocked as many of the blows as he could, counterpunching several times. Allie's fear exploded from her lungs in a scream.

King glanced her way, and that moment's inattention allowed the man's next blow to catch King on the head. He fell like a tree.

Allie lost her mind, coming up out of the cocoon of covers and exploding in a frenzy. She grabbed a broken piece of wood and struck the intruder over the head. He stumbled, but King was down. She hit the man again and again and again until someone pulled the wood from her, wrenching her around.

She kicked out, her foot connecting with a gut, and then heard someone yell her name once more. Fire licked up the walls of the suite, and a huge hole had been ripped into the side of the hotel. The crackle of the wood reverberated through the smoke-filled room. She heard people yelling, screaming in terror, and in the distance sirens. This was bad. Really bad.

"Allison Redding?" a man yelled again.

She didn't answer. She had no idea who these men were. They'd attacked King, and that alone made them enemies. Allie went to her knees, searching for some sign of King. She found him lying in a pool of blood, eyes closed, face white. But the initial intruder was down too after a single shot to the throat. He was about two feet from King.

"King," she called out.

He didn't move.

"Allison Redding, your father sent us," the voice called out.

Her father? No way. Her father had no idea where she was. The smoke was thick, choking her. She grabbed at the bedding, tugging a sheet off the bed, and ripping off two strips. She wrapped one around her nose and mouth before she did the same with King. He was breathing, but she had no idea the extent of his injuries.

Someone had blown a hole into this hotel. But she wouldn't run anymore. She'd told him she wouldn't run. And so she wouldn't. Unless she was running with him.

She glanced around, searching for an out. The man continued to call her name. He couldn't see past the smoke and fire, but Allie could see daylight. She'd only seen one thing do what had been done to this room—a rocket-propelled grenade. And she'd never been more grateful for its hole-punching capabilities than she was right now.

It had blown a hole through to the next room. Her side was on fire and her throat was clogged with smoke, but she got to her feet, grabbed King under the armpits, and began to pull him.

"Allison, your dad sent us," the voice said again.

"Bullshit," she murmured. Her dad would never have allowed somebody to use an RPG anywhere near her.

She'd just gotten King into the other room when a big shape rose out of the smoke. She dropped him and turned to confront the threat.

"My name is Brody Madoc, ma'am," the big man said.

Brody Madoc, Brody Madoc… Wait, he'd been one of King's men killed in Beirut.

"You're a dead man," she garbled.

Madoc smiled and shook his head. "Not anymore." He stooped down and grabbed King up in a fireman's carry. "I need you to follow me if you want to live."

He met her gaze unflinchingly, and for some reason, she believed him. He reached for her hand, and they ran through the room, hitting the hallway outside and taking the stairs down.

Allie followed him, unwilling to lose sight of King. They blended as casually as possible into the sea of fleeing patrons, settling into a wide stream of humanity that poured onto the sidewalks outside the hotel. Trucks were everywhere, water streaming into the smoking building.

"You have two choices. Follow me or get caught," the man said in a deep, broken voice.

Allie followed. They reached a single, unoccupied car, and the man identifying himself as Brody Madoc put King in the passenger's seat before turning to her and handing her a sat phone. Once that was done, he threw King's duffel into the back and gave her the keys. Madoc had thought to grab King's duffel and was now giving them a way to flee.

"I don't know where to go," she said around a cough.

He nodded to the phone, and she saw it was ringing. She'd not heard it.

She answered it. "He-hello?"

"Follow Brody, the man who pulled you out, Ms. Redding. If you don't, the men who attacked you will catch up." It was a woman's voice. Soothing and fervent.

The man nodded at her. Allie got her ass in the car. She watched as he pulled away from the curb and stopped, obviously waiting on her to follow. She glanced at King, whose head lolled to the side. He was bleeding badly, but she couldn't tell where the wound was on his scalp. She reached for his duffel and rummaged without looking until her hands fell on a large metal object. She pulled out a wicked-looking matte gray pistol.

King needed help. She had no other options at this point. The phone was ringing again, a distant sound like a cell phone left beneath a pillow on a couch.

"What?" she demanded.

"Follow Madoc, Ms. Redding. Time is running out," the woman urged her in a soft voice.

The man was waiting in a Mercedes ahead of her.

"I'm not the enemy, Ms. Redding. In fact, I think you'll be interested in hearing what I have to tell you."

Allie hung up, not interested in anything other than getting King help. She put the car in gear and took off after the man called Madoc.

They swerved through traffic, not rushing but moving quickly. After a half hour of driving, they came to a beautiful villa on a hill. Allie pulled through the gates and watched as those gates closed behind her.

King still hadn't come to, and she was worried. She pulled up to a large main house and parked the car, rushing out and training King's weapon on Madoc. A woman built for sin and with eyes the color of frost walked slowly down the steps.

"Ms. Redding, it's nice to finally meet you," the woman said and held out her hand.

Allie swept the heavy gun back and forth between the woman and Madoc, who just continued to stand there patiently. His eyes were kind, but he was another big man, capable of bad things Allie was sure.

"Who are you?"

The woman lowered her hand and inclined her head. She was dressed in a cream linen pantsuit, her dark hair swept up into an elegant chignon. There was a scar, similar to a burn mark, along her left temple. She must have caught Allie looking at it, because she gave a small smile and traced it with a trembling hand.

The gesture was inherently self-conscious, and it

soothed something inside Allie. It made the unknown woman with the frostbitten eyes vulnerable.

"I won't ask again," Allie said.

"My name is Ella Banning, Ms. Redding, and I'm here to help you."

Chapter 18

MADOC PLACED KING ON THE ENORMOUS, ORNATE WOODEN bed and stepped back.

"Someone's coming," he said gruffly.

Allie stepped in front of Madoc, training the gun on him as she moved backward, closer to King's position on the bed. She'd be damned if she'd let anyone hurt him.

A small, low laugh sounded from the doorway. "Not to harm him, Ms. Redding. To stitch his thick-ass head up, I assure you."

Allie's gaze moved from Madoc, who stepped back and turned to the side, to the woman who'd changed her clothing to black cargoes, black T-shirt, and black combat boots. She walked with a grace few women Allie had ever known could claim. More to the point, she floated over the carpeting, making no sound as she was at the door one minute and by the bed the next.

Allie stepped to her, and within two seconds, the woman had Allie's gun in her hand, barrel pointing at Allie's forehead.

Fear shot through Allie, bitter and biting, as a bead of sweat congealed on her spine. She opened her mouth, frozen for precious seconds, her mind unable to comprehend that the woman had even moved.

"I don't want to hurt you, Ms. Redding. I told you I want to help you. But you can't go around pointing a gun at me and expect me not to react," Ella said smoothly.

"Get the gun out of my face," Allie responded evenly. "Now."

Ella smiled, and once again Allie was caught up in the woman. Smooth, pale skin, unmarred with the exception of the mark at her temple. Her eyes were the clear, light blue-gray of the sky after a snowstorm. It was eerie. Her eyes told a story of cold death, while her smile spoke only of the warmth after the storm.

She'd kill you but hold you afterward. Lovely.

Ella lowered the gun and handed it back to Allie, handle first. "It helps if the safety's off."

Allie simply glared at her. It was becoming her rote response to an unspoken threat. King was rubbing off.

Ella simply inclined her head. "Madoc, please bring the physician in."

Madoc left to do the woman's bidding.

"Who the hell are you people?" Allie demanded.

"I'm a member of Endgame Ops. That man on the bed is my team leader." Ella glanced once at King, her face pinching in pain before her expression blanked.

Allie recognized the emotion rolling through her at that moment—jealousy. "You're the one who betrayed the team," Allie dropped into Ella's silence.

Ella's elegantly arched, brown eyebrows drew down before she cocked her head and stared hard at Allie. "Is that what he said?"

Allie didn't reply. She'd not give anything away. Besides, the little she knew could fill a thimble. It's not like she and King had exchanged deep, dark secrets during the few days they'd been together. Wait, maybe they had. He had told her he'd killed his father, then changed his name. And she'd told him about her mother. She'd never told another soul about her mother.

A discreet knock on the door broke the tension. Allie stiffened.

"Francisco is here, Ella," Madoc said in that deep, rusty voice.

"Send him in," she replied and glanced at Allie as if daring her to naysay.

Allie shrugged, flipped the safety on the big Kimber, pulled back the chamber loading a round, and pointed it at Ella. "Safety's not on now."

"Touché," Ella said with a grin.

That grin soothed Allie, much as the gesture earlier had. This woman had stories to tell, but not to Allie. And it was obvious by the affection in her voice when she'd called King her team leader that she wasn't going to hurt him.

Allie kept the gun focused anyway as a slight, raven-haired man stepped into the room. He appeared harried, his gaze darting to and fro and a veil of worry settling on his shoulders.

"Francisco," Ella said in a soft voice. "It's so good of you to come when we need you."

Francisco's entire demeanor changed when he saw Ella. A smile broke on his swarthy face as his brows rose to his hairline, and he hurried swiftly to the stunning spec ops soldier.

"It's been too long, Ella-Bella," Francisco said with a smile, grabbing the slender woman and hugging her tightly before his face tightened and he stepped away. "You're good?"

"I am, but King has taken a pretty hard hit to the head."

Allie had no idea who this Francisco was, but he nodded and set a small bag on the bed. Allie took a step back, lowering her gun but keeping it firmly in her grip. One wrong move, and somebody was going to have a serious case of lead poisoning.

Francisco got to work, checking King over and wincing when he found the wound on his head. He checked King's pupils, his pulse, his breathing and blood pressure. Then he set about suturing King's head. The bleeding had slowed dramatically, but the gash was at least four inches long, splitting his scalp viciously.

Francisco didn't acknowledge Allie in any way, and that was fine with her. The fewer people she knew, the less she knew *about* them. It was preferable. For a moment, Allie mourned the loss of her anonymity. She was onstage now. She'd hidden behind her father's cloak of invisibility for years, but all of that was over.

So regardless of how many people she avoided in this game, she was a player now. Her heart hurt, and she rubbed her chest. So much had changed on that fucking plane in Cameroon. Silence fell, and once Allie noticed it, she glanced up, meeting kind black eyes.

"He'll be fine. His head is much harder than we suspected," the doctor said with a smile.

All these people smiled. Except for King. Their mouths curved as if they weren't all killers and liars. Except for King. The levity in every expression made even his occasional smiles precious to Allie.

"He does have a hard head," Allie ruefully acknowledged.

Francisco looked at Ella. "He's no doubt going to have the mother of all headaches. He should probably take a few days to rest, but we're talking about His Highness so it won't happen. What the hell's going on, Ella?"

Ella shook her head, glanced at Allie, then back at Francisco. "Endgame business. The less you know, the better off you are."

Francisco nodded and finally turned to Allie. "Your father is a fine man."

Allie didn't say a word. She didn't know these people, didn't trust them. How the hell did he know who her father was?

He laughed. "Just like her father, isn't she, Ella?" He turned then, gathered his bag, handed Allie a bottle of pills, and walked out whistling.

Ella sighed and motioned to King. "He'll rest for a bit. This place should be safe for another twenty-four hours, but it won't take them long to track us down. I think we should talk."

Allie put the pill bottle beside the bed, pulled the chair beside the bed closer, and sat down, making sure to keep the Kimber on her thigh and her hand on the grip.

Another sigh from the woman with the cold, cold eyes, though she too pulled a chair up and sat down.

Silence held them tightly wrapped in its embrace. Allie refused to be the first one to speak. The woman had secrets? She could share them on her own. Allie neither wanted nor needed them.

A rough breath shuddered through Ella. "They think I betrayed them?"

Allie maintained her silence.

A bitter laugh, another sigh, and then the torrent began. "Of course they think I betrayed them. I took a bullet for them, gave up the last year of my life for them. Of course they think I was the leak. Tell me, Ms. Redding, have you met Jude?"

Something in the woman's voice tugged at Allie's heart. Allie shook her head.

"I wanted to know if he was safe." She rubbed a hand over her eyes. "Your father is a bastard. Francisco said he was a fine man. I agreed until Beirut."

Allie remained quiet, waiting. Something monumental was about to happen. She wanted nothing to do with it, became desperate to stop it.

She held up a hand. "Ms. Banning, Endgame Ops business is Endgame Ops business. I have no dog in this fight."

"Oh, but I think you do, Ms. Redding. Your father is one, and if the looks you keep throwing at our fearless leader are any indication, you've another to feed now."

Anger brushed the edges of Allie's mind, painting her vision red for a moment. This woman saw things Allie didn't want her seeing. "Just say what you have to say."

Ella sat back in her chair. "They think I betrayed them, but the truth is, I was not the betrayer but the betrayed, and I've paid a thousandfold for putting my trust in a man who gave me over to the wolves."

Allie remained silent. A shiver danced over her arms, lifting the hair and making her stomach cramp. For some reason, she knew where this was going. "You worked for my father." Statement, not question. She knew Ella had been a CIA liaison. But she was asking a deeper question. Ella Banning had the look of many others she'd seen come and go from her father's house—broken but rebuilt harder, with less of a conscience. Yet the woman's voice couldn't hide her secrets. The men of Endgame Ops had become her family.

Ella raised a brow and nodded slowly, her gaze trained on the man lying silently on the bed. "I was recruited out of high school. I went through my training during college, graduated early with a dual degree in international finance and foreign languages, and went on my first op at the age of twenty. Your father had me trained personally in the art of espionage— getting close to a target for more personal kills. He's really good at his job, your father. Can kill you with a smile on his face."

Ella's words echoed Allie's earlier feelings about the woman herself. Despite her beauty—and no doubt she'd been targeted for both her intelligence and her physical appearance—she was a killer. Hadn't she just held a gun to Allie's forehead?

Yes, she had.

"Your father was the single largest influence in my life until I met Kingston McNally. Your father taught me how to kill. King taught me how to wait for the exact right moment to deal death. King tried to teach me trust, but your father indoctrinated me, showed me that no one is trustworthy—not family, bosses, lovers—nobody."

"Sounds like you've had it rough, Ms. Banning, but I'm not sure how any of that relates to me," Allie said softly.

Ella's gaze moved to Allie, and she felt pinned, hemmed in by the brevity in those frigid orbs. "Why are you with King?"

Allie pushed down her ire. "I don't think I owe you any answers."

"You'll answer me or…"

"You're threatening me? Oh, this is rich!" Allie stood then and began to pace, the weight of the Kimber a growing familiarity that brought a measure of peace in the midst of this shit storm. She stopped and leveled her gaze on Ella Banning. "I get it, I do. You hate my father, and you're angry at your team for leaving you wherever the hell they left you. Yet, for some reason, here I am, watching you tend your team leader.

"You speak of betrayal. You speak of hating my father. Your voice softens when you talk of this Jude character, which by the way, screams of emotional connection that most CIA operatives shouldn't let leak into their voices. I think you need to give me some answers before we go much farther because, Ms. Banning, I haven't heard great things about you, and you should probably plead your case before you start demanding shit out of me."

"You've got more of your father in you than anyone realizes, don't you?" Ella let several moments pass between them. Allie remained standing, unwilling to give up her tactical advantage. Sure, the woman was as badass as King and could incapacitate Allie before she blinked, but with Allie standing and Ella sitting, Allie had the advantage. At this point, she'd take whatever she could get.

"Your father trained me, inserted me into Endgame Ops as a CIA liaison, and then used me as a way of keeping tabs on Horace Dresden's operations. He saw an opening to insert me as a double agent into Dresden's operations and did so without my prior knowledge, giving Dresden information about Endgame Ops he

never should have had. In the process of his grand machinations, your father got a man on my team killed and
both myself and Madoc labeled traitors. He also got his
double agent, though I'm not reporting to your father. I
wonder how he feels about that. I wonder if he worries
I've gone off the reservation."

Allie held up her hand, desperation slicing through
her gut. "I don't need to know this. Please just be quiet."
She'd known her father had a tough job. The world of
black ops and spying was murky. No sun shone in the
land of spooks and goblins. But to hear anyone say her
father had led them intentionally into danger, while that
might possibly be the truth, made Allie doubt who her
father was. That he could so easily play with other people's lives, maneuver them like players on a chessboard.
It disgusted her.

"The truth hurts, right? Thing is, your father has
repeatedly denied he was the one to do this. But I know
the truth because I've been mired in Horace Dresden's
operations for a year now—having to prove I'm loyal to
a murdering bastard who takes innocents and destroys
their souls before they've had a chance to live. Your
father put me in the Endgame Ops situation, and if he
isn't the one who pulled the strings that got me into
Dresden's grasp, there's a much bigger problem than
any of us realize, Ms. Redding."

"Why are you telling me this?" Allie practically
yelled her question at the woman. Part of what she'd said
snagged in Allie's mind. "You think it's possible it wasn't
my father who wanted to use you as a double agent?"

"I'm telling you I don't know the truth, and my
lines are blurring. I'm telling you I've endured hell the

last year and a half. I've lost pieces of myself while in Dresden's clutches that I'll never get back. But I'm also telling you that I didn't betray my team, and no matter what happens, their safety is my number one priority. That's why you're here right now, Ms. Redding. I'm a watcher, an information gatherer. It was my niche on the Endgame team, and it's my niche with Dresden."

"What does that have to do with me?"

"You were put on the radar a year ago by Vasily Savidge, Ms. Redding. He has known who you are for a while and has been waiting for the right time to use you."

Shock ghosted through Allie. All those last months in Africa, someone had known who she was—and she'd been out there alone, a sitting duck. She shivered, feeling footsteps over her grave. She wanted to do the things she wanted to do, but she didn't want to die doing them.

The knowledge she could be used against her father was always there. It was why he'd hidden her so deep. And now people knew. Bad people.

"How did he find out who I was?"

Ella shook her head. "That has eluded me. But someone knows, and all roads lead to the White."

Confusion banked Allie's fear. "I don't know what that means."

The sheets on the bed rustled, and Allie knew then King had heard everything.

"Shut your mouth, Ella. Not another word." King growled the command, and Ella did exactly as she'd been told. She shut the hell up.

Allie glared at him, even as her heart thumped heavier. He was sitting now, his black sleeveless T-shirt hugging the heavy muscles of his chest and exposing his defined arms. Her mouth dried. He winced as he raised a hand to his head.

Then he speared Ella with an icy, green look, and she lowered her head. He never met Allie's eyes. It pissed her off.

"Why stop now? Why not just tell me all of it?" she demanded.

"You can't handle the truth," King told her bluntly. "Give me the Kimber, Allie."

"Go fuck yourself," she responded acerbically.

His gaze did rise then, and everything that was woman inside Allie sat up and took notice. His lids lowered slightly, and his cheeks went ruddy. Oh, he was pissed but at something else, something even more dangerous to Allie in that moment.

King McNally was hot for her.

"I won't have to, once I've got my hands on you," he murmured before he stood, swayed, and then sat back down heavily.

"You're screwing up here, sir," Ella said in a rough voice.

King cocked his head at the woman and narrowed his gaze on her. Allie swore the other woman shifted nervously beneath that glare. "Have I screwed up as much as you have, Banning?"

That straightened Ella's spine, and her head snapped up. "We're keeping score?"

"Yeah, I guess we are," King replied.

Allie heard it then, the weariness in his tone. He was in pain, probably had the mother of all headaches, and he had Allie to take care of now. She rubbed her chest again. Her heart hurt.

"I didn't betray you," Ella whispered.

King shook his head. His disbelief in her statement clouded the air around them all. He glanced at Allie. "Give me the gun before you shoot one of us."

"If I wanted to shoot either of you, I've had a million chances so far, McNally. I know how to shoot."

King eyeballed her—no other description for it—just stared her down until she flipped the safety on and held the gun out to him handle first. He put it in the waistband of his cargoes and crossed his arms over his chest.

"Don't do that," she snapped.

Ella gave some unrecognizable grunt-slash-snort-slash-wheeze, and King just raised an eyebrow.

"That either," Allie bit out. Dirty, delightful things. That's what she wanted with him when he crossed his damn arms or, hell, pretty much whenever he breathed.

He pointed at her. "You, I'll handle in a bit. We've got some settling up to do." He turned to Ella, and for some reason that rankled Allie. She had no doubt he meant about her use of the word *fuck*, but for him to dismiss it so easily? It bothered her.

To Ella he said, "I don't trust you any farther than I can throw you. Where are we?"

Ella's face tightened before smoothing like someone had waved a wand over it. "We're in a house on a hill."

King nodded. Allie had no idea what that meant. All these people spoke in a code she couldn't decipher. She knew they were in Spain—had no idea where in Spain though. For someone who didn't trust Ella, King sure didn't seem in any great hurry to get away from her.

"I've got questions you're going to answer," King said to Ella. "How much time do we have here?"

"I'll give you what I know, but nothing that compromises myself or Madoc," she replied. "And we should be clear for at least forty-eight hours. Savidge thinks I'm in Morocco."

King went still. It was the eerie stillness that spoke of bad things headed your way. Allie didn't relish being in Ella's position.

"Madoc?"

"We survived. Did you not think to make sure we were dead before you saved your own asses? So much for no man left behind, right, Master Chief?"

Allie noticed two things. One, she'd called King Master Chief. Two, the temperature in the room had dropped to subzero. She didn't want to be involved in a shoot-out. She'd just survived an RPG through her hotel room.

"This is nice, huh? Catching up and stuff? Tell you what? How 'bout I just mosey my happy ass on a plane and go home? Then you guys can handle whatever misunderstandings are coloring your black ops world, and we can all just moooove along." Allie nodded and smiled vacantly.

Neither one paid her a bit of attention.

A hand touched her shoulder, and her heart dropped. She fell to the floor a nanosecond later, sweeping back with her leg, then grunting when she encountered an immovable object. The hand on her shoulder tightened. She heard King shout, but she was up by then, reaching for the hand and twisting it around. On a smaller man, her maneuver would have surely broken a finger. On Madoc, it did nothing.

"Let me go, or I'll break it," Allie threatened.

Madoc smiled, and Allie wondered if he was crazy. "You can try, little bit," he said evenly.

A breath later, she was out of Madoc's space, well to the side, as King got in the other man's face with his pistol, saying nothing but letting the gun speak volumes.

"We survived, Your Highness," Madoc ground out.

"You put your hands on her again, and I'll make sure that state changes real quick, Brody. We clear?"

"As glass," Madoc, first name Brody, replied with a smile.

"Go sit by the bed. I'll be back in a few," King said.

Allie waited for Madoc to do what he'd been told because although he had several inches and more than a few pounds on King, the big man looked like he was absolutely subservient to his team leader. None of that helped the fear reverberating through Allie.

King's head swiveled to her, green eyes frosted over as he raised a single eyebrow.

"You mean me?" she asked inanely. "Wow, okay. I'll go sit like a good dog then. You hurry back, and be sure to bring me a treat or something, okay?"

Anger wound through her, but she did as he asked, all the while categorizing escape options, entrances and exits, windows and doors. She'd gotten away from him once; it could happen again. Wait. She'd promised him she wouldn't run. Damn it.

King grunted, then stepped back, waiting for her to sit before he motioned both Ella and Madoc out of the room. The door slammed behind them, and Allie heard the distinct sound of a lock being engaged.

She took several deep breaths. She'd saved his ass. Okay, Madoc had saved their collective asses, but she'd watched over King when he couldn't watch over himself. She'd returned the favor he'd had done for her when she'd been shot. They were even.

He could tell her all day long she had no rights, that she was under his command, but the truth was that she wasn't under anyone's command. He wasn't her team leader or anything else. *Liar*, her heart whispered.

Her gaze roved the room, landing on the phone by the bed. King had left the room with two people he clearly didn't trust. What if something happened to King, if they ambushed him or something? Based on Ella betraying her whole team—whether intentionally or not—Allie knew the woman wouldn't bat an eye about using her, *especially* since she considered Allie's dad responsible for her problems. Out of the frying pan and into the fire, indeed.

She hesitated for several seconds and then picked up the ancient handset and was surprised to find it operational. She dialed a number and waited.

"Hello?" Her father's desperate voice had tears springing to her eyes.

"Dad? I'm safe. I don't know how long it will be until he comes back," she said in a rush. "Is this line safe?" She had no intention of striking up a lengthy conversation, and from what she'd seen of tracing a call—and to be honest here, her knowledge came from action movies— she had to assume some minimal amount of time was required to route the call. But if she was wrong…

"Yes. This line is secure." Her father breathed deeply. "This is bad, Allie. Keep your head, girl, and know that I'm doing everything I can to get you back here. Has McNally hurt you? He's a dead man if he's hurt you."

"He's done nothing worse than get on my nerves. He also saved my life on that plane, Dad. They were looking for me. They weren't looking for him."

"They were looking for you because of me. Listen to me, Allie. Someone is willing to use you to hurt me or get to Endgame Ops. You've got two choices."

She was beginning to hate choices.

"You stay with him, or you get away and go deep."

Panic knifed her gut. "Those aren't really choices. What do you want me to do?"

"I'd prefer you stay with McNally, but if push comes to shove, you survive. Get the hell away from him and go deep. Trust your gut, girl."

The same gut now sliced into tiny pieces? She closed her eyes and took a deep breath. "I got it, Dad. Look, he's good and he's motivated. He also says you're responsible for his team being in the position they're in." She heard him preparing to rebut that information. She cut him off. "I don't have time, Dad."

He said nothing.

"You taught me how to play the game, and I opted out. I don't have a choice now. But this man is honorable. I don't know what you know about him. I don't care. I can take the measure of a man, and I've taken his. Whatever he and his people are involved in is theirs. I don't want any part of it. But, Daddy, if you have them hurt before you know the truth, I'll be disappointed."

"Allie girl, you be safe. Remember the trail home. Skip, hop, and jump, but trust no one. I'll have money waiting for you if you need to separate from McNally."

"No! Somebody knows every move you make. Boko Haram knew about me first—they used me as a pawn.

I've been shot, run to ground, and now my hotel has been ripped open by an RPG. Whether it's to leverage you or for some other reason, I get the feeling Savidge or Dresden don't want me so we can play Parcheesi. So until we know why, I don't want you sending anything anywhere. It's traceable and opens me up. They've got eyes inside your organization. I've got this," she said in frustration.

"This isn't what I wanted for you," her father said, and his voice was thick with unshed tears.

"It was inevitable though, wasn't it? You are who you are, and I'm a part of that no matter how badly I don't want to be. Watch your back, Dad. You get to King, you give him a chance. He saved my life, and for that alone he deserves your mercy. You do that for me, we clear? I'll see you soon."

God, now she was really starting to sound like King. She closed her eyes and felt the hot lick of a single tear down her cheek.

"Come home, Allie. I'll keep you safe," her dad replied.

In spite of her father's reassuring words, Allie knew she wasn't going to be safe for a long time. With that knowledge in her mind, her eyes fell on the bathroom door and the light streaming underneath it. She took a deep breath and hung up.

Chapter 19

"Tell me everything," King demanded.

He watched as two people he'd thought dead sat down on the delicate settee in the middle of the elaborate room. Ella Banning looked as beautiful as ever, her face model-worthy with the exception of a ragged, raised scar at her temple. Brody Madoc was still the same behemoth he'd always been, though a bit rougher around the edges, and there was a look in his brown eyes that spoke of mayhem and a driving need for retribution.

"Where should I start?" Ella asked softly. "Maybe where you left Madoc and me to die in Beirut?"

She was trying to bait him, and there was dangerous anger in her tone that had brewed for over a year. King wasn't going to rise to it.

"Yeah. Start there," he commanded her.

She took a deep breath, and King could see the struggle play out on her face. His gaze skirted to Madoc, who remained impassive, even though a shudder ripped through his large frame. What had they been through? Who were they working for now? Dresden? Broemig? Both?

"There are things I can tell you and things I cannot," Ella began.

King had both of his guns out that quickly, one aimed at her, the other trained on Madoc, who still hadn't moved.

"You'll tell me everything, and we'll move on from there. I don't like liars, Banning." King waited for her to acknowledge who held the power here. She nodded, and King lowered his weapons.

"I was put into Endgame by Broemig for the sole purpose of monitoring your activities and making sure the balance was held. Your Piper plays games that get all sorts of people in trouble. Broemig was worried about his interests, so he made sure I was the liaison for Endgame," she said. Bitterness flavored her tone.

King shrugged. "I knew when the Piper put a liaison on the team, even if you were under the guise of intel gatherer, you were a plant. Hell, we all knew. Even Jude." She flinched at the man's name, and King realized she was nowhere near over Jude Dagan. "It didn't stop us from making you part of the team. It didn't keep us from trusting you, because at the end of the day, you were Endgame even though you'd started as Company."

He let that sink in and reined in the need to hurt her. Her eyes glittered in the falling light, and King might be a first-rate bastard, but she'd been one of his at one time. He didn't like that she was hurting.

"Did you kill Nina?"

Her gaze shot up. "What? No! She was my—"

"Your what?" King asked in a dead voice.

Ella shook her head, then sighed. "My partner."

King had suspected as much. The CIA had master intelligence gatherers. Why would Broemig stop with one when he could have two? Endgame Ops was the cream of the crop. The elite of the elite. Soldiers taken from every armed force by virtue of their exceptional talents in their respective units. SEALs, Rangers, Force

Recon—the men of Endgame had been handpicked by the Piper because they were stone-cold killers and they did it well. The shadows held them, and they moved within them. Their intelligence gatherers needed to do the same.

The Piper allowed CIA into Endgame because its agents were the best at what they did. What he hadn't controlled was their leader.

"Doesn't surprise me. What does is why Nina was killed. Could she not have instigated Beirut the same as you?"

Ella's face drew down, mouth flattening, eyes going blank. "I don't know what you're talking about. She got sick, I stepped in, and we went on the mission you initiated. I didn't *instigate* anything."

He laughed. "Priceless. Company to the end, huh, Ella-Bella? We trusted you. The man you were fucking trusted you. When Dresden rose up and shot you, we mourned. Then, when we went over the mission, shit started not adding up. Nina was dead. I put you on the mission. We went down, and there was Dresden, staring at Jude as he kissed you on the cheek before he blew your ass away. Or so we thought."

Ella swallowed hard. Madoc stood up and began pacing. King let him, understanding the man's need. Memories of that night, the senseless slaughter and devastation, the…loss… It haunted them all.

"I didn't do this," Ella said firmly, but in her voice was doubt. King recognized it, but instead of it reeking of subterfuge, it tasted of confusion.

"You didn't know," King said into the silence.

"I can't give you—" she began.

King raised a hand. "You can't give me what? The goddamn truth? Not even for the man you loved and led into ambush? What about Jude, Ella? Let's say you didn't give a shit for me, Rook, Black, Chase, Madoc, Knight, or Samson, but what about Jude? You're a cold bitch. I'll give you that."

She stood then, cheeks red in her rage, hand reaching for the piece she carried at her side.

"Don't do that, Ella. I'd hate to put a hole in you," King said in a near whisper.

It took her a second to gain control. Madoc stood to the side, a silent sentry, and King wondered about their connection. Had Madoc been in on it too? Did Loretta not know Madoc had survived, or had she kept that information from him?

"No, Madoc would have killed me if he'd known anything about my other mission. Dresden shot us all, but Madoc survived and I begged for his life. Dresden granted me that in exchange for other information," Ella whispered.

She'd been tortured, King thought. It was in the trembling lines of her body, the hitch of her breath. Lust for Dresden's throat in his hands nearly overwhelmed him. At the same time, he wanted to knock Ella to the floor because he had a sneaking suspicion about the information she'd given up.

"Allie." King's heart slowed, even as his body chilled. She'd given up her boss's daughter to save her teammate.

Goddamn, what a choice to make. An innocent for her teammate.

"I would have stopped her," Madoc said. His voice was broken, as if he'd screamed for days from pain or anger and finally his voice had deserted him. Or maybe the bullet he'd taken to the throat had destroyed his vocal cords?

"He couldn't have stopped me. Broemig is a bastard. If his daughter had to be given up for my teammate, I'd do it again. Besides, I only gave them verification of what they already knew to be true."

King had her throat in his hands before he knew what he was doing. "You won't give her up again. I'll kill you first."

Ella smiled. "I learned from the best, Your Highness. Team comes above all, even an innocent."

He swallowed hard, his words coming back to him from the past. He'd taught her that, and she'd done it. But now? King couldn't do it—use an innocent to meet an objective. Or maybe he just couldn't use Allie.

Madoc standing in the room with them was living proof that Ella had done exactly as she said.

"How did Dresden get to you?" King asked her, putting a little more pressure on her windpipe.

"Broemig had to have set it up. Feeding him information on Dresden was my mission. I was inserted into Endgame because you had the track to him. If I could ensure he was eliminated, or if it got screwed up, it wouldn't fall back on the CIA or Broemig, but on the private entity that was Endgame Ops. It's all about deniability," she responded.

Her pulse beat slow and steady under his hand. Madoc still stood, watching everything, waiting for something, though King didn't know what that was.

"The Piper had no idea, Ella. He had no idea what was going on. You had a mission within a mission, and at any moment you could have come to me—or hell, Jude—and you didn't. You let us go straight into that ambush without a hue or a cry. Samson is on you. That you saved Madoc by giving up an innocent woman is a true sign of a guilty conscience."

"If you think the Piper wasn't aware of what was going on, you're blind. His ideals are even more convoluted that Broemig's. Talk about giving up your firstborn? The Piper would not only give up his child, he'd go have another and do the same thing. If you hear nothing else I say, hear that. I did what I had to do, McNally. I saved you all because without me giving over that information about Allie Redding, you'd all be dust in the wind today," she responded faintly.

"That was your bargaining chip? Allie Redding? Why the hell did he want her so bad?"

"It isn't her, it's her father. Dresden knew Broemig had a daughter, and no matter how badly Dresden hates *your* guts, he hates Broemig even more. If I hadn't given Dresden verification right then, it was only a matter of time before someone else did. Broemig has secrets, but he's also trusted some people with those secrets and he must have royally pissed them off."

King released Ella's throat and stepped back, running a hand over his pounding head. They'd used an RPG to enter the hotel room and then attacked him. He'd been desperate to save Allie, but the steel pipe had taken him out after several blows. He should thank Ella for getting them out alive. Instead, he felt nothing but hollow.

"Who has he pissed off?" he asked.

"I don't know," Ella spat out as she rubbed her neck.

"You've been following me?"

She nodded. King glanced at Madoc. "How deep are you?"

"They let me follow Ella as protection. Dresden thinks I'm a bit off after being shot, but I've also proven my allegiance by ratting on others so he trusts me to tell him if she goes off the deep end."

King walked to the huge bank of windows in the large room. "If you gave them the information they wanted, why have they let you live?" He prayed she didn't answer as he knew she was going to.

"I continue to give them information," she replied.

"Goddamn," he whispered, the implications of her statement making the hair on the back of his neck stand on end. "What information?"

"Random, innocuous information."

He grunted. "Yeah, I really believe you." He ran a hand down his face. "So they just let you roam free?"

"Not so much. I'm here, but I have to go back soon or I'll be missed. I've been watching you, keeping track of what's going on, and I followed Ms. Redding to Spain," she told him. "When I realized some of Savidge's goons had the drop on her location, Madoc came after you and brought you here."

"Yeah? Moving pieces on the board? Or you wanna kill me to my face instead of stabbing me in the back?"

She winced. "I came to warn you and to save the woman I gave up."

He raised his hands. "I'm waiting."

"Dresden is moving. He wants you, but he wants Rook and Broemig more. The White is involved—someone high up is giving away Endgame and CIA secrets. We have no friends in this, King. They know who we are, all of us, and they're coming after us. The first sortie was Allie Redding. They want her desperately, if for no other reason than to cripple Broemig. Now that you have her, they're even more interested. A two-for-one if you will."

"Broemig isn't a part of Endgame. I don't understand how we got pulled into his shit. What about Savidge—what's his goal?"

"If I had to guess, it's to make Dresden the most powerful man in the world and then take him out. But he's a deep well of hate I haven't dared dive into. Dresden has been enough. I do know Savidge has set a bounty on Allie's head. It only pays if she's brought in alive, and from what I understand, he's actively coming after her."

"Tell me, Ella, what's your mission *now*?"

"To take Dresden out. To help my team."

King nodded, completely okay with that. His gut, which was rarely wrong, screamed at him that this was Ella—he could believe her. His head screamed he was a moron. "I don't trust you. There's still so much you aren't giving me."

"It's something I'll have to earn back. But after I've accomplished what I set out to accomplish," Ella responded firmly.

"You get in my way, I'll kill you and keep moving." King infused just enough truth into his statement to get his point across.

She nodded. "Clear."

"Jude will have to know."

"Not yet." It was a plea.

"I won't keep this from him. In fact, he may already know."

She nodded again, clearly miserable.

He turned to Madoc and raised a brow.

"I've been Endgame Ops since I walked through the doors, and I will remain so until I die. Protecting my teammate was the only reason I haven't let you know I was alive. And if either of you think Jude doesn't suspect Ella is alive, you're both dumber than a brickbat."

King nodded and walked to the big man. They grasped hands and pulled toward each other, slapping each other on the back. "Glad you're still with us."

"Keep Jude away from her," Madoc whispered. "I don't know what's up her sleeve, but it's big and it could be the end of all of this. Jude is batshit right now, and he'll fuck it all up if he runs in guns blazing."

King couldn't promise that. Jude had loved Ella— been immersed in her like nothing King had ever witnessed. "I'll do what I can," he promised instead.

As he stepped away, his gaze fell on an ancient desktop phone and his heart stuttered. "Tell me you disabled phone service," he whispered.

"No, why... Oh shit!" Ella shouted.

King was on the move, throwing open the door to the room he'd left Allie in.

It was empty.

Wait! No, there she was, huddled on the bed, a tiny lump under the covers.

He wanted to breathe a sigh of relief, but his chest constricted.

King glanced at Ella. "If he gets her, I'm holding you responsible. Know that. If he hurts her, I'll be hell on earth," he said as he headed to the bed.

The woman lying on it was a nuisance. Drop-dead

beautiful but a nuisance nonetheless. He said he'd never seen anything like what Jude felt for Ella, but truth was, when he looked at Allie, tasted Allie, *smelled* Allie, he understood the sentiment all too well.

What bad timing she had. Horrible timing.

"Call Broemig. Tell him what you've told me if you haven't already." Ella looked ready to dispute his order. "Do it. I don't care what you've set in motion, that woman is innocent. She's been brought into Endgame business, and it's my job to keep her safe."

"No, it's your job to find out who sold us out," Ella pointed out.

"Call Broemig, Madoc. Tell him," King ordered the man, even though he stared at Ella. "You betrayed us. Whether intentionally or not, we're in this because of you. Dresden has grown in power, Savidge is now the tool of a madman, and we had our sights on him over a year ago. You played with the truth, Ella, and now an innocent could pay the price. Don't fuck with me. I will eliminate you."

He waited for them both to leave and rolled his head on his shoulders to ease the tension. Allie had finally succumbed to the strain and was knocked out, her breathing deep and even.

What he'd learned just now was game changing. He needed time to process it, but his head was pounding. His gut said to trust Ella.

He lowered himself to sit beside Allie on the bed and rested against the headboard. The need to close his eyes was pressing.

A little rest, and he'd figure it all out. They had to move soon. He'd relocate to London with Allie, meet up with the source on Dresden, and then get her home. Whatever happened after that, at least she'd be wrapped in all the cotton her dad could provide.

She'd be safe, and ultimately that's what King wanted more than anything, even more than Dresden.

Chapter 20

"WE'RE GOING DOWN, YOUR HIGHNESS!"

Chase's voice was loud in his ear mic. The dying whine of the bird's rotors screamed through his mind.

"Brace for impact!"

Then hell unleashed as they hit the ground. His world split apart, and flames covered them. Fuel was a stench in his nostrils.

"Check in," he demanded.

Nothing.

"Goddamn it, check in!"

Still nothing.

The crackling flames were reaching for him so he reached for his boot, grabbing his knife and cutting through his harness. His left arm was numb, his head splitting. He coughed and felt the heat and smoke singing his lungs. "Chase! Check in!"

Not a sound. Then a groan and, "Jude, check."

"Chase. Check."

"Rook. Check."

"Black. Check."

"Knight. Check."

Nothing from Ella, Samson, or Madoc. Where were his people? King coughed again, the fire licking toward him as the black smoke choked. He crawled, ignoring the pain in his body.

The bird had been taken down. Thank God they'd

been flying low. Nobody should have known they were coming. How had they known?

"Ella!" Jude was screaming his lover's name, a wail of pain and confusion, desperation.

King saw Jude then and pushed to his feet, heading toward his man who was holding his right arm to his chest. He dragged Jude from the wreckage and went back in for the rest.

Black met him carrying Chase. "The pilots are dead. I can't find Ella, Samson, or Madoc."

"Get them to safety," King ordered Black, who nodded.

Then he saw them, Ella, Madoc, and Samson, on their knees in a line, a single man holding a large rifle on them.

Savidge.

When King met Savidge's eyes through the smoke, he knew his team members were going to die. He lifted his rifle, but before he could clear a shot, Savidge turned and fired.

King went to his knees, pulling his sight up and taking aim. Then his world ended. Another boom and the rush of a fireball blasted over him. He went to his back, but not before he witnessed hell.

Vasily Savidge stepping up, shooting each of King's men before Horace Dresden kissed Ella on the cheek and shot her too.

They fell, one by one, and by the time what had happened registered, by the time Jude's cries had dissolved into whimpers, Dresden and Savidge were gone. And so were his people.

Allie was warm. Cozy, even. But something had woken her. She moved closer to the heat source, let the moan building in her throat free, and smiled.

Then it hit her…she was in Spain. She'd been attacked with an RPG and was now in a *house on a hill*, whatever that meant. Panic replaced the smile and she opened her senses, everything but her eyes, to get a track on her surroundings.

Someone was beside her, definitely the source of the warmth. Tension snaked through the room, bleeding off the large man who thought he could sneak into her bed. Okay, technically not her bed but the one she was occupying.

He grunted, as if taking a hit, and her eyes opened. He was laid full out beside her, less than six inches separating them, but more like a miles-wide chasm, if his closed eyes and tense body told the story.

Allie lifted up and took his measure. His lids were closed, but his eyes moved rapidly beneath them as another inhuman sound ripped from him.

He was having a nightmare. His body was a rock. She lifted the covers and glanced down at his hands. They were fisted at his sides. Then he let out a cry that lifted the hair on the back of her neck. Loss. That's what his cry spoke of.

What the hell was haunting him?

She wanted to wake him, take him in her arms, and soothe him. She wanted to press herself against his body and return the warmth she'd borrowed moments ago. She wanted to ease him.

Instead, she reached for his fist, carefully wrapping her hand around it.

He woke instantly, knifing up in the bed and pulling away. His movement was fluid, and he now stood staring down at her, his green eyes murky with his memories.

"What?" he barked.

She looked down at the space he'd just occupied and said nothing. He knew what had happened. The moment stretched taut.

"Did I hurt you?" he finally asked.

She lifted her gaze and saw the torture on his face. He wiped a hand down it, and the look disappeared. In a split second he became His Highness once again.

"No."

He turned away from her. She heard him rummage through his bag and then head to the bathroom.

Allie heard the shower come on and rose from the bed, taking her shoes off and stretching. What was she thinking? King was beyond her scope of experience. She didn't want a hardened spec ops soldier.

Did she?

She closed her eyes and huffed. Yes, she did. She wanted him—all of him.

The shower shut off, and she sighed. This wasn't good at all. She had little to no control of her hormones around him already. Giving in to the emotions he roused was sure to rip her apart.

"Bathroom's yours."

She nodded. "I left my bag in the hotel."

"I brought your stuff from Serbia," he bit out. "It's in the bag you managed to grab at the hotel."

From the corner of her eye, she watched him leave the room. Her shoulders drooped. She was fighting an uphill battle. Oh, King McNally wanted her as much as she wanted him, but they were in for quite a fight, it seemed.

She did her own fair share of rummaging through his bag, and her heart damn near melted in her chest when she discovered what he'd brought—the Yves Saint Laurent dress and heels, all the bras and panties, and another pair of jeans and a T-shirt.

The refrain repeated—she was in trouble. Big. Large. Huge.

She showered quickly, putting her hair back into another ponytail. She brushed her teeth with a brand-new brush she found in one of the drawers and then headed back to where she'd left her clothes on the bed.

As soon as she stepped into the room, her skin tingled. He stood across the room from her, leaning against the door, arms crossed over that…damn it, that *chest*.

She finally acknowledged the truth. There wasn't a word to describe the amount of trouble she was in. Her gaze stuck on his forearms, traveled up his biceps, and finally tracked back over his pecs, now encased in olive-green cotton.

Her mouth watered. She continued her journey, drifting up over the strong, tanned column of his throat, across the stubborn chin to that delicious mouth.

He smiled. Another of the rare grins she'd grown desperate for.

Damn.

She stood there like a moron, covered in a towel and nothing else, the taste of mint and the remembered flavor of his evergreen taste sliding down her throat.

"Um," she stammered. "I need to dress."

His smile widened. "Go ahead."

That smile was going to make her do wicked things. The same wicked things she'd been envisioning for a

few days now. Her inner hussy reared its head—Who
knew she even had one?—demanding she play the game
he seemed to be taunting her with.

"You think I won't?" she asked, desperate to recall
the words but picking up the gauntlet he'd thrown down.

He shook his head.

It was her turn to smile. She reached for the edge
of the towel tucked between her breasts and slowly
removed it, letting the towel fall to the floor.

His green eyes glittered, narrowing on her body.
Never had Allie felt more feminine. Never had she seen
that look on a man's face before.

Pure, unadulterated lust. And something else she
couldn't name but that made her heart jump and her
soul hope.

"Never dare me," she whispered.

He came for her then, reclining against the door one
second and in front of her the next. That glorious heat
he always brought seeped into her skin, marking her in
subtle ways and branding her definitively.

She backed up and met the wall. He put his hands on
either side of her head and leaned down.

"Do you think I *won't*?" he asked, returning her
words from moments ago.

She sure hoped he *would*. But she shook her head just
as he had.

He smiled once more. She had enough time to draw
in a small breath before he took her mouth and mind in
one fell swoop.

It was another branding, but this one was wrapped
inside a promise. What he'd started in that hotel room
yesterday was going to find fruition today.

Her body sang, rising to meet and press against his. His hands pulled her ponytail free, and the feel of her hair falling over her skin was so erotic that she moaned. His presence was enough to sensitize her skin; the hair was overload.

Her hands tangled in his shirt, pushing and pulling it from his cargoes, and then she was touching him, pressing her fingertips into the satin of his skin and feeling his strength as his muscles bunched. He lifted her in his arms and brought them to the bed. He sat down, never relinquishing her mouth as he stood her before him.

Then he pulled away, letting his hands drag slowly down her sides, barely skimming the sides of her breasts before they cupped her hips.

"This is a bad idea." His voice was guttural, and it did things to her best left unsaid.

"I disagree," she countered, right before she moved closer to him and took his mouth.

He hissed in a breath but made no protest, allowing her to plunder and pillage as she would. He wrapped his arms around her, and Allie wondered if this was what home felt like.

His fingers smoothed the flesh of her ass and then pressed deep into the globes, holding her still for whatever he would do.

Allie ached and then decided she had no idea what that was once he settled his mouth on the tip of her breast. He watched her the entire time, his face hard, his eyes soft. Her mouth opened as he drew the tip inside the heat of his mouth, and then she exhaled as one of his hands found the flesh between her legs.

He tugged at her nipple, lightly taking it between his

teeth as he stroked the inside of her thighs and finally, oh sweet baby ducks in a pond, finally touched the folds of her pussy. Her knees weakened and he caught her, laughing softly as he spread her legs and sat her over his lap.

He let her nipple go with a pop, and then he pulled her flush with his body. The contact between the hard ridge of his erection and her swollen flesh sent lightning flashing down her spine.

Her eyes crossed and she moaned. He laughed again and then pushed her back slightly.

"This is madness," he said.

"Beyond," she whispered. "And I want more."

"Look at me."

She obeyed—she hadn't realized her eyes were closed.

"This won't end here."

More electricity scampering across her nerve endings. "I should hope not."

He touched her again, running his fingers along the exposed lips of her pussy, stroking gently and then circling her clit until her hips were gyrating for deeper contact.

"You like that?"

She couldn't answer. Between his deep voice praising her and his wicked fingers working her body so eloquently, she was nearly insensate with need.

"You need to come?"

She nodded. "Yes," she groaned, but he responded, giving her deeper contact, delving inside her with a finger and then slipping back out.

He groaned. "You are so tight. You'll burn me alive."

She thought perhaps they'd burn each other and it would be beautiful. "I need to touch you."

"Leave your hands there. Let me do this for you, Allie."

She met his gaze again. Once again, he was showing her that he was a caretaker. And she could no more help giving herself to him than she could have stopped the sun from rising.

"Please," she whispered.

He took her with his hands, one toying with her breasts as the other took her to a place she'd never been...ecstasy. The world lightened with the colors of the rainbow as her body crested into orgasm under his touch.

Her internal muscles clamped on his fingers, and he praised her once more, stroking her through climax and petting her until she thought she'd go mad. He built her up again and took her over gently, circling her clit and making her keen.

He seemed to know her body better than she did. He shifted them, laying her across the bed, then standing.

"Allie?"

She opened her eyes, meeting his electric gaze and smiling. "Yeah?"

"I'm going to take you now," he whispered.

"About time," she responded.

He removed his pants, boxer briefs, shoes, and socks in one fell swoop. Then he covered her body with his, settling himself in the cradle of her thighs. The feel of his impressive length pressing against her pussy had sparks showering through her belly.

So much heat he generated. So much desire.

"I would kiss you more..." he said as he placed a nipping bite at her collarbone.

She remained silent.

"I would lick you more…" He followed this with the blazing trail of his tongue in the valley between her breasts.

Again, she held back from speaking. Doubted she could anyway. This was seduction, pure and simple.

"I would take you high again with my fingers…" he promised as he lowered his hand to her clit again.

Allie waited, breath held, lungs screaming for oxygen.

He moved then, the head of his cock nudging her entrance. "But it would prevent me from finding heaven."

He surged inside her then, all heat and male and velvet-covered steel. He pushed deep and she moaned. He retreated, and a plea formed on her lips.

But there was no worry. King was not going to stop.

"I'll take you there, Allie," he promised.

She reached for him, pulling him all the way down to her and taking his mouth, desperate for everything he had to give and more.

He lifted her leg, and she wrapped it around his hips. He stroked her with his hands, his eyes cataloging her every response. It was erotic, his taking. He watched her and she watched him, the bond forged so deep and sure that she knew she'd never be the same.

Over and over he took her, higher and higher, to a heaven she hadn't known could exist, much less between two people.

And when she crested the peak, he was with her, groaning her name and spending deep inside her body.

King wrapped her in his arms, still joined to her, and pulled her into his embrace. And there she rested on top of him, surrounded by him, mind whirring but knowing only him.

Chapter 21

HE'D TAKEN HER. BUT IF HE WAS TRUTHFUL WITH HIMSELF, King knew she'd taken him. He had decided in Belgrade he was going to make her his—if for no longer than it took to get her home to DC. King wasn't a safe bet. Bad things happened to the people around him. He had his men to protect, and he didn't need another burden.

But they were safe here for at least a day, and his mind churned with the war he was having with his body.

Never had he felt this emotion. It settled inside him, warming him, making him want the impossible, forcing him to crave the woman lying in abandon beside him.

He closed his eyes, opened them, and focused on the ceiling. His head hurt, but it was a pain he could breathe away. Instead, he focused on his surroundings. A house on a hill. Ella had taken refuge in an Endgame safe house.

He shook his head. Thoughts of Ella and Endgame had no place here. Not right now.

Right now was about Allie Redding.

He turned to his side and rested his head on his hand. She was incredible. Beautiful with her large, blue eyes and upturned nose hinting at stubbornness. Her hair was all over the place, the sunlit strands stroking everything they touched, including King.

Her smell was wildflowers—delicious, addictive.

He'd touched her now. The smudge on her neck, barely peeking out from between the strands of her hair, marked her as his.

How in holy hell was he going to keep her safe? He couldn't even keep his own men and women safe. How would he prevent the holder of his heart—

Oh shit.

He'd fallen for her.

Five days in her presence, and he was talking the l-word.

He was fucked.

"You're thinking incredibly hard," she murmured.

He glanced at her, meeting her blue gaze and feeling everything in him settle. "Nah, that's not possible."

She stretched luxuriously, giving King glimpses of her silken skin, the skin he'd wanted to revel in. She turned to face him, resting her head in her hand like him. He grazed a fingertip down her neck to her breast, circling her nipple.

She inhaled deeply, and the tip puckered. King's mouth watered.

"You make me want, King McNally."

He sighed. "It's only fair, since you do the same to me."

"I don't know if there's enough want in the world to explain what this is." Her gaze held his captive. She was telling him something.

King was a master at reading between the lines. Things unspoken were his world. No matter what Loretta Bernstein had said, he could see through the smoke to the fire—hell, he lived in the fire.

And now he had a brand-new flame to deal with.

"Maybe we shouldn't talk about it," he urged. "Maybe we should just feel."

She smiled then, gamine and teasing. "You're a wimp." Apparently he wasn't the only one who could read between the lines.

He shrugged. "I'm a big, bad spec ops soldier, baby. Ain't no wimp."

She laughed and the sound trilled through King, tinkling to settle right in his heart. "Okay, okay, but before we go in for round two, can we have a little get-to-know-you session?"

He groaned and fell to his back dramatically. "Can't I just give you an amazing orgasm, and we'll call it square?"

She laughed again, and his heart lightened.

"You aren't going to let this whole talking thing go, are you?" he asked with a grin.

She scooted over to him and wrapped her leg over his hips, grazing his erection as she climbed on top of him and rested her head on his chest. "Nope."

"Okay, but I get first question," he said.

She nodded and smiled. He wanted that smile for eternity. Nothing was like it. Nothing made him feel more alive.

"What's your favorite color?"

She raised an eyebrow and frowned. "That's what you're going to ask? Did I mention you're a wimp?"

He tapped her lips. "Unh-unh-unh… I'm asking the question. We gotta start off small and work up to the big things."

"Green."

"Green? Why?"

She shook her head. "That's two questions. It's my turn."

He wanted to laugh but she looked so serious, contemplating what to ask him. For a second he was fearful of what it would be.

"What's your favorite food?"

King barked out a laugh. It almost dislodged her from his chest. And there was that smile again. "That's what you're going to ask?" he parroted her earlier comment.

She nodded. "Yep."

He gave it serious thought, but only one answer kept pounding his brain. "You." And if she moved over his hard cock anymore, her entrance teasing him mercilessly, he was going to prove it to her.

She shuttered her eyes from him, but he saw the gooseflesh rising on her skin. She liked his answer, no doubt about it.

"My turn." He stroked along her sides, glorying in her indrawn breath. "What was the name of your first pet?"

"George." She drew in another roughened breath. "What was yours?"

"My what?"

She chuckled. "It's my turn for questions."

"I never had a pet." His father had abhorred animals, and by the time King left juvie, he was in the service. The navy frowned on pets too.

"That's sad," she murmured softly.

"That's life, princess. Big, bad spec ops boys don't have pets." He let his hands continue to rove her body, cupping her bottom before rising to stroke the sides of her breast. "My turn. Why the Peace Corps?"

Allie placed her hands on his chest and rested her chin on them. Her gaze took a faraway path, and he mourned that his question took her away from him. "My mother was a Peace Corps fanatic. She was the single most giving person I've ever met and used her influence as an ambassador to UNICEF to further their agenda. She believed in sharing knowledge and medical care and anything else that would make the less-fortunates' lives better."

King brushed a strand of hair off her forehead, then wrapped it around his finger. She kissed his chest.

"Okay, what do I ask now? Do I go for the deeply meaningful questions, or keep it banter-like?"

"That's two questions, maybe three. Which do I answer first? I feel like you're cheating at this game."

She frowned at him but couldn't hold it. "Why did you kill your dad?"

King almost shut down, but something in her eyes told him this was important to her. If opening himself up to the greatest pain in his life would make her happy, he was discovering he'd damn well do it. "My mother died giving birth to me. Thomas Sacco Sr., my sperm donor, was a bastard. Being stuck with a baby wasn't his idea of a good life, but for the first few years, until I got big enough to hit, he might have done his best to raise me. He taught me to hunt, cook, grow my own food. But he drank. A lot. And he was a mean drunk. Eventually, I got big enough to protect myself, and one night, I gave him back what he'd given me. Unfortunately, he did something I'd longed to do for years—he died."

Allie was gripping his shoulders, her fingers digging into the muscles there. Then she laid her head over his heart, and he felt the hot sting of her tears.

"Don't cry for me, princess," King pleaded. "I'm not worth your tears."

Long moments passed in which King debated with himself about telling her about his dad. Then she raised her head, and on her face was an expression he'd never seen before…acceptance.

She rose, leveraging with her hands on his chest until she was straddling his hips. His cock rose like a brand between them, begging to be seated in her warmth. She did this to him. No matter his horrible memories, no matter the dire nature of their situation, she made him *want*.

"Green is my favorite color," she said softly, lifting up and placing his cock at her entrance. "Because it's the color of your eyes."

He hissed in a breath as she seated herself on him, taking him to the hilt and shifting so she could rise and fall with ease.

King gripped her hips as her words tore through him. He loved her.

A man who'd only known hate now knew the ultimate fear of love.

She rode him with his help, lifting and gyrating and sinking down over and over until King lost what was left of his mind.

He switched their positions then and proceeded to show her with his body everything he couldn't say with his mouth. He worshipped her until the sun rose.

───⁕───

Allie woke to King's mouth at her breast. She smiled and opened her eyes, seeing his wavy, brown hair, feeling the soft strands brush her skin.

"You make me feel things I didn't think possible,

McNally." She didn't question her need to voice her conflicting thoughts. She trusted him.

"That's a good thing, right, princess?" he asked as he looked up at her, his face relaxed, the smile she'd grown to cherish flirting with his lips.

She started to answer when, for the second time in as many days, her world exploded.

"Allie!"

It was King yelling her name, but all she could hear was that damn strange ringing in her ears.

He picked her up and set her on her feet. "Get dressed!"

She shook her head, everything unclear until he grabbed her face in his hands and forced her to look at him.

"Allie! Baby, listen—we're under attack. Get dressed, take this bag, and hide in the bathroom," King ordered.

She shook her head as the staccato impression of gunfire splintered in her ears. All she could think was, again?

She did as he demanded, dressing hastily, her body still humming with the pleasure he'd given her, though it was rapidly disappearing under fear.

Whoever Dresden and Savidge were, they were not giving up.

"Be careful," she said as King pulled gun after gun from his bag.

He paused for a moment and looked up at her. He handed her a gun and said, "I will. Use it if you have to. I'll be back for you. Hunker down in the tub and I'll be back, I promise."

She nodded and moved to do as he commanded.

She locked the door behind her, praying for his safety

as every shot pierced the veil of what had happened between them.

Another loud explosion and she yelped. In the aftermath, she heard one voice among the falling debris. King.

"Run, Redding. Run!"

Chapter 22

ALLIE SKIRTED THE CITY, DOING HER BEST TO BLEND IN, though her shirt had a bloodstain where she'd cut herself on the glass in the bathroom and her hair was a ratty mess. She looked like a street person, and while that would have suited her purpose inside the city, in these hills it was a slight detriment. People were giving her sidelong glances, and she was drawing notice she couldn't afford.

She had no idea how much time had passed. King had told her to run, so she'd escaped through the small bathroom window. She'd been half afraid of being shot as she shimmied out, while the other half of her had been afraid she'd be shot if she didn't. She was numb, the feeling running deep and making her cold.

Fear held her hand now. Was King okay? What about Ella and Madoc? She didn't want to run. She wanted to go back and find them.

Instead, she continued putting one foot in front of the other, doing her best to hide her tracks but this running-from-danger business was for the birds. She wasn't a professional, and she was desperate.

The hair at the back of her nape rose and she brushed a hand over it. Nerves, she told herself. She glanced back anyway, assuring herself no one was paying any undue attention to her. The small village on the outskirts of the larger city in the valley below was going to be her home tonight. If she had to bed down in a stable, she'd damn well do it.

Her stomach growled, and there was that feeling of being watched again. She had limited funds, no phone, and was hurting. She had to hope she'd come far enough to hide because she also had no more energy.

She was a mess.

Maybe she should venture down into the village she could see below, find a small hotel, and use some of the money she'd found in the bag King had tossed to her to reserve a room. Most places required some form of ID even with a prepaid room, but given her appearance, she could claim she'd been mugged. Lord knew she looked like she'd been through something traumatic. Once she settled into the hotel, she could shower, tend her wound, and eat. Light was falling, the sky darkening to deep pinks and oranges. Just a little over two days ago, she'd been in Africa.

It seemed so long ago.

People were beginning to close up shop. She needed to make up her mind. She saw a bus pulling away from the curb and flagged it down.

"*¿Puedo conseguir un paseo a la ciudad?*" she asked the driver. She needed to get somewhere that had people, and she needed to do it quickly.

"*Sí,*" he returned with a smile.

Allie walked around to the door and had just stepped on when she glanced to the back of the bus. A man sat there, taking up most of the rear seat, his gray hair shorn close to his scalp and his eyes vacant.

She shuddered, given a moment's pause by the absolute nothingness in his gaze. Is that what she looked like right now? Empty? Her stomach growled again and she made her decision. No matter how much of a mess she was emotionally, she needed to take this bus to the village below. King would find her. She'd hold on to that.

Spain was a beautiful country, but she spoke limited Spanish and couldn't read the signs all that well. She recognized that she was heading toward the village of Alcala de Henares, but that was all she knew.

Allie sat wearily in the seat and did her best to slow her racing heart with deep, even breaths. A woman a few seats behind her conversed sparingly with the driver, who glanced at Allie in the rearview mirror, then laughed. She shook off the feeling of impending doom and just prayed the ride was over swiftly.

Thirty minutes later, the bus stopped, pulling along a street that was dark and didn't look all that safe. Allie got off the bus and began walking, her side burning, her stomach trying to eat her spine, and her mind whirling.

Fatigue pulled at her. She came to the first hotel she saw, a dirty, run-down building, but it had a vacancy according to the sign, so she ignored the shady folks lingering outside the entrance. She didn't make eye contact and avoided touching anything.

"*Cabida*?" she asked the old woman at the desk. She was asking for a room, but in reality she needed so much more that this woman and this place could never provide. Safety. She wanted King and safety. In that order.

"*Sí*," the woman replied in a hard voice, not looking at Allie, just waiting for the money.

"*¿Tiene una habitación disponible*?" Allie asked, hoping the woman wouldn't ask for identification.

"*Sí, aquí*," the woman responded and held out her hand for money.

Allie handed her the money. The woman handed her a key, and Allie thanked her.

"*Farmacia*?" Allie asked the woman.

She pointed and Allie headed back out the door, searching for a pharmacy. There was no CVS or Walgreens in this country, nothing but mom-and-pop stores. Half a mile from the hotel, she located one that was about to close and gathered bandages, cleaning solution, and tape, as well as aspirin. She needed to clean her wound and rewrap it.

She stopped by a small bar that served *patatas bravas* and grabbed an order before setting off for the hotel. Again, she didn't make eye contact, shutting herself off from anything other than food and cleaning her wound.

Allie locked her door, set her food on the tiny table in the room, and pulled a small dresser in front of the door for added protection before she turned to face the room. It was small, the lone bed sagging sadly in the middle but covered with a colorful quilt that at least looked clean. The windows were closed so Allie ventured over and opened them, taking in the smell of coming rain and letting it calm her as the thought of rain never had.

She left the windows open. She was on the fifth floor after all, and unless someone could scale the side of a wall or, God forbid, shoot another RPG into her room, she should be safe. Plus, those fragile panes of glass weren't going to be much of a deterrent to anyone. The bathroom was relatively clean and sported a large claw-foot tub that she hastily began to fill with warm water.

She took her clothes off, washed them out in the sink,

and hung them on the curtain rod to dry. The stain on her shirt wasn't coming out, but at least it was muted now, and her pants and underwear were clean. For a second, she mourned the loss of the gorgeous lingerie King had bought for her. Then the thought disappeared as her stomach yelled at her again.

She patted it gently. "I hear you," she promised.

She ate quickly, shivering in the aftermath of her fear, and she wondered if King was okay. Her eyelids were heavy, but sleep was a commodity she couldn't afford right now. So instead she tried to wrap her mind around how the hell she was going to get out of this country and get home.

King had no idea where she was, and though she desperately wanted him to just show up, she knew that wasn't likely. Her safety net was gone now. She was going to have to go deep like her father had urged her.

She was going to have to save herself.

Allie breathed in deeply, her belly full and her mind raging.

She could do this.

She had no choice.

King sat gingerly on the bed and just watched her. Relief poured through him as he saw she was alive and well. Unfortunately, she'd left a trail a blind man could follow. But she needed rest, so he was hoping against hope he had at least a few hours before they would need to be on the move again.

Her clothes were drying as they hung over a curtain rod, but she was knocked out, dead-to-the-world asleep.

He didn't have the heart to wake her. How much fear and pain would she know because of him?

He watched her, his gaze traveling over her nose, to her bow mouth, over the curve of her cheek, and down her neck. Everything about her was graceful, from the arch of her brows to the upper globes of those luscious breasts. Her skin glistened in the low, yellow light. He wanted to touch her...to take her. He beat the impulses back. They needed to move soon, so sex was a luxury they couldn't afford.

The taste back at the villa hadn't been nearly enough.

But he continued to watch her breathe, thanking God she'd heard him yell at her to run, even as he assured himself she hadn't managed to get herself killed on the wild trek down the mountains above them. He, Madoc, and Ella had laid down cover fire as she'd retreated, but then they'd been swarmed and it had been hand-to-hand combat for them both. They'd taken out every man who came for them, but King was sure more were on the way.

The villa was destroyed, but they'd found and eliminated each of the twenty men who'd attacked the safe house. Then Ella and Madoc had gone their way and King had gone his, intent on finding the woman who'd stolen the biggest piece of him.

His heart had been pounding when he came to this hotel on the outskirts of the small city. She'd picked the seediest joint she could find, and all he wanted to do was congratulate her.

Savidge's reach was long, and he was actively seeking them. King wasn't about to let that bastard get anywhere close to her.

Still he watched her. This tiny woman had burrowed inside him, turning everything upside down for him. It both angered him and made him nervous. Her safety was his priority. Nothing else. Endgame business could wait.

He blinked down at her, unaware he'd even moved. Like an iron filing to a magnet, he was drawn to her. She was beyond beautiful. And he wanted her.

"Allie," he called softly. "Baby, wake up."

He wanted her in his arms, so he reached down and picked her up gently. She moaned and curled in to his body, coming to rest in his arms as if she'd rented space there.

Breathless. She made him breathless.

His dick was hard, and his hands wanted to fist in her hair, to pull her up to accept his mouth in whatever way he wanted to give it to her. The desire she stirred in him was madness.

She moaned, and he realized he was an inch away from taking her mouth. So he stood up and covered her. Temptation was living and breathing fire—and its name was Allie Redding.

"King," she whispered before she winced and settled back down.

He'd had Madoc contact Francisco once King knew where she was holed up. His sat phone rang.

"Cisco?"

"Your Highness." The man's voice held laughter. "You should be resting."

"Shoulda, coulda, woulda. I need you up here. Room 1502, La Jolla Hotel."

"Coming."

Thirty minutes later, a discreet knock sounded at the door. King pulled out his gun and opened the door.

He smiled when Cisco lowered his weapon. "I trained your ass well, didn't I?" King asked him.

"Sometimes, I think too well. Where is she, boss?" Cisco asked as he walked to the bed.

A few minutes later, he'd determined that Allie simply needed more Steri-Strips on the wound at her side. She also had a small cut on her arm, probably from where she'd broken the window and crawled out. "She heals fast. The wound is completely closed, and she shouldn't even need the Steri-Strips in another few days. That cut on her arm will heal on its own."

"Thanks," King said on a rough exhale.

"This woman means something to you, boss?" Cisco asked.

"This isn't her fight. I need to get her home safely," King responded.

"Right. Got that. You don't want to talk about it."

King shook his head and sat down heavily beside the bed. Allie hadn't roused at all, even though Cisco had poked and prodded at her wound. "She doesn't deserve what was brought to her door, Cisco."

"Do any of us?" Cisco asked as he packed up his stuff and stood.

"Some of us, maybe," King replied in a low tone.

"And some of us do all we can to make amends. Be careful, boss, that you don't confuse your guilt over the past with this woman's future."

"You finished?" King asked suddenly, unwilling to let Cisco's words wrap around his mind.

"I am. I'm heading to Burundi. Chase said a village there is in need of medical help. I'm out tomorrow morning." He stopped before he opened the door and turned back to King. "She's nothing like her father. I told her she was, but the truth is, that woman doesn't have an ounce of subterfuge in her body. Remember that, boss."

King didn't reply, just watched Cisco leave before he got up and locked the door.

"King?"

Her voice whispered in his ears, and he turned to her, going to a knee beside the bed. "Yeah, it's me."

"How did you find me?"

"I will always find you," he all but growled. "I need you to dress, Allie. We could have to move quickly."

She pushed her hair back and did as he asked. He winced that the clothes were still wet, but there was nothing to be done for it. Just like there was nothing to be done for his heart when she looked up at him and asked, "Hold me?"

It was what he wanted, but what he could not give her. He shook his head. "Rest, Allie. We've gotta head out soon. I need you alert."

"Jerkface," she murmured. She closed her eyes, but not before he saw the hurt in them.

"You'd do well to remember it," he whispered. "For both our sakes."

Holy shit, he was done for.

Chapter 23

KING CAME TO IN A RUSH, THE TASTE OF BURNING FUEL AND smoke in his mouth. Even knowing Ella and Madoc hadn't died that day, the scene was still fresh. He'd allowed himself thirty minutes of rest time. It hadn't been enough.

"Bad dream?"

Allie's sultry voice was balm to his fraying mind. He'd lost so much that day in Lebanon. Even if Samson was the only one gone, his loss would haunt King.

"Bad memories," he corrected her as he sat up in the chair and wiped a hand over his eyes. "How long you been awake?"

She was sitting against the headboard, head cocked to the side, a book of some sort on her bent knees. Her hair was a waterfall of white-blond strands, and he wanted to sink his hands in it.

She grimaced. "Long enough to hear you yell your men's names in terror."

He hissed in a breath and glanced at her.

"You should really let me go," she said, and there was a plea in her voice. She closed the book and looked at him.

"I know." And he did, but he couldn't. Not until Dresden and Savidge were six feet deep. Not until she was safe.

"I'll never be safe again. This crusade is fruitless," she dropped into his silence.

"I would imagine being Gray Broemig's daughter is fraught with all manner of danger. But Savidge is after you, probably to get at your father, maybe to get at me. Either way, I'm a bonus, but he also wants you for things you don't want to know about."

Her breath hitched, and he felt it in *his* chest. "So we're back to me blindly following you?"

"It might be easier if your eyes are wide open. But however it works best for you is how we'll do it," he said.

"Can I ask for one thing?"

Her chest rose and fell, and the sheet she'd been holding for dear life earlier was dipping lower with each exhalation. He wanted it to fall. He wanted to pull one of those beaded nipples in his mouth and taste her.

"One. That's the limit."

"Kiss me," she said aloud. "I need to know if it's as good as I remember."

Or maybe that was wishful thinking. Whichever it was, he gave in to the need.

He took her mouth, sinking deep into the warmth of her, tangling his tongue with hers, and sipping from her the only way he'd allow himself right now. Her fingers wrapped in his hair, tugging as she became desperate. He held her head still, tormenting her lips, evading her demanding tongue, and giving what he wanted and nothing more.

Until she sighed his name and he was lost. A knock on the door, a louder bang moments later, and King pulled away from her. Their time was up. King didn't question how Savidge's men had found them so quickly.

He trained his gun on the door and said, "Allie, take the gun on the bed. Now."

"Who is it?" he asked through the door.

"Room service" came the muffled response. King didn't question his instincts. Savidge's men were here. There'd be time later to figure out how he'd found them so quickly. For now, King had to get Allie out safely. He glanced at her. He was glad he'd had her dress earlier. He watched her settle the gun in her waistband. He nodded to the balcony.

"Get there now. There's a rope ladder to the roof. Take it and wait for me there," he ordered her. She hesitated. "Now!" he demanded.

She moved, fear a tattoo on her face before he said, "They're here, Allie. Trust me, and I'll get you out of this."

She scrambled to the balcony as shots began to pelt the room through the door. King grabbed his pack, strapped it over his shoulder, then meshed his back to the wall, checking the rounds in his gun and taking a single deep breath. Out of the corner of his eye, he saw Allie heading up the ladder.

He counted to ten, stepped away from the wall, and began firing in return, steady shots in a pattern that would keep them guessing—through the wall, through the door, whatever it took to buy them some time.

He dropped the empty cartridge and reloaded, firing again, dodging sporadic return fire, and watching as the thin wooden door began to splinter from the gunshots.

King saw an arm through one of the holes and fired, hitting the man and hearing him scream in pain. Two more shots, and he was on the balcony. Instead of climbing up the rope to join her, he waited for them to make entry.

Could be suicide, but he had to buy her time to hide on the roof, and he'd do whatever was needed to accomplish that. Another few shots from the men on the other side of the door, and it broke down the middle.

King aimed and dropped the first man with a shot to the head. He fell but two more stepped over his body, firing continuously. King drew back behind the balcony doors, waiting for them to reload. Bits of wall and wood pelted him, and above was Allie, yelling his name.

Something in her voice tugged at King but he had men on his ass. He heard a brief silence, knew it was his moment, and stepped out from behind the balcony wall, firing and dropping two more men.

From the corridor came a sound that had the air in his lungs freezing—rifles being locked and loaded. He had no idea how many men were in the corridor. He reloaded and took off up the ladder, turning to fire below. Keep them guessing, and they might not get a clear shot.

His head was clear. Adrenaline coursed through his body, and he climbed to the roof faster than he'd ever climbed in his life. Allie was there at the top, up and over the small ledge.

A single shot fired, and pain ripped along his calf. It was a graze, but it stung like a razor blade.

He crested the roof and turned to shoot at the men attempting to scale the wall. "I've got you," he said through gritted teeth.

Allie didn't respond, and as he looked around, his heart leaped to his throat.

Allie was on her knees, a large man behind her holding a gun to her head. Her eyes were wide, chest rising and falling rapidly. The look in her eyes nearly destroyed him. It was acceptance.

"No," he responded to that look. Then he lifted his gun, and with a move he'd perfected long before he'd ever joined the SEALs, he fired a single shot to the forehead of the man holding her. Blood splattered in her hair, and she fell forward as the man fell back, his hold on her hair broken by his sudden death. King couldn't stand anyone having their hands on her. He'd kill anyone who tried to hurt her.

She scrabbled to him, tried to crawl into him, and he was up, tugging on her arm and refusing to let her stop moving.

Her sobs were silent, though no less vicious because of it. He felt her trembling even as she ran with him, and when he jumped to another rooftop, she followed him, never breaking stride.

They fled over the rooftops with the report of gunfire ripping through the early morning until he pushed her behind a metal shed on top of one of the buildings. She fell to her knees and released one of the sobs she was holding on to.

King winced hearing it, a part of him wanting to soothe her pain, but knowing that if he didn't kill whoever pursued them, he'd never be able to comfort her. They'd both be dead.

He unstrapped his pack and placed it beside her. He reloaded his Kimber and handed it to her. "Shoot sporadically, enough to keep them guessing. It's got a wicked recoil. Be careful," he said in a rush.

She nodded and wiped her eyes with the back of her hand. He looked at her then, noticing her pale cheeks, the circles under her eyes, and the fear darkening her gaze.

"I'm here, baby," he promised.

She nodded again, hiccupping but chambering a round. She put her free hand on his face, rubbed her thumb over his lips, and smiled. "You've got this."

Her faith staggered him, took him right out of his element for a precious moment before the sound of shots peppering the metal in front of them brought him back to the present.

He reached inside his pack, pulling out his rifle.

"Put your hand around the side and shoot three times, Allie," he urged her.

A muffled scream echoed back to them.

"See? You're a better shot than I thought," he said as he assembled his rifle, loading the big killer with ammunition.

She didn't say anything, but she fired five more times, her face grimacing with each shot, and his heart ached.

"I've got it now, Allie. Get behind me. I'm going to step out. You stay here. If something happens to me, you run. Do you hear me? Run hard, run fast, and don't stop until your heart does," he urged.

She gazed up at him, eyes unfocused and filled with tears.

"I'm afraid if you fall, my heart will have already stopped," she whispered.

His calf burned, his head pounded, but in the space between them, her words reverberated in his soul.

"Then I won't fall," he told her.

He took a deep, fortifying breath, sinking into that space inside him that was all killer. The air became heavy, his vision sharpened, and his hearing became keener. He heard the pounding footsteps and muffled wheezes of the three men following them. Peeking around the structure he and Allie were hiding behind, he located the men. Two rooftops away now.

He counted their steps, used his hearing to guide him as he set his scope to his eye, and stepped from behind his cover.

Boom! Boom! Boom!

Three shots. Three kills.

Silence reigned, and King was left with cotton in his ears until the adrenaline cleared for a moment. He slung his rifle over his shoulder, grabbed his pack, and reached for Allie.

Her hands were over her ears, and tears streamed down her face.

"No time for tears, baby. Let's go," King demanded.

She got up, as he'd known she would, and they were once again running over the rooftops, sirens cutting through the air and people shouting below. When he knew she could run and jump no more, he took them down to the ground and located a car.

Like the Yugo in Douala, this car was nothing special but it responded to his attempts to hot-wire it, so they had wheels. He stowed his gear in the back, settled Allie in the passenger's seat, and they were heading away from the village of Alcala de Henares toward Madrid.

Chapter 24

ALLIE WATCHED THE COUNTRYSIDE DARKEN UNTIL FINALLY the green grass turned black, the shadows creeping along the land until they covered everything. She'd killed another man today. That made two since she'd met Kingston McNally.

It wasn't fair to link the two, and yet it was the truth. She glanced at him, his face illuminated by the dashboard lights. His grim countenance made her stomach churn. He hadn't said much to her since he'd hot-wired this vehicle and started driving.

They'd been on the road for hours, and she'd wondered if they were traveling in circles. Then he'd confirmed that, yes, they were traveling in a way that should throw off anyone following them. They were now headed to Bilbao, on the coast.

The silence was deafening, and yet for the first time in her life, Allie didn't have the desire to fill the void. She felt broken inside. Fear had been her companion for four days, and it had finally locked her down inside herself. She was unwilling to venture out.

"Allie?"

His voice sliced through her reverie. "Yeah?"

"We're close to Bilbao. You okay?"

"Sure," she replied laconically. She didn't know if she'd ever be okay again.

"Talk to me, Allie." Deep and dark, his voice held a

slight hint of the South in its tones. She'd not noticed that until now.

His words seemed like a plea to her. In her heart, she wanted to give him what he asked for, but her throat was clogged with tears and her emotions were warped. If she started down that path, she'd splinter into a thousand pieces, and he'd be left to pick them all up.

"I will, Allie. Goddamn but I will pick up every piece," he murmured.

Her gaze met his, and she realized she'd spoken aloud. "I'm afraid."

It was the second time she'd admitted this to him. Would he use that against her?

He slowed the car and pulled to the shoulder, shoving the car in Park and reaching for her. Allie unbuckled her seat belt and went into his arms willingly, ignoring the pull in her side as she scrambled over the small middle console and folded herself against his body. He was so warm, so alive. His heart under her cheek reassured her as nothing else ever had.

"Shhh, baby, I'm here," he said in her ear, his warm breath trickling down her neck and over her collarbone, sinking into her skin.

"I know, King. It's what's holding me together," she whispered at his neck.

His smell, evergreen and mint, teased her, but it too was a comfort. She inhaled slowly, deeply, letting his scent linger in her nostrils before it tripped over her tongue and she swallowed. She wanted to taste him.

In the middle of God-only-knew-where, on this two-lane road, she wanted to taste King McNally. She wanted his lips on hers, drowning her fear and making her feel clean.

"We're close to Bilbao. I'll get you something to eat, and you can shower and rest, okay?" he asked her as his hands roved over her back and hips.

She was spread-eagled on his lap, her body pressing into his, and she pulled away enough so she could look into his eyes and see him.

He smiled ruefully. "I'm beginning to really like it when you sit on my lap."

Her gaze tracked the planes of his face, watching as her hands rose of their own volition, framing his masculine features. Her fingers traced the contours—over the slashing dark-brown eyebrows, down the patrician nose with the crook in the bridge, and along lips that begged to be kissed. Her thumbs rubbed across his cheekbones, and she reveled in the strength of the man who held her.

He wasn't classically handsome. He surpassed that taking it straight into beautiful. She touched the area over his heart with one hand, feeling his heart beat steady, strong. She dropped both of her hands, searching for his. He allowed her to pick up his hand and twine her fingers with his, and then he hissed in a breath when she touched her lips to his.

She held his green-black gaze, leaving her eyes wide open as she licked along his delicious bottom lip and demanded entrance.

His mouth moved, but he didn't pull away. She didn't care what he said; he would kiss her now and give her ease. She'd earned it, and he was the man to give it to her.

She hovered over his mouth, waiting.

He untangled their fingers and framed her face with

big hands that held her still. "If you let me in, I'm not leaving, Allie," he said in a guttural tone.

She didn't respond to his declaration. He'd said basically the same thing at Ella's. He was a soldier, and soldiers always left. It was part and parcel of who they were, what they did for a living. Her heart turned over in her chest though, his words stealing her breath and making her blood hot.

Because while he probably wouldn't be able to keep his promise to not leave, the intent was there and she wanted it.

She wanted him.

So she leaned closer, hoping his heat warmed her. He wound his hands through her hair and tugged her even closer, mouths only a breath apart now.

"Don't let me in, Allie," he begged.

She smiled, forgetting where they were and what had led them to this place. "It's too late," she murmured, and she closed the remaining distance.

His lips were firm on hers, and there was no doubt that while she'd instigated the kiss, he was the one controlling it. He gave her his breath and she returned it, unwilling to let him pull away though he held her securely.

King turned her head to the angle he wanted, and then he consumed her. Lips, breaths, tongues, teeth—they all met in a conflagration of desire. She sank into him, the tips of her breasts finding rest against the hardness of his chest.

She groaned into his mouth, and he hissed when she shifted her hips over his. Still they didn't break apart. Over and over their tongues dueled, sparring to pull away and venture once more inside each other's mouths. He tasted like home. Like forever.

She knew as he finally lifted away from her that he alone had the ability to wrap around her dreams, to hold her safe and keep her grounded.

And that scared her. This man had things following him that went bump in the night. She loved staying off the radar, but for a totally different reason than he did.

She didn't want his life, and he seemed to fit so well into it that he might never change. Hell, he might not be able to.

"I don't know if I'll survive you," he said at her lips.

"At least you'll go smiling."

He chuckled and the sound moved through her, tugging at her belly and making her even slicker between her thighs.

"Just a little farther, and then we'll take this back up," he assured her.

She shrugged but carefully moved off him, buckling her seat belt and staring into the night outside the windshield.

She wanted him, and if he moved toward her again, she'd give herself to him in a way she'd never done before. Completely.

—∾—

His dick throbbed like an open wound. Her scent was in his nostrils, in his mouth, and by God, he wanted her like he'd never wanted another person in his entire life. This was so bad it defied definition.

And his intent had morphed the minute she'd crossed the console and folded herself into his arms. Yes, he'd keep her safe. Hell, he'd already killed for her. He had no problem doing it again. If she were hurt, it would destroy him, but somewhere along the way these last four days, she managed to sink deep inside him.

He was going to have her again. Come hell or high water, he was going to rest inside her body and reclaim the parts of him she'd stolen.

She sat now in the passenger's seat, quiet, eyes turned to the darkness outside the car, and he wondered what thoughts were walking through her mind. Was she still scared? Or did she trust him to care for her?

So many balls were in the air, plans being initiated that would bring down Dresden's conglomerate and ensure that more innocents stayed that way. Dresden was a fucking monster, and it was going to be a joy to bring him down.

King pulled into Bilbao and located a hotel that wasn't a shithole but wasn't a five-star either. He registered under a burner name with a burner credit card and had them in a room on the seventh floor of the modest hotel in less than fifteen minutes.

"Grab a shower, Allie," he said as he lowered his duffel to the floor.

She walked to the window and opened the curtains. It wasn't the safest move, but he allowed it. No way Savidge knew where they were—not yet. Hell, he barely knew where they were.

Her hands settled on the glass as she looked over the city lighting up the darkness. Her hair was a mess, tangled and stained brown in places with someone else's dried blood. Her T-shirt had seen better days, and her jeans were equally stained. Her shoes were the brightest thing about her right now, and for some reason that made King sad.

Her expression was wan, her skin was pale, and he wanted to hold her. But he had to procure food and medicine, and he was sure she'd want another shower.

"I'm going to grab some food. Don't answer the door for anyone. I'm leaving my backup pistol under the pillow. I'll knock twice before I enter, okay? Now go get in the shower," he urged.

She just stood there, and he realized she might be in shock. If anyone had reason, it was Allie. He walked behind her, gently grabbed her shoulders, and directed her to the bathroom. He sat on the edge of the sunken tub and ran the water as hot as he could stand it, then stood when the water almost reached to the top.

He lifted her chin with his finger, and her gaze met his. What he saw there made his breath catch.

Goddamn, she was potent. But she was hurting.

"I'm going to grab us some food. Remember, don't open the door for anyone."

She nodded, and he left the bathroom. He waited until he heard the sounds of her getting in the tub before he left.

Twenty minutes later, he'd scored food, aspirin, and a change of clothes for them both. Jeans and T-shirts, but that was better than nothing. He knocked twice before he entered, and the first thing he noticed was the sound of the shower running.

He'd left her in the bath, and now she was showering? He pulled a quickie alarm from his duffel, rigged it, and set the food on the table. The shower was still running, so he opened the door, and that's when he heard her break—a sob.

He threw back the curtain, and there she was, huddled on the floor of the tub, forehead on her knees, shoulders shaking as hot water beat down on her. She was crying so hard that it hurt his chest.

He stepped in, picked her up in his arms, and held her there under the spray of the water. He was soaked, but that didn't matter.

He lowered her until she was standing, but her face was buried in his neck and her hands were clawing at his back. So much pain.

"Baby, please stop," he implored roughly.

"C-c-c-can't," she mumbled.

His hands moved up and down her back, holding her as close as he could. Her skin was wet velvet under his touch. He wasn't a praying man, but just then he shut his eyes and prayed.

He wanted to soothe her, to offer her succor with his body and help her forget she'd been shot, had taken lives herself, and was now the target of an insane son of a bitch.

She grabbed his back, nails digging deep, and then she looked up at him, and he lost himself in her blue eyes.

Kick-me-in-the-nuts for real, he thought.

"Please don't cry," he pleaded, his hands along her sides aching to mold the breasts presently pressing against his chest.

"I can't seem to stop," she whispered, her gaze hooded. Need was in that gaze—need and something he dared not attempt to decipher.

"Let me help," he responded as he lowered his head. "I can make it all disappear except for you and me."

"I trust you," she said.

And he was lost in her. It was too late to hold back.

King took her mouth, breaking contact only to rip off his sodden T-shirt. Her hands rose, and she began molding the muscles of his chest, her eyes bright with need, her cheeks rouged with lust.

"You shouldn't," he told her. One last effort to derail the inevitable.

Her gaze cleared, and she shook her head as her brows lowered. "Shouldn't what?"

He palmed her cheek, brushing a thumb over the soft skin. "Trust me."

She opened her mouth, closed it, and opened it again, but no words came out.

King smiled at her, even though his body ratcheted with need as her fingers played over the muscles of his chest, then drifted down over his nipples. "Cat got your tongue again?"

Allie rose on her tiptoes, fingers digging into his abdomen, the silky press of her skin on his ratcheting King's need for her. She lifted her face, her mouth hovering beneath his, and whispered, "I really, really hope so."

He kissed her then, taking her, owning her mouth in the way he'd wanted to since the first time he saw her on the plane. When he'd caught her looking at him, he'd had no idea she was the one his heart had been looking for.

Right now, as his hand dove into her hair, holding her still, he was grateful. So fucking grateful.

He moved forward until her back met the wall, and still the warm water poured over their bodies. Her tongue played hide-and-seek with his, and she moaned into his mouth as he cupped her breasts in his hands.

His thumbs stroked over her hard nipples as he lifted her breasts higher. He broke from her mouth, moving his intentions lower. He glanced up, gauging her reaction.

Her breasts rose and fell with her swift inhalations. Her hands clenched on his triceps. Her body was wound so tight. Allie shifted sinuously in his grip, her body begging. She wanted this. She needed him.

He'd give her everything he had. He was going to walk away from her once he got her to safety, but for right now, right here, she was going to be his.

"Need you so much, King," she moaned.

He bent to a nipple, teasing it with his teeth before he sucked it into his mouth. Her breath hissed in as her eyes widened and she locked gazes with him. That look went straight to his cock. He was beyond controlling this ravening need for her.

"Then you'll have me," he told her.

Chapter 25

KING'S GREEN EYES BURNED HER. EVERYWHERE HE LOOKED, she felt it like a tactile caress. His hands were on her breasts, kneading, as his mouth suckled and teased, flipping a switch inside Allie and making her wild.

Her body ached deliciously. The sharper pain in her side had long since been eclipsed by the overwhelming need between her legs. He was light in her darkness, and she wanted to rest inside him, to feel his warmth overtake her.

Never had she needed like this, with every touch ratcheting up the desire until it was almost too much.

She grabbed his hand, stepped gingerly out of the tub, and pulled him behind her. She wanted him flush on top of her, his body resting on hers. He followed her, this big man she'd only met four days ago. This beautiful man who promised her so much with his kiss and his touch. This strong man who had taken care of her when she'd been shot, then done his best to keep her safe.

Allie turned once she came to the bed, and he stopped within inches of her. She was naked, soaking wet, hair dripping on the carpet, and her body was cooling in the air-conditioned room.

She watched as he cocked his head and very deliberately ran his tongue over his bottom lip. The he followed each drop of water as it dripped down her neck, sipping the droplets from the tips of her breasts and drying her with his mouth. She moaned, couldn't have stopped it if she tried. There was no shame. Her body was trembling for this man.

Slowly, so slowly, her pussy clenched in demand as he unbuttoned his cargoes, revealing the silky trail of hair from his belly button down. He toed off his boots, then pushed his pants and black boxer briefs down, stepping out of them and then just standing there, gloriously nude.

His cock stood out from his body, thick and hard, the rounded head glistening. "I wonder if you want me as much as I want you?"

"I do, maybe more," he said harshly.

He fried her synapses consistently, reducing her to a blubbering, stuttering mess. "Not more. It just isn't possible. There's no backing out for me, King."

He reached for her, one of his large, warm hands cupping her shoulder before he stepped close and ran that hand down her chest. He caressed the valley between her breasts, flaring out his fingers to grip one before tugging on the nipple.

Her hands wrapped in the softness of his hair, tugging.

"Show me what you like, Allie. Show me, baby," he pleaded in a voice so gravelly that she could barely make out the words.

"I'm sure with you, I'll like it all," she returned in a breathy voice.

He pressed on her shoulders, and she lowered to the bed. He came over her then, and she pushed back on the bed, letting his big body cover hers the way she'd wanted for what seemed like forever.

"You're beautiful," he said reverently as he lifted up on an arm, using his hips to spread her legs.

"Show me," she whispered, parroting his earlier comment.

He settled his head against her core, and her hips rolled against his, a plea for the action she hoped he'd agreed to.

King's gaze rose to meet hers, and in his eyes, she saw his promise. Felt it notch in her soul as surely as his cock nestled against her pussy. She wasn't cold anymore; he'd warmed her completely.

"I need you to say it," he demanded, his voice gravelly.

"Fuck me."

His hips flexed, and she laughed softly. He growled.

"Yes."

And then Kingston McNally took over.

He kissed down her body, licking her collarbone again before he lavished his attention on her breasts, moving lower to bite the skin of her navel. He lightly kissed over her wound, the bandage hanging on for dear life. His tongue was wicked clever, dipping into the hollow of her belly button and shooting sparks of heat through her abdomen. They centered in her clit, and then he was there.

He hissed in a breath as he stared at her. "Goddamn, Allie, you make me want to come, and I'm not even inside you."

Her hips shifted restlessly. "Stop teasing, King."

"Tell me you want this," he said gruffly.

She looked down her body, meeting his green-fire gaze. "I want you."

He held her gaze as he lowered his mouth to her. A

swipe along her cleft, his tongue rimming her opening, and then he found her clit.

And when he found it, he gave it his undivided attention. She grabbed his hair, directing him, showing him what she wanted and where.

"I wanted to do this yesterday. Take my time and lick you, taste you, drink you in and never stop." He kissed her like he was worshipping her body, and then he bit lightly on her clit and she exploded, stars coalescing behind her eyes, breath locking in her chest.

She might have screamed his name, but all she heard as she floated back to earth was his throaty chuckle.

He let her catch her breath, and he was there once again, sliding up her body and leaning on a single arm. King brushed a strand of hair from her eyes.

"You are delicious, Allie Redding," he said matter-of-factly. "My very favorite food."

The long, slow slide she'd been taking into him ended with her heart firmly in his hands. It was too soon. She didn't know this man in all the ways she wanted to, but she'd taken his measure the first time she'd seen him.

No matter how rash her decision might be. No matter that he could be using her for his own ends. She'd just given him the biggest piece of herself.

Wonder sifted through her, making her drunk on her brand-new feelings for this warrior. He watched her and smiled as if he knew exactly what she was thinking.

But he didn't. If he did, he'd run screaming for the hills. Four days, and he'd stolen her heart.

"It's your turn," she whispered, pushing those feelings down deep, concentrating instead on the heat in her body, the desire to feel him deeply seated inside her.

"Are you hurting?" he asked as he motioned to her side.

She shook her head. Nope, absolutely zero pain—he'd given her too much pleasure. Then another thought struck her. It was something she'd never even thought of yesterday. "We should have talked about playing safe sooner."

"This is no game, woman. But I know where you're headed. I'm clean. Last checkup was over a year ago, and I haven't had sex since then," he told her.

His cock was a brand on her thigh, teasing, delighting her with all the possibilities.

"It's, um, been a while, and I've got an implant," she said, pointing to her arm, "that prevents pregnancy. I'm clean though, last checkup two years ago, before I took the Cameroon position. Definitely no sex since then." She laughed nervously.

"How many?" he asked, and the question seemed to be pulled from him.

"Not that it's a bit of your business, but you will be number two," she told him and winced.

Did he really need to know that? From the small smile on his face, she guessed so.

"It damn well is my business," he responded in a low tone.

That was his you're-about-to-get-mad-crazy-sex-from-me tone. Well, that was a nice change, she thought. "Carry on."

He pulled away slightly, and the cool air moved in. She shivered in response, nipples tightening even further, and he watched it all like a predator.

"I've already had you, but this feels like the first time. It'll be a slow ride at first because I want to give us both time to feel me deep inside you. You're tight, your taste is in my mouth, and your moans are ringing in my ears. It could get real rough, real fast, so tell me if I do something you don't want or like. Make sure I hear you," he demanded.

She nodded.

"Say my name," he ordered. "Tell me you want me."

"I want you, Kingston McNally."

He glanced down her body, and fire was everywhere his gaze touched. He took his cock in his hand and ran it along her cleft, and his eyes closed.

She breathed in sharply—so good. Just that fleeting touch was so good.

He pushed into her, his thick, broad cock breaching her walls and bringing fullness and heat.

"Look at me," he urged.

She hadn't realized her eyes were closed, but when she opened them, she went liquid. The sight of him above her, his large, tanned body covering hers, was foreplay all its own.

Her body softened, and he sank in deep. She hissed, he moaned. He found her mouth while sinking into her another way, pulling all of her inner desires up from hiding, and demanding she take the ride with him.

He withdrew, and she felt every inch of him, then mourned the loss a scant second before he sank back inside her and rotated his hips. Her eyes crossed. His pubis rubbed against her clit, and the feel of his cock buried inside her almost tripped her into another orgasm.

"Not yet," he murmured at her neck.

"Not a weapon," she said in return.

He rose up on both hands, and she glanced down

where their bodies were joined. It was perfection. Nothing else mattered but right here, right now with this man.

"Never a weapon with you, Allie," he ground out.

"Take me," she demanded.

He pulled out again, hovering at her precipice before he dove back in, a little harder this time, his action making her breasts bounce. His eyes keyed on them, and he licked his lips. He leaned down enough to swipe his tongue over both nipples before he lifted away without withdrawing his cock.

She couldn't say anything. His actions had buried him so deep inside her that he'd taken her voice. So good. So full.

He shifted his hips, finding all the places inside and out that needed him, and rubbing against her clit while he flexed his cock deep within her. Then he took her.

Over and over he sank into her, pulling out slowly, then coming back quickly to repeat it again and again. She spiraled, seeing the blaze of her orgasm hovering so close, and he would slow. She sobbed for him to finish her, but he just laughed, letting her ease down so he could take her higher the next time.

"Please!" She was a madwoman, needing release, reduced to begging. Sweat covered her flesh. He licked it away, feasting on her with everything in his arsenal — mouth, hands, and cock.

"Give me everything, Allie," he snarled.

"You already have it," she said.

Her voice deserted her because he pushed as she lifted her hips, and he hit the spot she needed to reach climax. Her vision went black, hazing as the pleasure coursed through her, ripping her apart at the seams and piecing her back together.

He shouted, and she experienced continued ripples of her climax as he came inside her, his cock pulsing, his hips bucking.

She didn't know how long they stayed that way. It could have been a minute or an hour. Allie came back from the edge of ecstasy slowly. King lowered her legs but remained inside her. She felt him slide her back up fully on the bed, and then he was lying on top of her, making sure not to put all his weight on her but definitely staking a claim.

He was warm. She was sated. Sleep called to her, but there was something she needed to say.

Allie cleared her throat, trying to find the words he kept stealing with the small kisses and tongue flicks he was placing on her face and neck. "Never would have believed it, but you're better than fries for sure," she murmured.

Chapter 26

ALLIE CLOSED HER WORD SEARCH BOOK AND PLACED IT ON the bedside table. It was in Spanish, but hell, beggars couldn't be choosers. When she'd seen it at the store where she'd purchased her medical stuff, she'd snagged it. Engaging her brain kept her mind off her current dangerous situation.

Between her legs was sore, but it was a nice kind of ache. She wasn't complaining. Cold air tickled her back and she lay down, squirming to get closer to the heat at her front.

King grunted and pulled her closer. She closed her eyes and breathed him into her lungs.

She lay there, quiet and introspective, taking it all in. His bare chest rose and fell steadily under her cheek, the firm skin like heated silk against her.

"You awake?" he asked, and his voice rumbled through her body.

She lifted her head and rested her chin on his breastbone. "I am."

"How do you feel?"

"Hmmm, I feel pretty damn good, all things considered," she murmured.

He smiled, that panty-melting smile, and she couldn't help but smile in return. "Yeah?" he asked.

She raised an eyebrow at him. "Seriously? You need me to tell you how good you are?"

He laughed, and the motion almost shook her off his chest. His arms wrapped around her, and his hips rolled up. He was hard. "Nah, you said I was better than fries. That's enough of an endorsement. Not that the 'Please' and 'So good' weren't enough of an indication."

She bit his pec, and he laughed again. "You were doing your fair share of moaning and groaning, if I remember correctly."

"Touché," he whispered. "Why were you crying?"

She took a deep breath and met his gaze. "I can't cry?"

He shook his head, and his eyes glittered in the low light from the lamp. "Obviously you can. I just don't want you doing it."

She snorted. "I'm a woman. I reserve the right to cry. Besides, I've had a rough few days. Not sure if you remember."

He palmed her face and rubbed beneath her eye. "I don't like it when you cry, Allie. You're too strong for that."

"Look, McNally—"

He put his thumb over her lips. "King."

"Look, *King*, I can cry if I want to," she said, beginning to push up and off his body.

He locked his legs around hers and refused to let her budge.

"You've been through a lot. I get it. But no more tears, Allie. They rip me up."

She laid her cheek on his chest again, unwilling to look in his eyes when she admitted her weakness. "I only cry when I hurt."

"Damn, baby," he said as he shifted until she was on her back with him leaning over her.

"I killed two men, King. Two. I've never killed anyone before."

"It was them or you. I'm personally pretty happy it was them," he bit out. "If I could raise them from the dead to kill them again, I would."

His response sent a shiver through her. Her alpha, hear-me-roar male. And when exactly had he become hers?

Silence reigned for several long, comfortable minutes. They hadn't had this at the house on a hill—the time to relax into each other. She had no idea how long they had now, but she was going to enjoy every moment with him and catalog every word and touch so when he left, as she knew he probably would, she could pull out the memories and keep warm.

"You need to rest," he said.

She yawned, lending validity to his claim.

He smirked. "I knocked you out with one shot for the rest of the night, didn't I?"

"You know what I like best about you, McNally?" she asked as she rolled away from him before he anticipated the action. She really had to use the bathroom.

He grunted as he lay back, watching her. "No idea."

"Me either, but it's absolutely *not* your humility," she said with a groan as she stood.

She made her way to the bathroom, handled her business, took a quick shower, and came back out wrapped in a towel. He was on his stomach, facing the bathroom, asleep. Not asleep like he'd been in Belgrade. She doubted he'd allow himself that luxury again with her around.

Allie covered him with the sheet more for her sanity

than his comfort. The man had a delectable ass—taut, muscled, and just mouthwatering. Her stomach rumbled, and she followed her nose to the table where he'd set out the food.

Cold burger and fries, but it was one of the best meals she'd ever had. Apparently, great sex made everything *better*. She gazed out over the city of Bilbao, Spain, and wondered what their next move would be.

She wanted to go home. She wanted King to go with her. It was bizarre how quickly she'd grown attached to the man. But it wasn't something she was going to question. Not right now.

She towel-dried her hair and got lost in her thoughts.

King shifted on the bed, and she heard him get up and pad over to her. He took the seat across from her and, butt-assed naked, began to dig into a burger. The fries, he left alone.

"We'll have to move soon. Within the next few hours. You need to grab some sleep because I need you alert and ready to move, Allie," he said between bites.

"Where are we going?"

He eyeballed her, and though his face was completely blank, she knew what he was thinking.

"I'm taking you home."

"And then what?" she asked. She couldn't keep the hope from her voice.

His brows lowered. "What do you mean?"

"What happens then?"

"Then I go back to my business, and you go back to being safe."

She jumped in. "What about us?"

He grimaced, and her heart sank. "What *about* us?"

"Seriously? That's all you've got, McNally?" She bit out her question.

"There can't be an 'us' if you aren't alive," he returned in a hard voice.

"So you want there to be an 'us'?" She didn't care much for this vulnerability.

"I want you safe" was his response.

"Again, didn't have you pegged as a coward. Since you're such a wimp, I'll step out on the limb. I've never been much for hiding from the truth anyway. What happened in the house on a hill? What just happened there?" She pointed to the bed for emphasis. "Made me want more. Not just of your body, but you. You've got the goods, McNally, and I've seen your heart now. You might think you can hide it, but I've touched it, tasted it in your kiss. You want me safe, but I have a sneaky suspicion neither you nor I will feel that way unless you're with me."

"Don't—"

She held up her hand, cutting him off. "Just tell me you feel it."

He met her gaze, the hard green of his eyes shredding her.

"Tell me, McNally. Give me something," she pleaded.

"I feel it. But it doesn't matter. What does matter," he said bitterly, "is that you're safe."

For some crazy reason, she wanted to refute that. She didn't want safe. Okay, she did. But what she really wanted was King.

Insanity. She was a lightweight at running from the baddies. She should be jumping for joy that he was taking her someplace safe. Instead, she went cold at the thought.

"Thank you," she responded inanely. "Now, what's the plan?"

"This is a mess. Savidge is a dog with a bone. I need you someplace safe so I can get to him before he gets to you." King threw his napkin down and ran a hand over his head. She noticed he did that when he was frustrated. He had tells and probably wouldn't be happy to know she knew them. "I'm going to get you home, Allie. I don't want to play Fifty Questions while we do it, okay?"

She gave in to her brewing anger. It didn't help that her insecurities made the frustration worse. "If it wasn't for you, I wouldn't be in this anyway."

His face blanked. A shiver raced up her spine. "I know you might want to find some refuge in that statement, but the truth is, you were in play long before I came looking for you on that plane in Cameroon."

She knew that. Ella had told her as much yesterday. Didn't help rationalize her anger toward King at all. He was going to leave her at her father's and probably not return. Ever.

"You said you didn't want to play games, Allie. I'm getting you home so you're off the board. Out of the field of play," he said as he stalked to the bathroom.

Allie remained silent, keeping her gaze averted. If she watched his fabulous ass as he left the room, she'd drool and it would ruin her mad. She needed to stay mad.

He showered quickly, coming back into the room and dressing almost silently. The jeans he now wore molded to his thighs and ass but hung low on his hips. The black T-shirt he pulled on saved her life. Her eyes glued to his chest ruined any hope of holding on to the flickering flame of her anger. She was reminded of how a little less than a week ago he'd pulled on another T-shirt in Cameroon. Then he'd walked to her and pulled her in to him, using his body to chase away the cold.

"You gonna get dressed or fight me on that too?"

"You don't understand," she said as she stood, feeling the rage bubble to the surface. "This is who you are—the games, the running, the shooting, the killing! It's not who I am. I stay far away from my father because I hate what he is. I hate who I have to be when I'm with him," she said bitterly.

He stilled, and the air in the room seemed to cool. "And what is that?"

"Dead on the inside. You asked me why I was crying earlier. It's because I have a heart, damn it. So you want to know if I'll fight you anymore… The answer is no," she bit out as she pushed past him, grabbing the clothes he'd placed on the bed for her and stepping into the bathroom.

The door was almost closed when she heard him take a deep breath. "I'm not dead on the inside," he said so quietly she wondered if she'd imagined it.

She placed her forehead on her side of the door and sighed. "I know. And that's why I won't fight you. Whatever you tell me to do, I will."

Then she closed the door and dressed, braiding her hair and brushing her teeth. She opened the bathroom door ready for anything, but unprepared to find Harrison Black and another man she'd never seen before in the room with them. King was closest to her, and his head rose as she walked out.

She fought panic, biting her bottom lip to hold in any

words that might valiantly try to pass. She wouldn't do this—fall apart in front of these men she barely knew. Not King or the other two silent sentinels who looked at her as though they were dissecting her soul.

King's green gaze locked on hers, holding her tight. He had to recognize her struggle.

"Allie, you remember Black. This is Jonah Knight," King informed her, pointing at the smaller of the two. And by small she meant that Black had maybe twenty pounds on the new guy.

Jonah Knight was scary. Where Black was light, Jonah was darkness. Though shorter than Black by maybe two inches, his face would have been classically beautiful, were it not for the large scar splitting his left cheek. He had pitch-black hair and a devil's look in his blue-gray eyes. Trouble, those eyes screamed. Then a smile bisected his face, easing the hold the scar had as a look of mischief appeared in his eyes. Beauty came in all forms, and Jonah Knight had been blessed.

She nodded, still fighting to maintain her silence. She didn't know what the hell would come out if she opened her mouth.

"Ms. Redding, it's a pleasure. Don't mind His Highness. He gets a bit uptight sometimes," Knight said as he inclined his head.

She snorted, surprised at the old-world charm Knight brought to his words. "I can safely say I've noticed."

King groaned, cutting her off. "Not again." She cut her eyes at him and scowled. He shrugged, but a smile played about his lips.

Harrison Black looked askance at Knight. "Did he just smile?"

Knight rolled his eyes. "I guess?"

"I didn't think he knew how," Black said.

Then it was back to awkward silence. Allie's mouth literally itched to speak, ask questions, sing a song. Anything to break it up.

"We're going to help get you home, ma'am," Knight said, his intent in his voice.

Allie waited for Black to mention Serbia. He didn't. "Well, then, that's nice," she said finally. "Just so you know, I could probably get myself home with no problems. In fact, I didn't really have any issues until McNally here came on board."

Neither man knew what to say, their shock conveyed by the looks they leveled at King. His gaze slid to her and narrowed. He was getting frustrated.

"What happened to you won't fight me?" he asked in a low tone. It was his don't-fuck-with-me-on-this tone. Similar to his we-ain't-moving-'til-you-answer-me tone but equally as somber and dire as his do-what-I-say-and-you'll-live tone.

She wasn't swayed by any of them at the moment. Yes, she needed help getting home, but that didn't mean she had to love the fact. "I'm not fighting you, McNally," she said with a slow smile.

His gaze narrowed even further, and everything that had happened between them last night was in the air. "Looks like it. Sounds like it. Walks like a duck, quacks like a duck, it must Allie."

She clapped her hands and laughed. "Clever, McNally. A duck I am then. But this duck is going home, and though she'll have help, she wants you to know she isn't all that happy about it. I don't want anyone hurt because of me."

He was within inches of her a second later. He moved like water—silent and fluid. Over his shoulder, she saw the other two men step to the door and leave.

"When I saw you on the plane, I think I knew what you could be to me," he said after a long, pregnant moment. "I knew you were dangerous. To me. But I had no choice, because once that bastard hit you, there was no way anyone else was going to. Not on my watch. Then you were shot, and goddamn but you're the bravest woman I've ever met. It's in everything you do and say. I want that, Allie. Even though you deserve better than me, I want you."

She had no words. Surely she hadn't known him long enough to fall in love. Yet it had happened. And he might not love her as she defined it, but his desire to hold her, to keep her safe, told Allie everything.

"I don't know that there are any better men than you, Kingston McNally," she said softly. She lifted her hands, wound them in his hair, and pulled him the scant inches she needed to take his mouth.

He pulled back, stepping away before she could see her intention through, and ran a hand through his hair. "We have a flight to catch," he said, and his voice was tortured.

He turned then and walked to the door, opening it and murmuring to the men outside. He walked back in the room and handed her his duffel. It was much lighter than she remembered.

"We're leaving on a private flight from the local airport. You'll be in Little Creek, Virginia, before the sun sets tonight. Knight and Black are accompanying you to your father's house." He gave her the itinerary in rapid-fire succession.

She held back the tears that threatened. Nowhere on that list of things she was about to do was anything related to King's next move. "Where are you going?"

"I can't tell you that."

He was hurting her, and for a second, fear warred with the burgeoning love. He was a protector. It was what he did.

She glanced up, aware she'd been having an internal struggle for a while. His face was hard. He was shut down.

"Thank you, King," she managed to stammer out. "Thank you for everything." She wasn't going to make it harder for him. Not yet. Once they were on American soil though, all bets were off.

He stroked a finger down her cheek. "I'll keep you safe, baby," he said in that oceans-deep voice.

She nodded, and he turned away. Then he led Knight and Black back in. They spoke in low tones until King took her arm and they left the room. The men ushered her out of the hotel to a blacked-out SUV. None of them said a word. Black drove, and Knight sat in the back with Allie and King watching out the windows, no doubt making sure she "stayed safe."

It was too damn quiet.

"How long have you known King?" she asked them.

King glanced at her, confusion on his face.

Knight and Black gave her silence.

"Really? Interesting. I've known him almost five full days," she said into their absence of a reply. "So, um, you guys part of Endgame?"

Knight glanced at her from the corner of his eyes. Black kept his gaze on the road. She'd get nothing from them, not that she'd expected it.

"You know my father?"

Still nothing.

"You guys are getting on my nerves," she told them.

"We're here," Black said, and relief abounded in his tone.

She almost laughed. It hadn't taken long, only twenty minutes, to reach the airport. Black pulled into a secured lot, showed some type of identification, and was motioned to the private hangars.

They parked at a hangar, and Allie saw the plane they were taking. Another sleek Jetstream that spoke of money. Knight grabbed the duffel. King helped her out of the SUV and then took her right side while Black took her left. Before she could even breathe heavily, she was in the private jet, seated in a sumptuous leather seat, buckled up, and waiting for takeoff.

Allie leaned her head back, feeling like everything was moving along just a bit too easily. And then she heard a dull thud and a sound she'd heard enough of the last few days to last her entire lifetime.

Gunshots.

Not again, she thought as she unbuckled her seat belt. It had all started on a plane, hadn't it? She was beginning to hate this form of transportation.

Knight was there then, hurrying toward her as King headed to the front of the plane.

"Back of the plane, Ms. Redding," he said firmly.

She stood, and he handed her a gun similar to what King had—a SIG Sauer, if she remembered correctly. "Who is it?" she asked.

"Savidge," he bit out.

"He's breached the tarmac, Knight. Get her gone!"

Black's accented voice yelled. "I'll hold him off. King is taking lead."

"Get to the back, Ms. Redding," Knight said again.

She moved. The aircraft was being peppered with shots. She heard them bouncing off.

"Get in here," Knight said as he opened a door and pushed her into a tiny closet. "Stay here until I come for you."

She nodded, fear pushing under the skin and making her sweat. She was sick of this.

"Be safe, Knight," she whispered.

He stopped and cocked his head. Surprise flared in his eyes, but then he gave her a smile. "I will, Ms. Redding." He closed the door.

Allie sat down on the floor of the closet, her SIG Sauer ready. She tried to hear what was happening, but everything had gone dead silent.

There was a flurry of gunshots, then she heard Black yell that King was down. She heard Knight yelling, and then silence.

Her heart stopped. King was down. *Oh God! What did that mean?* Her skin prickled, and her mouth dried.

"Come out, Ms. Redding," an unknown man said.

Allie didn't move. This wasn't good at all.

"Don't make me hunt you, Ms. Redding. McNally and his men will pay the price," the man said. He had a nasally voice and a decidedly Serbian-sounding accent.

Was this Savidge? One of his goons?

A single gunshot report, and Allie jumped as a sound of pain came through the door. Black. He'd shot Black.

Allie stood then, opening the door and holding her gun out in front of her, ready for anything.

"Drop the gun, Ms. Redding," the man said from behind her.

"No," she responded.

Another shot and then silence. No more cries of pain, just nothing.

"Drop the gun, Allison Redding, and I'll let them live," he said.

She saw Black and Knight each on the floor of the plane, bleeding from their wounds, gazes pinned on her. Why hadn't he simply killed King's men? What was the point in not eliminating your enemies? There was something bigger at play here.

In the depths of their eyes, she saw acceptance but also apologies. Where was King? She shook her head. "Not your fault," she murmured.

"Drop the gun," he said again.

"You're a broken record. I'm not dropping the gun, not for you or anyone else," she said firmly.

It was bravado, and the smile the handsome, dark-haired man gave her was his acknowledgment that that was all it was. He turned calmly, casually, and shot Harrison Black in the leg. Black groaned, Knight winced, and Allie screamed.

She dropped the gun.

"Good girl," the man said, and he strode down the aisle to her, several large, thuggish-looking men behind him. "My name is Vasily Savidge. I have been looking for you, Allie Redding, indeed, waiting for you."

Allie's gaze was glued on Black's pale face. His eyes were closed now, and her heart wept. King had been right. She'd never have been able to handle getting home on her own. This man, this Vasily Savidge, was a monster. Monsters never stopped coming.

And he'd hurt King. King was down. Where was he?

Rage sifted through her fear, feathering along her mind and settling into her gut. These men had been hurt protecting her. And the monster responsible stood in front of her.

"Look at me," Savidge demanded.

She turned and did as she was instructed.

"You're hurt?" he asked.

Allie tried to process his words, but all she could see was the blood on Knight and Black. All she could hear were the gunshots and Black yelling, "King's down!"

"I asked you a question," Savidge demanded.

"No," she murmured.

"Good. That's good then. Come along. We've much to discuss," he said. His voice was filled with delight.

She hated him.

He started down the aisle, but Allie remained where she was.

"Go with him, Miss Redding," Knight mouthed. "We'll find you."

She saw him, she did, but rage had her now. From the muffled quiet of her shock, red flames emerged burning bright and hot. She reached down and picked up her SIG Sauer, cocked it and coughed to cover the sound. Her cough must have alerted Savidge that she wasn't following because he turned.

Allie was between him and King's men, and that was as it should be. To save them, she'd have to play this just right. She tucked the gun behind her back and began moving down the aisle to meet Savidge.

When he was within a foot of her, she sat down in a seat and tugged on his coat, pulling him off-balance. This left him sprawled on top of her. He tried to push off her, muttering an apology, but she had a firm grip on his coat.

She pressed the barrel of the SIG against his ribs and smiled. "They leave here right now, without being harmed any further, or I put a bullet into your side and follow it with one to the brain. You know who I am, Savidge. You know my daddy trained me. If you believe nothing else, believe I will kill you even if it means the rest of us go straight to hell with you."

His eyes widened, and the sick fucker grinned. "You're a strong one. I'll enjoy breaking you and sending you home in pieces to your father. Tell me, are these two men worth your life?"

Only two? Was King dead then?

"Yes." Unequivocal. Absolute. They were King's men; they were worth that and more.

"Holland?" Savidge called out. "Let our guests leave unmolested."

Her grip on the gun tightened.

"Sir?" his man questioned.

Allie pressed the gun harder into Savidge's ribs. He swore bitterly. Oh, she was pissing him off.

"Do what I said, Holland. Now!" Savidge's gaze pinned her. "You will owe me more than I think you're willing to pay, Allie Redding."

"Stand up slowly, Savidge," she instructed him and then used her hold on his jacket to follow him, never relinquishing her grip on the gun or its position against his ribs. "Now throw your other weapon on the ground."

"Don't do this, Allie," Knight said in a tortured voice.

"No choice, Mr. Knight. Now, please take Mr. Black and be gone," she urged.

Knight grabbed Black, hauled the big man over his uninjured shoulder, and began down the aisle off the plane.

"We're going to watch, Savidge. We're going to watch as they get in the car and leave, and once they're gone, we'll renegotiate," she said to him.

He remained silent, eyes burning with sickening lust and a need for vengeance.

Allie's gaze scoured the tarmac and found King being held up between two of Savidge's goons. His face was bloody, and it looked like he'd been shot in the shoulder.

Savidge leaned over her and sniffed her neck, running his nose over and up until he reached her ear. "I won't kill him this time. Dresden wants him alive so he'll chase us. The fun is in the chase."

Her breath hitched.

Several of Savidge's men lay fallen, blood soaking the concrete beneath them. Knight looked back once, and Allie nodded at him. The two goons released King but held a gun on him the entire time. His eyes met Allie's, and she could read the torture in their depths. She pleaded wordlessly with him to be safe. Savidge's men followed King to the SUV they'd arrived in and continued to hold their weapons on King, Black, and Knight as they pulled away, taking Allie's heart with them.

Allie stepped around quickly, which left her at Savidge's back with her gun still digging into his side. He'd been unprepared for her move.

"Well done, Allie. Your father did an excellent job with you," he said.

That wasn't true at all. She'd had bare-bones train-ing. This had been nothing but quick thinking and luck. "Walk down the stairs to the tarmac," Allie com-manded Savidge.

He did and, when they were at the bottom in the open area by the plane, his remaining men surrounded them. Savidge held up his hand, and they backed off. Before she could blink, he turned full circle, his elbow clipping her jaw and knocking her to the ground.

Her hold on her gun was lost, and it skittered to the concrete. Savidge was on her then, lifting her by the T-shirt. His face was mottled with rage, spit flying as he pulled her closer.

"You held a gun on me!" Then he slapped her. Once, twice, over and over until her ears rang and her eyes grew heavy.

He tossed her to the ground, and she crumpled at his feet. His shadow fell over her. She drew her arms and legs in, preparing for anything, but he just laughed as he straightened his coat.

"Get up," he demanded. "Get up right now, or I'll kill you."

The truth was in his words, though he wouldn't kill her before he had his fun.

He must have grown sick of her taking so long because he grabbed her by the hair and pulled her up himself. She cried out. Her jaw hurt, and her eyes were swelling shut, both of them.

"More than you're willing to pay, eh, bitch?" he reminded her.

She laughed then. It startled even her. Nothing about any of this was funny, but the sound continued to roll out of her. She had to be the butt of the universe's cosmic joke. She was heaving in his arms, laughing maniacally, and every man, including Savidge stepped back.

"She's touched," one man whispered.

"Crazy," another said.

"Sir," one man called out, "he is on the phone."

Who was? Allie wondered.

Savidge took the phone, and Allie went cold. The fact that he had the phone on speaker allowed her to hear everything.

She'd heard that voice before.

"Yes, yes. I hear you. I'll have my fun and ship her home to you then," Savidge said gleefully.

If Allie lived a hundred years, she'd never forget that voice. It was the same one the terrorist on the plane in Cameroon had been speaking to. The very same. She'd bet her life on it.

This thought triggered another round of laughter. Bet her life? She was playing the game after all, wasn't she?

"Shut up," Savidge yelled. To his men he ordered, "Bring her."

Then he turned and walked to a waiting vehicle. Two men stepped up and grabbed Allie under her arms, lifting her and ultimately dragging her to another vehicle. They pushed her into the car, and she curled into a ball, hugging herself close and wondering what the hell would happen next until her mind began to blank.

Hold on, Allie, she told herself. *Just hold on*. King was gone, but he'd come for her. She had no doubts. She'd survive this and be waiting for him.

Chapter 27

"WHERE IS HE NOW?" KING ASKED JUDE DAGAN IN A COLD, dead voice.

He'd taken a shot that grazed his shoulder. He'd been impotent in the face of Allie's danger, Savidge's two men assuring he made no moves against them. And now she was in that bastard's hands. She'd been taken.

"Heading to Dresden's headquarters in Beirut," Jude responded. "How are Knight and Black?"

"Alive. They'll be fine," King told him. "I want everyone in Juniyah, Lebanon, by nightfall."

"They're already moving," Jude replied.

"I need your head in the game, Jude," King said firmly. There was no room to fuck up on this op. Allie was at stake.

There was silence on Jude's end. "It's there," his man said with a sigh.

"There's time to figure all this out once Allie is safe." King ran a hand over his head. He'd left her with two of his best, and Savidge had found out their plans.

How? He'd told no one, and he knew neither Black nor Knight had. Nobody but Allie's father had known what King's plans were. He'd called the man last night so he could prepare for Allie's safety.

Allie's father…CIA…

Goddamn. There was no other explanation. Loretta

was the leak. King had tossed that around before and even asked Jude to investigate.

"Jude, what did you find out about Loretta Bernstein? Heard any chatter about her?"

"Not lately. I've had my ear to the ground, but there's silence around her. She used to be Broemig's enforcer. You went off the reservation, and Loretta was there to haul your ass back in," Jude responded warily. "Is she the leak?"

"I'm not sure yet. She told me she was no longer working for Broemig. I'm wondering if she's freelance now and has thrown in her lot with Dresden. I'll keep you posted. I'm relying on you to get Chase where he needs to be. He was heading back to Burundi two days ago."

"I've tried to raise him. I'll continue to do so, but if he's deep in-country, it could be days before I get him. Rook is heading to our meet point as we speak," Jude informed him.

"Keep trying Chase. I'll see you later," King said and hung up the sat phone.

He turned to Knight and Black. Cisco was stitching them up. Knight had a through and through on his upper arm. Black had taken the most damage—a pretty serious thigh wound.

Yet it could have been much, much worse. If not for Allie Redding's brave ass, it would have been. King clenched his fists and closed his eyes.

"Will they be operational?" King asked Cisco.

Cisco glanced up from swabbing Black's thigh, his face grave as he shook his head. "Knight is fine. Black is lucky he's alive, King. The bullet almost nicked his femoral artery. He's not going to be able to go."

"The hell you say. That pretty woman saved my life, and I'm going in," Black said viciously.

She had that effect on everyone, it seemed. Extremes. Allie Redding was all about extremes. But Black still wasn't going.

King's phone rang. "Yeah?"

"He's going to hurt her badly, King, if you don't get there to stop him," Ella Banning said. "I'm sending you video now—secure link to your email. She's in bad shape already. The woman likes to live dangerously. Baiting Savidge's type of crazy isn't advisable, but damn if she didn't do it."

"How the fuck do you have video of this, Ella? Were you there?" King bit out his question, the need to damage something locking down his muscles.

"I follow Savidge. He's mine, and I follow his movements when he isn't following mine," she murmured evasively. "You should also know that I'm not the only one who was there. There's another player."

King's skin went cold. "Who?"

"I'm not ready to divulge that quite yet, but when I know for sure, you'll have one of your traitors, and I'll be free to pursue my main objective," Ella said.

"Goddamn it, Ella. I need to know who," King demanded.

"Not until I'm sure, King."

She hung up and King cursed. It had to be Bernstein. Knight was watching him. "Ella's alive?"

King nodded.

"Interesting. You know then that's why Jude keeps disappearing," Knight murmured.

"Yeah. She claims she was betrayed. There are so

many entities in this shit that I'm starting to doubt any- and everybody. But I looked in her eyes, Knight. She saved Madoc. Madoc's alive too," King told him.

Knight rubbed his forehead before he shrugged on a shirt. "I don't understand why Dresden didn't kill them."

"Information," King bit out.

"Well, motherfucker. She is a traitor then," Knight said harshly.

"Degrees of innocence and guilt, Knight. We won't judge her until all the facts are in. She's been watching Savidge, and she's sending me…" A ding sounded, and King sat down at his computer. "Video."

He pulled up the link and watched as the scene at the airport unfolded. There was no audio, only video shot from a vantage point above the tarmac. The video was high quality, so when the bullets started flying, he saw their trails. He couldn't see what happened in the interior of the plane, but Knight and Black had filled him in. The mental picture was enough.

The howl that erupted from his throat couldn't be contained when he watched Savidge hit her repeatedly, then pull her up by her hair.

"He's a dead man," King said harshly as he closed the computer.

"Transpo is ready to roll," Knight said as he closed his sat phone. "Let's move out."

King nodded. No one had ever meant as much to him as Allie Redding. He hadn't even known her a full week, and yet she was entrenched in his mind and body. It was what it was, and there was nothing to be done for it.

They skirted Bilbao, traveling to an airfield on the

southern end of the city, and within an hour, they were on their way to Juniyah.

He'd meet his team. Then he'd go hunting. It was one of the things King did best. Leading and hunting were in his blood, and never had he been more grateful that he was Thomas Sacco Sr.'s son than he was right then.

His father hadn't done much besides beat the shit out of him, but in between those lessons had been the ones that taught King how to hunt and how to kill.

He was going to put those lessons to good use tonight.

Chapter 28

ALLIE'S HEAD WAS POUNDING. SHE WOKE SLOWLY, NOT moving lest she give away the fact that she was awake. She took stock of her surroundings. She was on a fairly soft bed, the feel of silk beneath her cheek soothing. The air smelled of sea and wind, and in the distance she heard gulls and the lilting sound of a muezzin calling Muslim believers to prayers.

Muffled voices drifted closer, but as she tried to focus on them, her vision dimmed and blackness threatened. He'd beaten the heck out of her. Her eyes were swollen, and as she valiantly tried to open them, she found she couldn't. The sun shone on her arm, and the skin felt raw there. She'd burn, not that this would be the worst of her injuries.

Where was she? What did Savidge have planned? Could she manage to escape him? *Probably not*, she thought. Not as banged up as she was.

Were Knight and Black safe? She shied away from thoughts of King. She feared she'd go mad if she contemplated his death. Even though Savidge had told her he was still alive, there were no assurances and King had had a lot of blood surrounding his head.

Instead, Allie concentrated on surviving. Was her father waiting for her in Virginia? What would he do when she didn't show up?

This could start a major international incident. Gray

Broemig was not just going to let his only daughter be kept by a terrorist. She knew next to nothing about Vasily Savidge. He was a horrible man who had no compunction about hitting women. His employer was Horace Dresden. Should have just put a bullet into Savidge's heart when she'd had the chance. Now she might not get that chance, and the thought was both sobering and frightening as hell.

"Is she awake yet?" Savidge's voice called into the room.

"No," a woman's voice, sounding frail and small, said from beside the bed.

She wanted to kiss the woman, thank her, and hug her, but Allie realized doing so would give away the fact that she was indeed awake.

"The minute she's up, I want to know," Savidge bit out.

Mentally, Allie flicked him off. A soft, cool, wet rag brushed her brow, and Allie sighed.

"You are awake, but I will not tell that devil," the woman whispered. "He hurt you badly, *habiibtii*. He is a bad man, but I will help you feel better."

Allie remained silent, but tears leaked from her eyes, stinging her cheeks and rolling into her hair. The woman wiped her face softly, then wet the rag again and placed it on Allie's eyes.

A long time later, she removed the rag and wiped some type of poultice over Allie's eyes. Immediately, the swelling began to go down. The woman wiped the poultice off and once again washed Allie's face.

Tentatively, Allie opened her eyes and saw the tiny, old woman. Her black hair was spun with gray, and her white hijab was slightly skewed. Allie smiled when she saw that. It would take a crazy woman wearing a skewed hijab to go against Savidge's wishes.

"They will be coming for you, *habiibtii*. Tonight, the big Americans will come and you will be safe," the woman whispered.

"Thank you," Allie said softly. "For helping me, thank you."

The old woman snorted and gathered her things before placing them in a pouch. "You listen to me. Bad men are here, and it is no place for one such as you."

Allie tried to sit up, but the woman hurried to her and pushed her shoulders down. "No, he will know you are awake, and that cannot be yet. The big Americans come, and then you can get up."

Confusion swam through Allie. "Big Americans? I don't know who you're talking about," Allie whispered.

"No matter. They saved my son a year ago, and I owe them a debt. Mr. Rook and my Vivi are diamonds in the sky. They will bring big Americans and save you. Maybe they will kill the devil too, eh?" The woman began to whistle softly.

Allie lay back and noticed where she was. The room was an older one, made entirely of stone, the light-brown color of the sand in the stones reflecting the light and making it seem like she stood in the middle of the sun. Big window-like openings had been cut out of the far wall, and elaborate silk curtains flowed in the breeze.

"Where am I?" she asked.

"Beirut," the woman responded as she brought Allie a cup and motioned for her to drink.

Allie did, suddenly thirsty beyond all reason, and

drained the cup in just a few swallows. The woman took the cup and pushed again at Allie's shoulders.

"Lie down, *habiibtii*. Rest," she crooned.

Allie's eyes were growing heavy again, and she rubbed her chest. She missed King. She missed her father. She was scared.

But now she was sleepy. Too sleepy.

"You gave me something?" she asked and heard the slur in her words.

"You must stay asleep. Otherwise, he will do bad things to you," the woman whispered and then proceeded to pet Allie.

Allie focused on the old woman's dark eyes, drowning in the black and feeling at peace. "Be safe, old woman. Do not get yourself into trouble for me."

"Trouble comes to us all, *habiibtii*. Trouble comes to us all."

Chapter 29

"DRESDEN'S PALACE IS OFF THE BEACH. THERE'S NO MOON tonight, but there will be several guards. Dresden isn't here, but Savidge is, and he'll have upped the number of guards, anticipating us," King said to his men.

He strapped on his thigh holster and slid in a SIG Sauer P226. He buckled the holster and then inserted a Kimber into the holster under his arm.

The sounds of his men preparing their weaponry for battle was soothing.

"My contact has left the compound but assures me that Allie is still out, helped along with a sedative. She's in bad shape, according to the old woman, but she's alive and decidedly spirited," Olivia Granger said from the back of the room.

She met King's gaze over her bank of computers and smiled. "Spirited, huh, King? You got a live one or what?"

"Be quiet, Vivi. And you too, Rook," King said, cutting off Vivi's husband before he even opened his mouth.

"There's chatter in the city, Your Highness," Jude Dagan said from his perch beside the window. Jude was already loaded down with enough firepower to take out an entire city block. Adam Babic had come through once again. Jude had met a boat earlier and retrieved the weapons the man had procured for them.

King almost winced. His munitions expert would definitely feel no compunction about taking out an entire city block and not looking back, just reloading for more and starting all over again.

Jude's gaze was flat, his tone equally so. His man was struggling with some heavy shit—mainly finding out that the woman who'd stolen his heart wasn't dead. Jude had assured King that he was all in on this mission, and while King didn't doubt him, he did wonder if Jude would be the same once all this shit was over.

Not just tonight's shit—all of it.

"Oh, Knight?" Jude called in a falsetto voice. "Heard you got a scratch today."

"Fuck you, Jude. Your mama said she'd kiss it and make it all better later," Knight said with a grunt.

"That's only after she's finished kissing mine," Black said with a smile as he grabbed his thigh and laughed.

"Fuck both of you. My mama wouldn't kiss either one of you," Jude said ferociously.

"Girls, girls, girls, we're all teammates here," Rook said patiently. "But there's a hierarchy, and if anybody's getting kissed by Jude's mama, it's me. I don't want anyone's sloppy seconds."

"My mama ain't sloppy," Jude said airily.

Rook chuckled and ducked as Vivi threw a pen at him. "Asshole," she muttered, but there was a smile on her face.

She knew she had her man on lock. No way was Rook letting anyone kiss anything when he had Vivi.

"Chase isn't gonna make it. We're two men down," King said into the silence. "Everybody clear on the mission?"

"Get in, get Allie Redding, and get the fuck out," Black intoned.

"Blow the place to smithereens after she's out," Jude threw into the mix.

"Kill Savidge," Rook said in a hard voice.

"Hooyah," King murmured. "He's mine, Rook. That motherfucker is all mine."

Rook nodded. Then they were all in a circle, Vivi included, locked and loaded for a mini-war on foreign soil.

"She doesn't get hurt," King reminded them, and his voice was harsh in the silence.

"We got it," Jude muttered. "She's important."

King pinned Jude with his gaze, and the man looked back at him before acknowledging the unspoken demand. If by some chance Ella was there, Jude had to stay on point. No running off to chase the woman who remained a ghost to him.

"I got it," Jude told him.

"I just received a message from Gray Broemig. He's got men ready to descend if we need them. He wanted me to tell you to bring his daughter home, King. He said it's your ass if you don't."

King shook off the anger, beating it back with everything in him. Rescuing Allie was the important thing here. Later there'd be time to deal with Broemig and his threats.

"Don't be brave," he said.

"Be accurate," everyone responded in unison.

They loaded up, leaving Vivi and Black to man their temporary headquarters for this mission. They would destroy all evidence of their presence and meet them at the extraction point in two hours. It would take them thirty-eight minutes to get to Beirut from Juniyah. From there, they had twenty minutes to grab Allie and make it to the extraction point an hour away.

They were cutting it close, but their team was an effective, well-oiled machine. They'd engage if they had to. If they were able to get Allie out quickly, Jude would set explosives around the compound and King would have the time to go hunting.

He breathed in deeply and clenched his hands into fists. King was in his element now.

"The satellite visibility corridor closes in thirty minutes, Endgame," Vivi said over the communication ear mics.

"Roger that," King verbalized.

They'd entered the compound's grounds via the beach, scaling an outside wall and hiding in the shadows. Savidge thought it was a source of a security, but when the men you had guarding that particular venue didn't know their assholes from their elbows, well, it ended up being the easiest point of access.

"Heat sig to your immediate right, King. Four men heading your way," Vivi intoned.

He held up a fist, and the men behind him stilled. He pressed his back to the wall and waited for the men to go by. They had no idea what was in their midst.

The guards passed, laughing and joking, and King opened his fist, showing all five fingers.

His men separated, staying in the shadows. Savidge's compound was set out in a square, surrounded by an outside wall. It was a large complex with the primary residence, a sprawling three-story structure with four wings, sitting in the middle. The house was surrounded by lush shrub barriers with a fountain sitting dead center in the ornate circular driveway. The place was lit up to the heavens, but this left the outside perimeter cast in darkness. Only one wing was being used as party headquarters tonight. The other three were dark.

"You're coming up on the west wing, Your Highness. There will be a corridor twenty feet off the entrance. Take those stairs and head up two flights. Your girl is on the third floor, second room on the left," Vivi directed him.

"Ten-four."

"Rook, you've got a tango coming up on your six," Vivi told her husband.

"Roger that."

Vivi sighed. "And now you have no more tango. Jude, there are five heat sigs to your left."

"Got it," Jude said. "King, this place is loaded for bear. He's knows we're coming."

"He's having a goddamn party," Knight's voice whispered across the links.

"Say again?" Vivi asked.

"There are a shit-ton of people here dressed in their finest," Knight bit out.

"Savidge gives parties once a month. This is standard. He's a cocky son of a bitch to still throw a shindig knowing we'll be coming for him. Stand by, second satellite comm coming online now," Vivi reported. "I've got visual. Best estimate, he's got up to two hundred people in the main house. Stay away from the main wing of the house, and you should be fine."

"Roger that," Knight and Black responded.

"Vivi, which door?" King asked as he moved up the stairs. He came to the second room on the left and found it empty.

"Intel said second on the left."

"Negative. She's not here," King reported. Fear was riding him now. It was entirely too quiet in this wing of the house.

"Hold for further," Vivi said. King knew intel was only as good as the source and the time that had elapsed since the information had been given. It made his hands shake.

He lowered his night-vision goggles and used the infrared scope on his rifle to go through the remaining five rooms. This wing was entirely dark.

"Nothing here. Party is in the main wing," Rook informed them.

Vivi came back. "Source says she was in the western wing when she left today, but that was over two hours ago. She should still be out. You'll have to hunt, King."

"I'm on it," King responded. "Meet at the origination point."

His men were right where they'd entered the dwelling, waiting on him.

"Directions, Vivi," King ordered.

"Main wing is to your right, up a flight and across a small courtyard. Place is packed. Be prepared."

"Roger that," King returned. "Vivi, how much longer on the satellite comm?"

"Fifteen minutes. Your window is closing," she told him.

He turned to his men. "Knight, stay here and be ready. Rook, Jude, quick, fast, deadly if need be. Find her."

It took them five minutes to make a two-minute trek. Guards were everywhere, and rather than kill and alert them to Endgame's presence, they avoided contact. But time was running out. King could feel it in his bones.

Adrenaline surged as he crossed the small courtyard, staying in the shadows. His men moved in the shadows, but the lights were bright tonight. Though there was no moon, the house was lit up like Christmas. He entered the main wing via a darkened window, Rook and Jude on his heels.

"Check in," Vivi demanded.

Her tone was business, but underneath King heard the nervousness. This was the unknown—this was what made everything dangerous.

"King, check."

"Rook, check."

"Jude, check."

"Well, well, well. I wondered when you'd show," a voice said from the dark.

King had his weapon trained and sighted in the space of a breath. Savidge. And beside him, sitting in a chair with her hands tied behind her back, was Allie.

Her head hung down, and her hair, which had been braided earlier, was hanging loose.

King flipped on his flashlight and skewered Savidge in the darkness. Allie hadn't moved to acknowledge anything. She simply sat there, a broken waif.

Savidge laughed. "I knew you'd come. You never disappoint, McNally. And look, you've brought company!" He clapped his hands like a kid and smirked.

"Step away from her, Savidge, and I'll let you live. I'm leaving here with her, and you're going to let me. Nobody dies. We just take her and leave," King said softly.

The lights went on then, and the sound of weapons being cocked reverberated through the room.

"How about this, McNally. How about you drop your weapon, and I don't kill you…yet," Savidge said with glee.

King didn't move. Rook and Jude had their backs to him, forming a circle. They'd come loaded for bear themselves.

Savidge walked to Allie and very calmly, very quickly slapped her cheek. "Wake up! The fun's just starting!" Allie didn't respond.

King was over the table separating him from Savidge in a split second. Savidge was faster. He had a gun against Allie's temple before King could get to him.

"For all your American special operations training, not even you are faster than a bullet, McNally," Savidge said with a laugh.

Allie's eyes were black and blue, her cheek had a long bruise on it, and her nose was now bleeding. She met King's gaze, and from what he could see in her eyes, she was both surprised and scared.

"Drop the weapon, McNally," Savidge said and pressed harder on the gun.

"I'm going to kill you, Savidge," King ground out. But he dropped his weapon.

"Now your men," Savidge ordered.

Rook and Jude both threw their weapons aside.

Savidge couldn't be that stupid. A single weapon gone when each of them carried more firepower than most entire units did? He must have something up his sleeve.

Savidge pulled his weapon from Allie's head. Her eyes closed.

"Release her," King ordered.

"You are not in a position to order me around. I give the orders now. You want her freed, you'll give me what I want."

King cocked his head and waited.

Allie glanced at him, and his heart wept. She'd had nothing but pain since he'd come into her world.

"I want Broemig," Savidge said casually.

"That's what this is about?" King asked snidely. "Her daddy?"

Savidge smiled. "It's about much more than that. She's a fine specimen, and I will look good between her thighs. But first I want her father."

King grappled for control. To lose it now would mean Allie's life, and possibly Rook's, Jude's, and his own as well. He wouldn't relinquish control to this cocky motherfucker.

"Call him. I'm sure he'll give himself up. She's his daughter. By the way, Savidge, how'd you find that out?" King asked.

"Your teammate, Ella Banning—she is ever a source of valuable intel. I look good between her thighs as well," Savidge said with a laugh and a glance at Jude.

King glanced at Jude, willing him to remain calm. If Savidge had been between Ella's thighs, it was rape. She would have never given herself up. Not like that. Jude's face was stone cold. His cheeks were red, and his eyes blazed.

Hatred had a scent, and King could smell Jude's from across the room.

"It wasn't Ella. Oh, she may have confirmed it, but someone else told you," King said.

"Lo-Lo," Allie moaned softly.

In King's ear came Vivi. "Ella just contacted me." King didn't answer her.

"What Ms. Redding is trying to say is that the lovely—" Savidge began.

"I told him," a woman said from the doorway.

"It's Loretta Bernstein," Vivi said through his earpiece at the same time.

Goddamn it, King thought before he had his backup Kimber out and pointed at Loretta Bernstein. "I thought it was you. I didn't believe it, but yeah, I wondered."

She walked to stand behind Savidge. King kept his gun trained on her. She lowered her head to Savidge's and kissed him. He wiped his mouth when she was done, but the smile lingered.

King didn't look at Allie, too afraid her fear and loathing would drive him to do something he couldn't take back.

"Buy me some time, Your Highness. Help is on the way," Vivi told him.

"Why?" he asked Loretta.

"My reasons are my own," she said simply, and again, just like in Cameroon, her voice was full of things that King couldn't get a grip on. She seemed to be telling him something, but for the life of him, he couldn't grasp it. "Dresden offered me an obscene amount of money, and I took it willingly. The CIA paid me nothing close to what Dresden does. She was expendable, McNally. Hell, in the end we're *all* expendable."

A soft sob ripped from Allie's chest. Loretta looked at her, and for just a moment King saw misery and regret on the woman's face. Then it was gone and she was the hard, cold Loretta she'd always been.

King nodded. "There's more."

"Dresden hates you as much as I do, McNally. And he knows your secrets, just like me."

"So this is about me? Well, then you can let her go," King urged.

She laughed and stroked Savidge's shoulder. "You're funny. Now I've got everything. Money, revenge, and you, McNally."

"You hate Broemig," Rook said into the silence. He was about ten feet behind King, hands at his sides. Keep her talking, and whatever Vivi had in the works could maybe bear fruit.

"With a passion," Loretta said and glanced once more at Allie.

Why did she keep doing that? Looking at Allie as if she wanted absolution. He didn't understand any of this.

"So much you're willing to hurt the one you helped raise to get at him?" King asked.

"I'd use anything to get at Broemig. I wondered for years whether or not he even recognized it. Allie was a pleasant way to pass the time, get into his good graces, et cetera, et cetera, but once I was there, it was easy to hate him."

"What did he do to you?" King questioned, feeling the buzz of movement at his back and hearing the throb and *whump-whump-whump* of helicopter blades in the distance.

Allie heard it too because her head lifted. How much longer could she hang in there?

"All manner of things that he needs to pay for," she returned.

"He didn't leave his wife," Jude said astutely.

Loretta's gaze speared Jude, but she smiled to hide the truth. "He was never anything to me, but he did make promises he never kept. His wife never even knew I was fucking her husband in their bed. She was pathetic."

"Not quite as pathetic as a woman sleeping with a married man," Vivi said in their ears.

Rook coughed to cover his laugh. King ignored them.

"Incoming in thirty seconds, Your Highness. Don't say I didn't warn you guys," Vivi called out.

The chopper was closer, but by the time Savidge and Loretta realized what was happening, and their men caught on that something big was headed their way, King had positioned himself beside Allie, cut her bonds, and had her on the floor covering her with his body.

The rush of the rocket blast in the courtyard shattered the windows and blew a huge hole in the wall behind King. He picked her up and was running with her as soon as the *whoosh* cleared from his ears. Fire rained down on them.

"Another hit coming in thirty seconds, men," Vivi informed them.

"Goddamn, woman! Let us get the hell out of here first," Rook demanded.

King ran for cover. The next blast took him off his feet, though he rolled with Allie, taking the brunt of the impact. Allie clung to him as debris fell on them.

"I've got you, baby. I've got you," he said in her ear.

Then he was up once more, carrying her slight weight over his shoulder and running through a ballroom full of well-dressed people who were now screaming and taking cover.

Rook and Jude were on his heels. When they came to the front door, Rook took Allie from King, who set up for cover.

Sporadic gunfire had erupted outside the ballroom, and soon Savidge's men were pouring out and heading King's way. He and Jude picked them off one by one.

King saw Savidge then, slipping on debris. He aimed and took his shot. Savidge fell immediately, but it wasn't solely because of King. At the bastard's back, holding a smoking handgun, was Loretta Bernstein. Her eyes met King's. She smiled and then she took off, disappearing in the smoke.

What the hell had just happened?

"You now have three minutes to get to the beach and head for extraction," Vivi pointed out.

"Damn, woman, you're killing me," King muttered.

Jude got up and started to make his way toward Savidge, but then he stopped as if he'd been shot. Proof of death was a valuable thing for the Piper and Endgame. King glanced at his man and then followed his line of sight.

Ella. One of the ballroom patrons was Ella. She held out a trembling hand, beseeching desperation in her gaze, and then she turned and ran. Fire licked up the walls of the ballroom, and more gunfire erupted.

Jude dropped to a knee, eyes closed.

"Get it together, Jude. We'll get her," King promised his man.

Jude opened his eyes and nodded, then stood and began returning fire.

"Bernstein is getting away," Jude muttered.

"Two minutes, Endgame. If you came to play and win, time's running out," Vivi counted down. "And Loretta Bernstein has much bigger problems than you, Jude. Those warbirds out there are courtesy of one very pissed-off Gray Broemig. She won't make it past him, I assure you. Once Endgame and the objective are out of the structure and clear, Savidge's entire place is going up."

"Move, Jude. Let's get the fuck out of Dodge," King ordered.

They ran, making it to the rendezvous point, jumping in the SUV, and beating a path away from hell.

King grabbed Allie from Rook, who looked at him with a knowing smile before he shut it down.

His gaze lowered to Allie. Her eyes were wide open, fear etched in the blue irises. He pushed her hair back from her face and winced at the multiple bruises.

Her sobs took him by surprise. Deep, racking cries that made his heart bleed and his soul yearn for revenge.

"It's okay, Allie. You're safe now, baby," he soothed.

Her cries were heartbreaking wails now.

"Allie," he said loudly. "Allie, look at me."

She did, but her eyes were swollen and the tears weren't helping. He needed her to calm down instead of cry. Her sobs were ripping him apart.

"Allie girl, you talk like a lovely loon. Keep going, please, until I go insane," he said desperately at her ear.

She stilled, then went quiet. Then she raised her head and stared at him as much as her poor eyes would allow.

He framed her face with his hands and lightly touched his lips to hers, and then she shuddered once and folded herself against him.

King held her through the entire trip. When they came to the extraction point and he started to get out, she held on so he didn't let go. He held her on the helicopter ride to Juniyah and then the plane ride to Little Creek, Virginia.

Whatever the old woman had given her in Savidge's compound had knocked her out. Cisco checked her out on the plane, cleaning her wounds, bandaging her side again, and making sure she was simply asleep.

She slept the entire way to Virginia. King watched over her the whole time. His team watched him watching her, and by their worried expressions, he knew they wondered what the hell was going on.

King wasn't inclined to share. Allie was in his arms, and in spite of everything that had happened, she was safe now.

She was safe.

Chapter 30

ALLIE WOKE UP TO SUN WARMING HER FACE. SHE OPENED her eyes and noticed the familiar surroundings. She was home. She took a deep breath as her chest threatened to rip wide open.

"Please don't cry anymore."

She closed her eyes and opened them again, sure she'd imagined his voice. There he was, sitting in a chair that looked entirely too small and dainty to hold his large frame. Beautiful. That's what he was to her.

He'd come for her, carried her out of hell, and gotten her home. Just like he'd promised.

"Okay," she whispered.

He grunted at that. Allie smiled.

Familiar ground all the way around. She needed it after the week she'd had.

"Where's Daddy?" she asked.

"Doing cover-up duty. He had some explaining to do to the President about why American military helicopters and personnel were used on Lebanese soil. Again," King said wryly.

Allie winced, felt her face pull, and sighed. "You guys aren't military personnel."

"Oh, not us. Your dad pulled in spec ops for your rescue."

"All he really needed was Endgame," she whispered.

He grunted again. "Your dad isn't Endgame's biggest fan right now."

"Yeah, well, my dad is obviously not the best judge of character, is he?"

"How are you feeling?"

She smiled. "Alive. Because of you, I'm feeling alive."

It grew quiet then, and Allie knew he was going to leave her. It wasn't in anything he said, but it was there between them.

He leaned forward and grabbed her hand, linking their fingers as he stroked the back of it. Yeah, he was leaving.

"I grew up in a little town in south Georgia. You know about my dad. He used his fists to correct me and his fists to praise me. He taught me how to hunt, fish, and survive in the wilderness for days on end, and he taught me that the truth is never simple.

"He attacked me in a drunken rage, but I'd gotten big enough to protect myself, and that night I did. I learned right then about control and how valuable it is. I told the truth to the cops, and they put me in jail anyway. I got lucky because the judge on my case was a retired SEAL who saw something in me besides the fact that I'd killed my father."

King took a deep breath, and Allie squeezed his hand.

"That judge made sure that I had a way out when I'd finished paying my time for a crime I'd been found guilty of as a juvenile. He helped me change my name, and I joined the navy. I wanted to be him. He knew my shame, knew what it meant to be the son of that piece of shit Thomas Sacco Sr., and he kept my secret, even pushing my past so deep that the secret was kept through every background check I went through for the navy."

"We do what we have to do for the ones we love," she whispered.

His gaze met hers and skirted away, and Allie wanted to cry. He was ashamed, and he had no reason to be. The shame of his youth wasn't his. It was his father's. He'd become a better man. A protector. A leader. Not many who'd been through what he had could claim they'd come out the other end a better person.

"I made the judge a promise that no matter what I did, I would do it with honor and dignity. I would keep my control and never put innocents in danger. I failed him, Allie. I failed you," King said, and in his voice was a wealth of pain.

"You saved my life, McNally. If you hadn't been on that plane, I'd have been in Savidge's hands even sooner. You also couldn't control that Lo-Lo betrayed us all. Don't hand me that bullshit. It's a pity party, and what I don't understand is why you're throwing yourself one."

She let her words hang in the air but felt him slipping away more with every breath.

"It's not a pity party, Allie. I'm giving you the truth."

"You're an honorable man. A man who risked his life to keep me safe. Where would I be if it wasn't for you?" she asked him, her voice edging to desperate, but that's how she was feeling.

"Safer."

A single word, and she had all the insight she needed into King McNally.

She wouldn't cry in front of him. Allie wouldn't do that to him because as much as it was ripping her up to watch him walk away, it was killing him to do it. He was that honorable. That loyal. He felt he'd let her down. She would have to show him that wasn't true. It was her turn to save King McNally, and to do it, she'd have to let him go. "I won't give you my permission, but I understand why you have to leave," she whispered.

He nodded, stroked his thumb over her skin once more, and stood. "I saw you in Savidge's ropes, and I knew that I couldn't survive if something happened to you. It's better for both of us if I go."

"It is, indeed, McNally," her father said as he entered her bedroom.

Allie hissed in a breath, anger flashing through her at his audacity.

"He's a wanted man, Allie. Even now, the Department of Justice is searching for him and his Endgame Ops team," Gray Broemig said. He turned to King. "Thank you for keeping her safe."

Allie shook her head. "Unbelievable." There was the anger lacking from the last few moments, bubbling over, and there Allie remained, unable to contain it.

King glanced at her. "What is?"

"That you think it ends like this."

He shrugged and crossed his arms.

"Don't do that, for God's sake," she snapped.

He grunted.

"You're home, Allie. That's what I promised. It's time for me to go," he said firmly, his voice infinitely deep with things unsaid.

She needed him to say them. She needed him to say that what was between them was more than adrenaline and fear and danger. But he wouldn't. So she did.

"It's more than what you're chalking it up to." She stood then, getting gingerly off the bed and standing before him. Her father was in the room, and Allie didn't give a shit. Right here, right now, was between her and King. "I gave you the pieces of me, Kingston McNally, formerly Thomas Sacco Jr. I gave them to a man with honor and dignity and a decided love of the word *fuck*."

His gaze went bright. At least they had that.

She wanted it all.

"You held those pieces in your hand, and now you're trying to give them back. Well, I'm not taking them. They're yours. I don't care how we met, I don't care how quickly it happened... I think I love you. Strike that." She made a downward chopping motion with her hand. "I know I love you. I wouldn't have given you those pieces if I didn't. You don't want to take the ride with me, walk out."

He reached out and rubbed his thumb over her cheek, wiping a tear away, pain and confusion in his gaze.

"It'll pass, I promise. I'm not who you deserve. I've got people dogging me. I'm not safe for you."

She wasn't going to sway him. And she was going to have to let him go.

Nodding, she stepped away. She cleared her throat and took a deep breath. "Good luck then, King. I wish you well."

She turned to the window and stared out for a long, long time, watching the trees blowing in a strong autumn wind. She felt like the leaves being blown about, tossed to and fro, no particular destination but a yearning to go higher so she could see over the trees and fly.

"I'm calling in my chit, Director," King said behind her.

Her father sighed. "I'll handle it."

King said nothing, and silence reigned.

When she turned back around, the room was empty

and she heard a car door slam. Then the car drove away, and King was gone.

—◦◦◦—

She showered, dressed, and went in search of her father. She found him in the den, sipping on a brandy and staring out the big bay window her mother had loved.

"Why?" Allie asked. Quick and to the point. No more games. She was refusing to play them ever again.

Her father looked at her, and for the first time in a long time, she saw him without the rose-colored glasses. He'd always been a handsome man—tall, with silvery-blond hair, his shoulders broad—and he'd always been in remarkable shape. Nearing sixty-five, he still maintained that effervescence she attributed to men half his age.

Yeah, his looks hadn't changed. On the outside, he was still the same man. It was the inside that she'd never known the truth about.

"Don't ask questions you don't need the answer to," he murmured as he took another sip of the amber liquid in his snifter.

"Don't you dare, Daddy," she spit out. "Don't you dare treat me as if I'm a six-year-old child with no brain. Loretta used to take me for ice cream. She taught me how to roller-skate. She taught me how to shoot and how to put on makeup. The woman you cheated with ended up being a stand-in for my mother. How could you?"

He maintained his silence. It infuriated her, and yet she'd expected nothing less. Gray Broemig, big, bad Gray Broemig—Vietnam vet, superspy, and CIA director—wouldn't lower himself to answer her questions.

"Intel says she's the one who pulled the trigger on Savidge. The same intel says she died at Savidge's villa," he said so softly that she almost didn't catch his words.

"You don't believe that though. I can hear it in your voice," Allie said through clenched teeth. "And I won't believe it until I see her body for myself. She had an agenda, and something about her betrayal reeks. Yes, she allowed Savidge to get his hands on me, but something about how she acted while I was there... It's just *off*."

"I loved her," he said, and in his words was a wealth of bitterness and pain. "And I never cheated on your mother. Ever. Your mother was gone before I ever took Loretta to my bed. I don't know what she said or her reasons behind it, but I never stepped out on your mother."

It was Allie's turn to be silent.

"You wouldn't understand. I could never explain it. But I owe you an apology, Allie, for everything you've been through. McNally is wrong. It wasn't his fault. It was all mine," her father said finally.

She nodded but went to sit beside him. Long moments passed as they both looked out the window, staring at a past that haunted them both.

"Your mother's death isn't on you either. It's on me. Those terrorists were using her to get at me, just like Savidge and Dresden tried to use you. I'm so glad you're safe."

She squeezed his hand, her only concession. She didn't know that she'd ever be ready to speak about Lo-Lo with him.

"I need your help, Dad," she told him. Because yes, Savidge—and through him, Horace Dresden—had been after Allie to get at her father, but other forces were at work here. Someone was also using Dresden to mask their own agenda with Endgame Ops.

Her father's gaze met hers, and she knew he was at least listening to her.

"Someone high up is going to do everything they can to make sure the men and women of Endgame Ops stay fugitives. That same person was in touch with both Savidge and the original terrorists on my first Air France flight."

"Allie, let this go," he urged.

"No. King saved me. Now it's my turn."

"I won't put you in that position. Whatever you remember, just let it go," he implored.

"You owe me, Dad. You owe Ella Banning. Yes, I know what you did to her—playing games with her life like you owned it. She's still out there, you know, trying to ferret out the truth of who's after Endgame and how you're involved in that. You owe the Endgame Ops team for putting their lives on the line for your daughter. You're going to help me, Director," she informed him.

"You're just like your mother, Allie. A spine of steel and a heart so strong nothing can rend it. You're my hero. That's what you are," he said right before he wrapped her in his arms.

She knew then he'd help her.

Chapter 31

ALLIE'S PALMS WERE SWEATING, AND HER STOMACH WAS in knots. It had been a week since she'd last seen King. She was struggling to eat, sleep... Hell, she was struggling to simply make it through her days without him. A week she'd been with the man. Seven days, and this was the result.

She'd lost her ever-loving mind.

Allie left her bodyguards at the door, telling them to remain outside. Amazingly, they did as she asked, though one went around to the back of the building. Her father had insisted she have two men looking after her at all times. She'd relented simply because she remained afraid, though she really trusted no one but King with her well-being.

She took a deep, cleansing breath and affected non-chalance like she'd been born to it as she walked into the bistro in the middle of downtown Washington, DC. She took a seat near the rear as she'd been instructed and ordered a double-shot espresso heavy on the sweet cream.

Allie tapped her foot impatiently as she waited for Olivia Granger. She'd badgered her father for a full twenty-four hours before he'd finally caved and given her Granger's contact information.

Olivia had worked solely for the CIA, but then her brother had been killed in an ambush in Mogadishu and she'd hunted down the man who'd been his commander. The man she'd ultimately fallen in love with, Anthony "Rook" Granger. Once Olivia gave her heart to Rook, she'd given her life to the endeavor of protecting him. Though she still did some consulting with the CIA, she was wholly, irrevocably Endgame Ops now. Allie's father remained slightly bitter about losing her.

Allie let her gaze drift over the various patrons, noting their positions in the bistro, what they were wearing, and what they had in their hands. Allie had never wanted to enter her father's world, but once it had been brought to her door, the intricacies came naturally to her. Oh, she'd never be a James Bond, but she was much better prepared now to take care of herself.

When Olivia Granger walked in, Allie had to do a double take. The woman was stunning. Around Allie's height, she wore her long, curly brown hair pulled into an elegantly messy chignon at the nape of her neck. Her large brown eyes were highlighted by the glasses she wore, giving her a college student look that served her well. The tote she had strapped over one shoulder lent even more credibility to that facade.

Were Allie not absolutely comfortable in her own skin, Olivia Granger could have been a woman to decimate her self-esteem. She was just that gorgeous.

Their eyes met, and Allie saw conflict in the other woman's gaze. She hadn't been happy when Allie contacted her.

"Miss Redding," Olivia said as she took the seat opposite Allie.

"Mrs. Granger," Allie returned, leaning back in her seat and watching the other woman.

Olivia stared at her. Hard. Allie returned the favor. Then a smile broke across Olivia's face, and she snorted. "I could hate that you do that so much better than me," she said with a grin.

"It's in my genes apparently," Allie replied with a shrug.

"Rook tells me I'll never be able to handle the field," Olivia said. "I think that sucks major ass."

Allie spewed espresso over the table. Those words from the innocent-looking woman's mouth had taken her by surprise. She liked her immediately.

"Didn't see that coming, did you?"

Allie shook her head and held out her hand. "I'm Allie Redding. It's a pleasure to meet you, Olivia Granger."

Olivia snorted again and lifted her hand to shake Allie's. "The pleasure is all mine, I can assure you. Anyone who ties His Highness up in knots is someone I want to meet. And please, call me Vivi."

Allie smiled, her first in a week. "Vivi it is." She took a deep breath. It was nice to meet more of King's people. "I appreciate you meeting me."

Vivi sighed. "Oh, honey, wild horses couldn't have kept me away. So what do you want to know?"

Allie stilled. There was so much she wanted to know, but first things first. "How are you?"

"Me? I'm doing great. And I'm willing to bet my brand-new Hyabusa that's not why you called me here today."

Allie's heartbeat tripled hearing that. "What's a Hyabusa?"

"Oh, you're good at this game," Vivi said with a small laugh, though the smile didn't reach her eyes. She shrugged. "It's a really fast crotch rocket. I love going fast, and my husband bought it for me to race at the track. It's heavier than most bikes, but I'm always up for a challenge."

"What game?" Allie asked.

"The don't-act-like-you-want-to-know-more-about-King game we're playing right now," Vivi returned.

Allie gave up. "How is he?"

Vivi nodded, and the smile breaking across her face was genuine this time. "I've only known him to be a surly bear on his good days. Lately he's been a raging ass. I'm guessing that has everything in the world to do with you."

Allie wanted to stand up and dance a jig. He was miserable? She was a horrible person for enjoying hearing that, but she couldn't help herself. "I sure hope so," Allie said.

Vivi laughed. "I'd hoped you weren't like your father."

Allie was brought back to earth just that quickly. "I'm not. At least not like you're thinking."

"So why else did you bring me here? I only have a little time before Rook is scheduled to meet me at the Smithsonian," Vivi relayed.

"Why the hell are you out and about in the middle of DC when they're all wanted men?"

"We're just that good at what we do," Vivi sing-songed. Then she smirked and said, "Harrison Black, uh, I think you met him in Spain—and by the way, you're going to have to tell me about Spain, Allie. Yep, I want deets, and before you open your mouth to protest, you owe me. I've yet to this day to see King McNally smile, and Black and Knight swear he did it for you."

Vivi took a breath, then started right back in. "Anyway, Black is great with identities and costumes. We get by very well. His work can beat even my own facial recognition software, and that is no small thing."

"So you hide in plain sight?" Allie asked. Was Vivi wearing a disguise right now?

"You could say that. We actually frolic our asses off in plain sight, and it serves us well. So our team members may be wanted, but they won't be caught."

Allie heard the underlying note of fear in Vivi's voice. It echoed in her own soul. "Someone is trying very, very hard to catch them, Vivi. And that's why I asked you here today."

Vivi eyeballed her. "Okay," she said finally.

To say Allie was startled at Vivi's easy capitulation wasn't doing the emotion justice. "Okay?"

"Yeah. I think His Highness is an ass, but he's our ass, and a better leader I've never met. He commands respect not with his words but with his actions. He's fair, loyal, and one of the best killers I've ever seen. King's team rallies behind him without question. He's the single most instinctive soldier I know. If he trusts you, I can do no less."

"What I want to do could get us all killed," Allie whispered.

"If you're here, you obviously have information that could also save us. Stop being such a negative Nelly, yeah? Now tell me what you need," Vivi said firmly.

"I need to know what went down in Beirut, who your team's contacts were. I need the mission's spec ops, all operational contacts, and communication audio from all sources. There was a communication to

Horace Dresden's phone within moments of Endgame's helo hitting Lebanese airspace. You were monitoring Dresden's sat phone."

Vivi didn't say yay or nay. That made Allie uneasy.

"You were monitoring his incoming and outgoing communications, and there was a call from a number traced back to DC. Yes, it was routed all over the world and back, but it ended here. Have you listened to the communication, Vivi?"

Vivi crossed her arms and stared at Allie.

Allie nodded. "You have. Does anyone know you have that?"

Vivi shook her head.

"I won't ask why you didn't tell your husband. None of my business, but you know what was said. I need that communication, and I need it soon. I also need the other information as soon as possible, Vivi. Today would be nice."

"You know who it is," Vivi said after a long, pregnant pause.

"I can neither confirm nor deny, and I think you know, Vivi, that at this point, you're better off in the dark."

"You are asking me for the moon. If King, or hell, if the Piper finds out I gave that information to Broemig's daughter, my ass is grass." Vivi blew out a rough breath and put her elbows on the table, settling her chin on her folded hands and just watching Allie. "You love him, don't you?"

Allie cocked her head. Vivi was solid; Allie knew it in her gut. "I do."

Vivi pulled a small slip of paper from her messenger

bag and slid it across the table to Allie. She took it and folded it gently before putting it in her pocket.

"That's an encryption key. I created a new email account for you, and that address is on there too. I'll have it to you tonight," Vivi told her softly. She sat back, breathed in deeply, and smiled at Allie. "You think you can fix this? Because if you think you can, I've got one more piece of information to, you know, just casually drop in your lap before you leave."

Allie grimaced. "I think I'm just going to make it worse. The person at the root of this isn't going to stop fighting just because little ol' Allie Redding is coming for him. But can I help get this immediate issue taken care of, get the men of Endgame Ops off the justice Tilt-A-Whirl, and throw that person off a little bit? You bet your fucking ass I can."

Vivi raised her fist. Allie did the same, knowing what she wanted. They fist-bumped and stood to their feet.

"What do you have for me?" Allie asked.

"A name. The CIA's deputy director, Grant Horner. He's an interesting fellow, likes to write things down, personal notes and such. You should look into him, and if you find what I think you'll find… Well, it should help all of us," Vivi said with a Cheshire-cat smile.

Allie nodded, an icy, numbing cold sweeping through her. How many people were going to betray her father? How widespread was this?

Vivi left, and Allie followed. They departed the bistro and headed in opposite directions.

Allie smiled to herself even though her throat was rapidly closing in the choking grip of fear. She was nuttier than a fruitcake to think she could do this.

Chapter 32

"THIS MEETING IS BROUGHT TO ORDER. FIRST ORDER OF business for the Senate Select Committee on Intelligence is the business of CIA Deputy Director Grant Horner. Mr. Chairman, I request permission to call Gray Broemig, director of the CIA, to the floor," said Herman Morton, the Republican senator from Virginia.

"Permission granted," Chairman Crawford Giles said.

He was a bastard of a man. His constituents voted for him year after year as if they were afraid that if they didn't elect the crotchety old son of a bitch, their great state of South Carolina would cease to exist in the Union.

"Turn that up, Jonah," Vivi said loudly from the kitchen. "And stop feeding my cat Twizzlers."

"It's C-SPAN, Vivi. Do we have to?" Knight asked. "And your cat likes Twizzlers."

"Turn it up," Rook said from his perch by the window. He was cleaning his guns just like King was.

Knight kept feeding the cat Twizzlers in between big bites of his own. Endgame was supposed to ship out next week. The Piper had a mission in the Ukraine, and all of them were going—except Chase, who remained in Burundi, and Jude, who couldn't be found. King's team was still flying under the radar, but when the Piper called, you damn well listened and obeyed.

King had signed on with the Piper, knowing he'd

done the right thing. The honorable thing. Endgame took missions the government couldn't sanction. The Piper remained somewhat of an enigma, but he'd never lied to King. Lately though, King had been wondering what the hell the Piper's true endgame was. One day, King was going to ask him what the fuck they were all doing. He was going to demand everything the Piper had kept from him. But today wasn't that day.

"Piper said we need to watch, so turn that shit up and shut up while you do it," Vivi yelled.

Knight turned that shit up in a hurry.

C-SPAN was carrying the meeting live. Director Broemig was sworn into the proceedings—a meeting called specifically in reference to his deputy director, who was now charged with espionage. King didn't personally feel that these types of meetings should be held in full view of the public. He was a bit hard core when it came to keeping secrets. The general public didn't necessarily need to know everything that went on behind their backs.

"Director Broemig, thank you for coming today. The council and I appreciate it. As you know, we're here to discuss the charges against your deputy director. Can you tell us, sir, just how far-reaching this problem with Horner is?" Senator Morton asked.

"Well, Sirs and Madams of the Committee, I can tell you that Horner was remanded into custody last evening, and the charges have merit. Just how far-reaching this case goes, I don't know yet," Broemig answered.

"It's your job to keep your people under control, Broemig. Can you not handle your duties? I find it hard to believe the head of the CIA had no idea what was going on in his own backyard. I want to know how deep this goes," Chairman Giles demanded.

"Chairman, as far as not knowing what's going on in my own backyard, well, I'm not the only one with issues in that department. What I can tell you is that apparently it goes very deep. People in our government have both aided and abetted DD Horner. The specifics will have to wait for the entirety of the investigation," Broemig bit out.

"You don't have control of your own damn agency, Director Broemig, and you're telling me I need to wait for answers?" Giles questioned harshly. "Maybe you aren't the man for the job. Just who are the people you're investigating?"

Giles's question was oily. King sat up straighter in his chair, glancing around the room to find every member of Endgame paying attention to the television.

"I'm glad you asked, Chairman. To answer that, I've brought in a witness with special knowledge about this case," Broemig said lightly.

And there she was, dressed in a prim pencil-skirt suit, light pink to contrast nicely with her long blond hair. Her heels made his mouth water, and that walk made him want to tell every man in the room to look away. She smiled at her father, was sworn in, and sat down beside him. Though King found it interesting she'd been introduced as Allison Redding.

Were they still trying to keep a lid on that?

"Take all the time you need," Senator Morton said with a smile.

"Thank you, sir," Allie replied in a lilting voice.

King was hard just that quick. He missed her. It'd

been over a week since he'd left her at her father's house, and he'd been lying low in Port Royal at Endgame Ops headquarters. They were back in the game, but King's head wasn't quite there yet. He was too wrapped up in what he'd walked away from.

Every man and woman on the council seemed to be staring at Allie. She cleared her throat and smiled again. With the exception of Chairman Giles, every man on the panel smiled back.

"I have names, but we still need confirmation on one. That's why I'm here today," Allie told them softly. "Deputy Director Horner had contacts in the government that he had cultivated over a long period of time. Unfortunately, DD Horner took his own life last night with a cyanide capsule, and Director Broemig lost the ability to question him directly. But we discovered, during the course of our initial investigation, that Horner took meticulous notes. Names, dates—he had it all in a notebook he stored in a safe at his home on Long Island. We are in receipt of that notebook."

She dropped that bomb and sat back, a placid smile on her beautiful face. She was holding a card, and King's breath locked in his chest.

Vivi gasped. "Hey, Rook?" Her husband stopped cleaning his gun long enough to glance up at her. "I should have told her he'd probably off himself, huh?"

"Nothing would have stopped him," Rook said dispassionately. "Nothing ever stops them."

Allie's voice pulled King's attention back to the huge television.

"I'm not sure if any of you are aware of the fact that Director Broemig is my father. My full name is actually

Allison Elizabeth Redding Broemig. Four weeks ago, I was a Peace Corps volunteer in Cameroon catching a flight home. My plane was hijacked, but thankfully there was a man on that plane who saved my life. I won't give you his name right now, because while it's important to me, it's not for the purpose of this meeting. Not yet anyway."

King wanted to shout at her to stop. Dresden and Loretta Bernstein were still out there. Whoever had it out for Endgame Ops was still out there. Putting herself in the public eye would take away any hope of safety for her.

"Goddamn, Allie," he whispered, but everyone heard and turned to glance at him. "Shut the hell up," he told them and looked once more at the screen.

"While I was on that plane, I was privy to a phone conversation between the lead hijacker and another entity, a man with an American accent. The American was giving orders, and he told the terrorist very specifically who I was and that he should either kill me or hand me over to Horace Dresden."

She took a deep breath, the serene look on her face never cracking. "I think you all know who Horace Dresden is."

King remembered the look on her face as the terrorist had taken that call. Her eyes had widened, and then she'd acted as if she'd heard nothing. She'd heard that conversation. Then she'd told him she had great hearing and now had proceeded to prove it.

King's palms began to sweat.

"I mentioned a man on the plane, also an American, who saved my life. I came to find out later that he was a member of Endgame Ops. You remember Endgame Ops, right, Chairman Giles?" she asked coquettishly.

The members of the council all turned to look at Giles, who simply shrugged. His face was turning red.

"I think you do remember them—a private entity doing contract work for the U.S. government. They were involved in a busted special operation in Lebanon. It caused a pretty nasty international incident, and you were the one who pushed the hardest to have Endgame team members tried as traitors in absentia for the events that occurred in Beirut on July 13, 2015. You were the one who demanded they be found and brought to justice. You were the one who had them put on the terrorist list."

She waited for several long moments before she started right back in. "I'm pretty sure you remember, but back to the hijacking. After he saved my life, I was hidden by this brave American who kept me safe and protected, but we were continuously pursued by people who wanted to capture me. One of those men finally succeeded, and I was privy to a conversation between the same American I'd heard on the plane and this new attacker."

Giles was sweating now. The camera panned over Allie, her father, and then the committee. It returned to focus on Allie, but King recognized fear and Giles was in the midst of a bad case.

"Go ahead, Ms. Redding. We're waiting," Senator Morton said kindly.

Her father reached for her hand and held it.

"The American told the new attacker—Vasily Savidge, who works for Horace Dresden—to do what he would with me as long as I returned to my father in pieces. 'That should put Broemig in his place,' the American said. Savidge promised to do that, but once again, the man from Endgame Ops saved my life. He risked his own to save me, and for that I'll be forever grateful."

"So what are you wanting here today, Ms. Redding? I thought we were here to discuss DD Horner," a female senator from Texas said in her long, slow drawl.

"Well, Senator Perry, we are here to discuss DD Horner, or more accurately the role he plays in all of this. But first I must address the issue of the voice. You see, I'm here because I recognize the voice from both the hijacking and my incident with Vasily Savidge. My hearing has always been excellent. And I've heard that voice here today."

Chairman Giles rapped his gavel. "Order," he said. "I can't believe this. You'd make a mockery of this meeting, Broemig?"

Broemig covered the mic and asked Allie a question. She mouthed, *I'm sure* and nodded.

Then she stood up and addressed the entire National Security Council. "I've heard the voice twice now, very distinctively on two separate occasions when my life was on the line. Of course mistakes can be made in the midst of terror-filled situations. I questioned whether or not I was right to be adamant about the owner of the voice, and then I was made privy to a recording from July 13, 2015. A communication placed from a residence here in DC to Beirut, Lebanon, and one Mr. Horace Dresden. I know the full contents of that communication, listened to it in its entirety, and once again I heard a voice that sent chills up my spine."

Giles was sweating now. The other senators were in an uproar, demanding to know what was going on.

"Ladies and gentleman, the voice I heard belongs to your chairman, Crawford Giles."

Silence fell over the room, then cameras began flashing.

Giles stood, face red, mouth falling open and shutting at a rapid rate.

Senator Morton stood and demanded order. "Ms. Redding, how can you be sure?"

"I understand your doubt. You cannot accuse based on my hearing alone, but once we knew what to look for, my father found it with ease. Remember the notebook DD Horner was hiding?"

Morton nodded.

"It lists the names of ten people, all in positions of power within the United States government and all people who have links to Horace Dresden. The notebook clearly shows monetary exchanges, account information, and dates the money was placed into these accounts. We do not know why the money was relayed from Dresden to these people, but we can assume it was payoff for favors. Since Osama bin Laden was eliminated, Horace Dresden has become public enemy number one. Why would anyone in a position of power for the United States take money from him? We are working on figuring out the specifics now, but four of the ten names are of particular interest to today's meeting and my own circumstances in Cameroon and after."

The smile never left her face, but King's heart was beating like a racehorse's. Fear tingled down his spine as his breathing slowed. His hands clenched, and the need for action had his adrenaline spiking. But he remained where he was because he couldn't do anything else.

"Well, young lady, we're waiting," Senator Morton reminded her.

"The four names belong to four National Security Council members, including Chairman Giles," Allie said.

King had been wrong. She didn't have a bomb; she had a goddamn nuclear weapon. Four members? Holy Christ.

"I would ask one thing," Allie said loudly, her father standing beside her.

"Yes?" Morton prompted.

"I would ask that justice be served, and I would request an inquiry into the events that led to the prosecution of Kingston McNally, Jonah Knight, Anthony Granger, Harrison Black, Chase Reynolds, Brody Madoc, Ella Banning, and Jude Dagan."

"Done." Morton hadn't hesitated, which led King to believe Allie and her father had given the man prior knowledge of today's clusterfuck.

"Woo-hoo!" Vivi squealed before she jumped into her man's arms. "I didn't think she'd do it. I hoped, but I wasn't sure. She must love your mean self a shit-ton, McNally, to risk her ass that way."

King stood then, fear racing through him. He was about to lose control. She'd gone to bat for him. He'd walked away from her, and she'd stood up for him... hell, for his entire team.

There wasn't anything else to do. He grabbed his keys and headed out the door.

Chapter 33

ALLIE PUNCHED IN HER SECURITY CODE, TOLD HER TWO bodyguards good night, walked into her apartment, and immediately stepped out of her shoes. She'd moved into this secure brownstone a week ago and still wasn't used to it. She loved her father, always would, but she couldn't see him everyday. Not yet.

The brownstone was completely modernized and as safe as one of Endgame's safe houses. She needed a pet or something...hell, anything to break the relentless emptiness of the sprawling apartment. She liked having her own space, but it was...lonely. She kicked her shoes to the side of the door, set her purse down, and locked the door behind her, setting the passcode.

Today had gone much better than she'd anticipated. It was another step toward freeing King and his men. She'd also partaken of a little "get-back" on one of the men who'd sold her out. Lo-Lo was still out there. Dresden was still out there, but Giles was sitting in prison. The other three senators were in the midst of heavy scandal and inquiries. Now, if she could get her hands on the person pulling their strings...well, things would definitely be looking up.

What she'd endured at Savidge's hands would haunt her for a long time. She shuddered at the thought and rubbed her hands over her arms.

Yeah, the bad guys were still out there, but so was King.

She missed him.

She poured a big glass of red wine and unzipped her skirt before she headed to her bedroom. She changed into a pair of yoga pants and a tank top before she picked up her wine and walked to the huge, empty living room.

She sank onto her only piece of furniture in the space, a huge leather couch, and sipped her wine, watching the lights of the city twinkle and wishing.

Wishing did no good, so she grabbed another glass and had just reached for the remote when a knock sounded at her door. She set her glass and the remote down, hurried to her bedroom and grabbed the SIG Sauer someone (a.k.a. Kingston McNally) had sent her the day after he'd left.

She chambered a round and flipped off the safety.

"Who is it?" she asked.

"It's me" came the voice she'd been missing so much.

She rested her forehead on the door. "Who's me?"

"Open the door, Allie," he demanded.

She frowned but did as he ordered. Then she stood there, door barely open as she peeked around it. "What do you want, McNally?"

"Open the damn door, woman." Exasperation flavored his tone.

She stepped back, her body going molten as he walked into her apartment like he owned it. "I'll ask again. What do you want, McNally?"

"I saw you today," he murmured, his green eyes burning as he caught her gaze and refused to let it go.

"I imagine a lot of people saw me today. That was the purpose of my visit to the Hill," she responded as she walked past him into her living room.

He smelled so good—evergreen and mint. She was mad at him for leaving her. She wanted him. She loved him. If the time away from him had done anything, it was to cement the latter. It wasn't adrenaline that kept her awake at night.

It was need for him. Those barely there smiles and the varying tones he used to get her to do what he wanted.

"Nobody has ever done for me what you did for me today," he said gruffly.

She sighed.

He grunted.

They seemed to be back where they'd started.

"So you saw me. That's nice," she said inanely.

"No, I mean I *saw* you," he said again.

"We still playing games, Kingston McNally?" she asked as ire wound through her body.

He shook his head and then shrugged out of his leather coat. He was wearing a black long-sleeved T-shirt and low-slung jeans.

"I'm done playing games, Redding. I'm all in with this one," he said firmly as he stepped out of his boots and pulled his T-shirt off.

Allie stepped forward, drawn by invisible strings of love and lust. She licked her lips.

"Yeah, do that again," he murmured.

She did. Hey, her mouth was dry. "What are you doing?"

He crossed his arms over his chest. "Staking my claim."

"You left, McNally," she murmured.

"I had no choice. Important thing is, I came back."

"Not good enough," she returned.

He made a beeline for her, scooping her up and over

his shoulder and heading to the couch. King placed her gently on the leather and came down over her. He grabbed both her hands in one of his and settled in the cradle of her hips.

"Don't say that, Allie," he ordered.

"Well, what should I say, McNally?"

"Anything but that," he said.

"Let me go, McNally," she demanded.

"Say my name, Allie."

"Let me go, *King*."

"No."

"Yes," she said immediately.

"You stood up there today, in front of the entire nation, and demanded that people look into what happened to Endgame."

"I think you're exaggerating. Not that many people watch C-SPAN," she whispered.

He chuckled. "I'm not leaving," he told her.

She squirmed beneath him, desperate to either get out from under him or get naked with him. "I don't want you to," she told him.

"I've got a lot to learn, Allie. I'm a tough man, and I really don't think I'm good enough for you. But you're mine. I've claimed you, and you're mine."

She was going to call that his you're-never-getting-away-from-me tone. She could dig it.

She nodded. "I missed you."

He dropped his forehead onto hers and stared into her eyes. It was the most poignant moment she'd ever experienced. He was hers; she just had to show him.

"More than McDonald's fries and mani-pedis?"

His hips rocked against her as his heat sank deep into

her bones. She cocked her head and played like she was giving it some thought. "*Fuck*, yes," she whispered.

He groaned, and she knew then that he was going to be hers and she was going to be his. There was still so much to deal with. Endgame was not out of the woods by a long shot, and she knew he'd be leaving on future missions. Dresden was still a huge worldwide threat, and so was whoever wanted Endgame Ops wiped off the face of the earth.

And this man she'd claimed was always going to fight for good because it's who he was.

"We have got to work on your language. You know what that word does to me," he said harshly.

She smiled, felt it echo as a song in her soul, and said, "Yeah, I really do."

He lifted off the couch and picked her up. "This is just the beginning. What you did today has stirred the hornet's nest. They'll be gunning for Endgame even harder, looking to eliminate us. I can't believe you did it," he bit out as he dropped his forehead to hers. A deep sigh, and then he squeezed her. "I'll keep you safe."

"I'll do the same for you, King," she said against his lips.

It was a promise that circled between them.

Then she laughed as he tossed her on the bed and followed her down. She'd landed the man with the lick-me-all-over lips...Mr. LMAO himself.

Ba-da-da-da-daaaa—better than her french fries, and she was loving it.

Epilogue

JUDE ADJUSTED HIS SCOPE'S SIGHT AND SETTLED DOWN in the slight depression between two trees. The wind had picked up an hour ago, and he allowed its bitter cold to seep into his soul. It was soothing to a degree, though Jude doubted anything could ever completely cool his rage. He'd been here for two days, following intel that would hopefully lead him to…*her*. He'd stopped even thinking her name six months ago. The sound of it reverberating through his mind caused unbearable pain that spread from his heart through every limb. It was debilitating, that pain. And unending. Instead, he remembered her face, the way her body had once moved beneath him, the promises she'd made that had inevitably been nothing more than lies.

Movement in the compound below had him tightening his grip on his rifle. He'd been trained to take down targets a mile away, but today was simply reconnaissance. When he'd seen her in Beirut six weeks ago, his mind had denied what his heart had immediately recognized.

El—*her*.

Then she'd disappeared in the smoke and confusion, and he'd had no choice but to leave her again.

In the desert of Lebanon.

A white Range Rover pulled up to the concrete warehouse that had once been a chemical engineering facility. Rumor had it that the facility's purpose was to conceal Horace Dresden's biochemical weapons stash. Whatever the case, those rumors had hit Jude's ears and his skin had prickled.

If he could find Dresden, he'd find *her*.

The left-side passenger door opened, and a dainty foot encased in a nude stiletto heel lowered to the ground. The leg attached to the foot had his gut clenching. He'd tasted the arc of that calf, tongued the indention of that knee, and had his hands all over that thigh.

She stepped out of the Rover completely, and his clenched gut released. Everything in Jude relaxed. It was a reaction he'd only had with her. Jude was a warrior, a soldier. He'd spent most of his adult life training, fighting, and killing. He was damn good at what he did. Had never even realized something was missing from his life until she'd stepped into his sphere and taken him over.

The wind caught her overcoat and tossed the ivory folds, allowing him a glimpse of a body that was thinner than he remembered but no less captivating. Through the scope, his gaze trailed upward over her hips and then higher across her breasts and up along the slope of her collarbone. Her skin was the same color as her coat but softer, glowing. Her taste was a phantom on his tongue.

The trees above him bowed to the wind, and in his spot on the ridge above the compound, Jude breathed in deep. He swore he could taste her on the breeze. She moved to shut the door and, in an instant, froze.

She slowly lifted her hand and removed the dark sunglasses that hid the frost of her gaze from him. And then she angled her head toward his location.

His heart locked in his chest. No way she had any

idea he was here. He hadn't even told King where he was headed—had kept the information about Dresden's supposed compound from the Piper, King, and his team-mates. This was what he'd been reduced to. Spying on a woman who'd betrayed him…betrayed them. Desperate for a glimpse of her.

The wind settled at that moment, but still she gazed up toward him. The man who'd gotten out of the Rover on the other side must have called her name, because she glanced at him and her lips moved before she began walking toward the building. Her long legs ate up the distance between the Rover and the building, and for a crazy second, Jude remembered her as she'd been the night before his world had been blown to hell. He saw her walking on their beach in North Carolina, the wind whipping her long ebony hair, the waves playing havoc around her delicate ankles. He saw her head turn as a grin broke across her face. He saw the flush of their recent lovemaking on her body.

A hawk screamed in the distance, and Jude was jerked to the present. Instead of seeing his woman through the sight of the scope, he saw *her*. A stranger. A traitor.

Jude's sight remained locked on her, his finger caressing the trigger as he let the anger flow through him. He'd heard the whispers—maybe she was a double agent. Maybe she wasn't the traitor he knew her to be. Maybe she was both and neither.

Maybe he hadn't given everything he was to a ghost.

He needed the truth, and he'd resolved that he'd have to be cold and merciless in finding it. She'd led them on this path. She could damn well walk it with him.

The man entered the building, but before she stepped

in behind him, she once again turned her gaze to Jude's location.

She couldn't see him, but for Jude, it didn't matter. She knew he was there. He knew she knew. She raised her hand—supplication or warning, he didn't know— but the sadness that passed like a cloud over the contours of her face in that moment had him swearing.

Then she lowered her hand as the soft curves of her mouth lifted in a travesty of a smile.

Jude cursed again, the wind taking the foul word and tossing it to and fro. As she moved out of his sight, his gut clenched again. King had warned Jude that all was not as it seemed, to give him time to figure it all out.

Jude hadn't been inclined to give himself that time. Until this moment.

Because there'd been one other emotion on her face just now that ripped a hole right in Jude's heart. He'd seen it many times over the course of their year together but had despaired he'd ever see it again. It had been the truest of all the emotions she'd ever displayed with him.

It was the one thing that stayed his trigger finger. It was the only thing that could save her.

Love.

About the Author

Lea Griffith has been reading romance novels since a young age. She cut her teeth on the greats: Judith McNaught, Kathleen Woodiwiss, and Julie Garwood. She still consumes every romance book she can put her hands on, and now she writes her own compelling romantic suspense. Lea lives with her husband and three teenage daughters in rural Georgia.

WILD RIDE

The Black Knights Inc. hero we've all been waiting for...

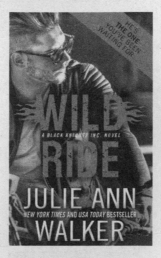

Welcome to the Black Knights, Inc.—deadly covert proceedings behind the scenes, custom motorcycle shop up front. Most of the bros are overseas on assignment, leaving the operation under the watchful eye of Ethan "Ozzie" Sykes, hacker extraordinaire, and one of the most memorable heroes you've ever encountered.

New York Times bestselling author Julie Ann Walker delivers a bombshell every time.

"Another exhilarating, not-to-be missed addition to the bestselling series!"

—RT Book Reviews for *Too Hard to Handle*

For more Julie Ann Walker, visit:
www.sourcebooks.com

DEVIL AND THE DEEP

A *USA Today* Bestseller! Second in
The Deep Six series from Julie Ann Walker.

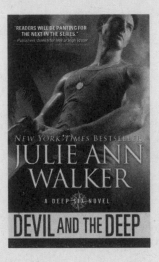

Former SEAL Bran Pallidino carries a dark secret—one that
forced him to push away Maddy Powers, the woman who
stole his heart. But when Maddy is taken hostage during a
trip to the Caribbean, the men of Deep Six Salvage embark
on a dangerous mission to save her. Passion boils in the
sultry sea breeze…but what good is putting their hearts on
the line if they don't survive the dawn?

*"Hot men, hot action and hot temperatures
make for one hot romance!"*

—BookPage

For more Julie Ann Walker, visit:
www.sourcebooks.com

SAFE FROM HARM

Book two in the Protect and Serve series of high-octane romantic suspense from Kate SeRine.

Prosecuting attorney Elle McCoy has been protecting her heart from cocky playboy cop Deputy Gabe Dawson. But it's hard not to notice a guy when he takes a bullet for you and seems determined to turn his life around. With terrorists at large and Elle a target, Gabe and his law enforcement brothers kick into high gear to take down the threat. And as they work together, Elle realizes she's losing her heart to a man who will risk it all to keep her safe from harm.

"Packed with nonstop drama and sizzling romance!"

—RT Book Reviews, 4 Stars

For more Kate SeRine, visit:
www.sourcebooks.com

RUN TO GROUND

First in Katie Ruggle's thrilling new
Rocky Mountain K9 Unit series.

Theodore Bosco lost his mentor. He lost his K9 partner.
He almost lost his will to live.

But when a killer obsessed with revenge targets a beautiful
woman on the run, Theo and his new K9 companion will
do whatever it takes to save Jules before they lose their last
chance at a happily ever after…

*"Sexy and suspenseful, I couldn't turn the
pages fast enough."*

**—Julie Ann Walker, *New York Times* and *USA
Today* Bestselling Author, for *Hold Your Breath***

For more Katie Ruggle, visit:
www.sourcebooks.com

HOLD YOUR BREATH

First in Katie Ruggle's celebrated Search and Rescue series of sexy romantic suspense.

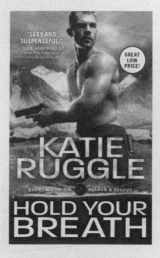

Lou's new to the remote Rocky Mountains, intent on escaping her controlling ex, and she's determined to make it on her own terms...no matter how tempting her new ice dive captain Callum Cook may be. But when a routine training exercise unearths a body, Lou and Callum find themselves thrust into a deadly game of cat and mouse with a killer who'll stop at nothing to silence Lou—and prove that not even her new Search and Rescue brotherhood can keep her safe forever.

"Vivid and charming. I love Ruggle's characters."

—Charlaine Harris, #1 *New York Times* bestselling author of the Sookie Stackhouse series

For more Katie Ruggle, visit:
www.sourcebooks.com

STEALING MR. RIGHT

First in a new romantic suspense "heist"
series, Penelope Blue brings you fast-paced
antics and a compelling caper romance.

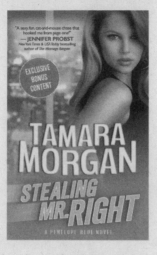

Penelope Blue has the perfect life, and the perfect husband.
Well, except for the fact that he works for the FBI...and
she's a jewel thief. It turns out that the only thing worse
than having a mortal enemy is being married to one.
Because in this game of theft and seduction, only one will
come out on top.

Good thing a cat burglar always lands on her feet.

*"A sexy, fun, cat-and-mouse chase that
hooked me from page one!"*

**—Jennifer Probst, *New York Times* & *USA Today*
Bestselling Author of *The Marriage Bargain***

For more Tamara Morgan, visit:
www.sourcebooks.com

HEART STRIKE

DELTA FORCE: The deadliest elite
counter-terrorism unit on the planet.

The newest Delta operative on the team, Sgt. Melissa
Moore has never met a challenge she can't conquer.
Technical wizard Sgt. Richie Goldman is Bond's "Q"
turned warrior, and a genius about everything except
women. When the Delta Force team goes undercover in
the depths of the Colombian jungle, surviving attacks from
every side requires that Richie and Melissa strike right at
the heart of the matter…and come out with their own
hearts intact.

"Phenomenal lead characters, with romance
as breathtaking as the action."

—RT Book Reviews for *Target Engaged*, 4.5 stars

For more M. L. Buchman, visit:

www.sourcebooks.com

FLASH OF FIRE

Fourth in M. L. Buchman's critically acclaimed
Firehawks romantic suspense series.

When former Army National Guard helicopter pilot Robin
Harrow joins Mount Hood Aviation, she expects to fight
fires for only one season. Instead, she finds herself getting
deeply entrenched with one of the most elite firefighting
teams in the world, who fly into places even the CIA can't
penetrate. And that's before they send her on a critical
mission that's seriously top secret, with a flight partner
who's seriously hot.

"A richly detailed and pulse-pounding read...
tender romance flawlessly blended with
heart-stopping life-or-death scenes."

—RT Book Reviews for Full Blaze, 4.5 stars

For more M. L. Buchman, visit:
www.sourcebooks.com